SCAM

G. R. TAPLIN

1

It had only been an hour since the sun had crept above the mountain tops, but the temperature was already soaring. Alistair MacDonald, Mac to everyone who knew him, stepped out of the air-conditioned hut that had been home for the last six months. Looking over the huge blast-proof wall surrounding the compound he scanned the barren hills in the distance. Somewhere in those hills shimmering in the heat haze was their destination for the day's operation. He walked across the dusty camp square watching his team load their equipment into the armoured personnel carrier that was their transport for the day.

After being stationed in Afghanistan for six months, todays patrol would be Mac's last while on active service. Although he knew he would miss his team he was glad to be leaving. The following day he would take a short helicopter ride back to the main base on the first leg of his journey home. The next leg would take him to Cyprus where there would be a short stopover, he could relax and catch up with a few friends then it would be onwards to regimental headquarters in Herefordshire. When he arrived back in the UK there would be some paperwork to complete then his time in the SAS would be at an end, and his time serving his country would finally be at an end. He would spend a few months with his fiancé renovating the farmhouse they'd bought before he was stationed in Afghanistan, then look for a job on civvy street, not something he'd ever had to do in the past and not something he was looking forward to, but it was time to settle down, time to get married and maybe time to start a family.

It promised to be another scorching day, something else he certainly wouldn't miss when he left Afghanistan. He longed to see the rolling green hills and forests of home again, to feel rain on his skin and spend an evening in front of the fire in his local pub.

Mac took off his sunglasses and wiped his brow on the sleeve of his uniform. *One more day,* he said to himself, *just get through today safely and I'll be home to start a new chapter of my life.*

Mac hated the thought of leaving his team behind, a team he'd built over the last few years, a group of men he considered not only as work colleagues but as friends, each of whom he'd relied on in life and death situations they'd encountered during his leadership. He took comfort in the knowledge that his replacement was a good officer, one with combat experience in both Iraq and Afghanistan, something that was vital to ensure your team would return home safely.

Special forces wouldn't normally carry out routine patrols such as the one they were about to undertake, but two of his team had been hidden in the hills for five days on an observation mission and needed extraction. The team's job today was to rendezvous with them outside the local village, talk to a few of the locals then return to base. Mac felt uneasy about taking his team out on patrol in a single personnel carrier, they would usually travel in groups of two or three along with armoured support, but all other available units were either already out on patrol or in the workshop for maintenance. They had no choice, if they were to meet the observation team on time they had to travel alone.

As the camp's huge gates slowly, opened Mac jumped into the back of the vehicle and pulled the door closed. Despite the fact they would be on their own today he was confident that this would be one of their easier trips. They would stop at one of the nearby villages for a hearts and minds visit, give the kids some sweets, chat to the locals, ask about any sightings of insurgents, a question he already knew the answer to, then pick up the observation team and return to base. It sounded straightforward but Mac knew nothing in this country was simple. If you wanted to survive while outside the safety of the camp walls you had to have your wits about you at all times.

As the vehicle left the compound Mac looked through the slit of a rear window, the heat haze was shimmering across the vast plain and dust thrown up in their wake further obscured his view. It was going to be another hot one he thought, not a day to be stuck inside an uncomfortable, noisy tin can like this being boiled alive.

HALF A MILE away in the hills overlooking the camp Omar raised his binoculars and watched the huge camp gates open. A single armoured personnel carrier slowly pulled onto the makeshift road the foreign army had constructed. He waited for more vehicles to emerge but as the vehicle pulled away the gates closed. During the countless months he'd been watching the camp he'd never seen a patrol vehicle leave alone. Normally there would be armoured support travelling with groups of two or three personnel carriers. He looked to the clear blue sky for any air cover the patrol may have but could see or hear none. They were becoming complacent. Although it would make today's operation easier, it would make it less fruitful.

Omar had been crouched below the crest of the hill for nearly two hours waiting for some movement from the camp, he was hot and had cramp in his legs. He stretched his limbs shaking out the stiffness in them, it would be good to be on the move again. Now the operation they had so meticulously planned could be put into action. With only one enemy vehicle involved it wouldn't reap the casualties his group hoped for, but any enemy deaths would be viewed as a victory. He put the binoculars down, took a mobile phone from his pocket and sent a text to his fellow freedom fighters, a luxury his forefathers never had when fighting invaders in the past. While he waited for his message to be acknowledged he wondered how they'd managed to communicate during their fight against the Russians during the last war.

The team Omar was part of had been preparing for this moment for the last two weeks. The final part of the plan, the landslide, had been completed the previous night, everything was now in place to decimate this patrol. The fact that the vehicle was travelling alone should make the task easier. They would hit it hard then disappear into the hills as they always did, ghosts the foreign army could never find.

The local villagers knew any collaboration with the enemy would result in trouble, some of Omar's group would return and exact a terrible retribution on anyone who cooperated with the foreign soldiers. The threat alone was enough to deter any collaboration. He put his phone, water bottle and binoculars into his rucksack, threw it over his shoulder and set off for the ambush site. He ran crouched below the crest of the hill, making sure he was invisible to the camp below, his AK47 rifle loose in his hand, a constant companion since returning to the land of his birth to join the fight. Omar hurried along the hillside knowing he had to get to the ambush site before the lone vehicle arrived.

USUALLY WHEN MAC'S team left the base on a mission such as this there would be a sense of nervous apprehension in the personnel carrier. Nerves would be wound tight, his team would be checking and re-checking their equipment, but because this was Mac's last mission everyone seemed relaxed and the banter was flowing.

"Last day then guv," Smithy said. "I expect you want to take us all to the mess when we get back and stand the drinks all night?"

Mac smiled. "Not the way you lot drink. I'll be skint by the time I leave. I may buy you half a shandy, if you're lucky."

"What's the plan for when you get home sarge?" Taff asked.

"I'm renovating a farmhouse I bought with my fiancé before we left on this tour. It should keep me busy for a few months. After that who knows. Find a job I suppose."

"You own a farm?" Smithy asked. "I can't see you as a gentleman farmer guv."

"It's not really a farm, more of a smallholding."

"Yes, that sounds about right," Smithy said with a big grin on his face, "I've seen you in the showers, it's definitely a small holding."

Mac knew he would miss this, the close-knit team and banter. He wasn't sure there was anywhere on civvy street where bonds such as these could be forged, but he knew once he found a job he would soon find out. The jovial mood also made him nervous. Everyone in the patrol needed to be alert, they all knew of the dangers outside the camp. Once they reached the rendezvous point Mac would remind them before they disembarked. He would never forgive himself if one of his team was injured and he hadn't done everything in his power to prevent it, even if it was something as small as reminding them to stay alert and of the dangers out here in the hills.

In a cloud of dust and diesel fumes the personnel carrier slowly made its way up the hill. "Looks like a landslide ahead," the driver shouted above the engine noise into the microphone attached to his helmet. The vehicle continued until it came to a stop in front of the obstruction, the front of the personnel carrier almost touching the rocks blocking the road. "There's no way we're getting around it," the driver said.

In the back of the vehicle Mac looked out of the window trying to assess their options, but it was so small and the angle so acute it was almost useless. There was no way he could make a decision about the situation from inside the vehicle.

"Call it in," he said to the driver on his helmet mic, "tell base we're going to check this landslide and clear the road if we can, if not we'll be returning to base."

The mountain of a man, Jock, sitting next to Mac looked at him. "Are you sure about this Mac? Don't forget we're on our own out here. If you really want to do this why don't we back up a bit, then we can get out and take a look. If there's any danger it will be close to the landslide. There's no need to take any chances, especially on your last patrol. Better still let's just go back to base and have a couple of beers, the guys can wait another day to be picked up and the locals are probably fed up of seeing us anyway. Maybe we can arrange for a chopper to pick them up if we can't clear this landslide."

Tempting as Jock's suggestion was Mac thought they should at least to try to complete his final mission. He looked out of the window again but could still see nothing that helped him come to a decision. "Got anything on the cameras?" he asked the driver and navigator in the cab up front.

"Can't see anything. All looks clear," the driver replied.

Mac decided to compromise as Jock had suggested. "Pull back about fifty meters then we'll get out and take a look."

The personnel carrier slowly retraced its journey along the dusty track coming to a halt roughly fifty meters from the obstruction blocking their path. Mac could hear the navigator radioing base with their location and what they intended to do.

In the back of the personnel carrier Mac briefed his team, the relaxed atmosphere and banter gone, replaced by the professionalism they had trained so long and so hard for. "Smithy and Taff drop down the slope behind the APC and cover the hills above. Jock, you and I will go up into the hills. If there's anyone up there we'll flush them out, and remember the rules of engagement, don't shoot unless you're engaged first. Gav, see how bad this landslide is. I don't like the look of it, this shouldn't happen in the summer. See if there's any way we can clear enough of the road to get through. If we can't we'll return to base and the Engineers will have to come up here to clear it with a bulldozer. Be careful everyone, radios on and stay alert." They exited the personnel carrier and swiftly headed to their assigned positions.

AT THE SAME time Mac's patrol moved away from the vehicle, Omar reached the hill above the landslide they'd painstakingly created. The bomb maker of their group, Hakim, lay waiting in the scrub for the perfect moment to detonate the bomb concealed beside the landslide. He acknowledged Omar's arrival with a nod. Everyone was in place, now it was a question of waiting until the patrol moved in range.

GAV WAITED for the others to reach their positions before slowly moving forward from the cover of their vehicle, sweeping the hills above with his rifle as he advanced. The landslide had come down the hill and carried on into the valley below, not unusual in these hills during the rainy months of winter but this was the middle of summer. As he neared the landslide Gav could see the road on the other side was clear. If they could move a few of the rocks from the edge they may be able to carry on and complete their mission. He put his rifle over his shoulder and clambered over the obstruction. After dusting himself down he looked up and was surprised to see a small boy walking down the road towards him. What was this little lad doing so far from the village he wondered? They could give him a ride back to the village if they could clear the road enough to get the personnel carrier through. It would be another small triumph in the hearts and minds campaign.

OMAR LOOKED on in horror as a small boy rounded the corner and walked towards the landslide. Nobody other than the soldiers were supposed to be here, the villagers had been told to stay away. He tapped Hakim on the shoulder and shook his head, this ambush could wait for another day. Hakim looked at him with cold dead eyes, his tanned weather-beaten face totally devoid of expression. What they were about to do was something he'd done too many times before. All the killing he'd been responsible for and witnessed had dehumanised him. Hakim didn't see people, loved ones who would be mourned, torn from their families by his bombs. Hakim only saw targets. He wasn't about to let a small boy get in the way of killing another foreign invader.

Omar grabbed Hakim's arm, staring into his black eyes. He shook his head again, vigorously indicating that they should abandon their plan for today, but Hakim pulled his arm free of Omar's grip and turned to face the road, waiting for the perfect moment to press the detonator.

Omar grabbed his arm again, "this can wait, we can do it another day," he whispered.

"No. The villagers were told to keep away. They all knew what was going to happen here today. We've spent too much time and effort creating this landslide to abandon our plan just because one little boy can't do as he's told," Hakim hissed back at him. He pulled his arm free of Omar's grip and returned his gaze to the road.

"We can't murder an innocent boy, it's not why we are here," Omar pleaded. "Killing just one foreign soldier can never be justification for killing an innocent child."

Hakim slowly turned back to Omar staring at him with his cold dead eyes. "The boy is not why we are here, but the others are. He may just be another unfortunate casualty of this war. One boy for the lives of some foreign soldiers is worth the sacrifice. If you can't stomach that you shouldn't be here with us. Now keep quiet and let us do our job. If you don't want to be part of this group leave now, we can cope without you."

Omar could sense Hakim's frustration; they had expected at least three vehicles but there was only one in the foreign army's patrol. More vehicles meant more soldiers trying to clear the landslide, and more soldiers meant more casualties.

THE BOY APPROACHED the landslide seemingly without a care in the world. Gav unknowingly walked towards the bomb hidden in the hillside, he squatted down to be at the boy's level. "Salam," he said, one of the few Pashto words he'd picked up during his time in Afghanistan. He reached inside his tunic for one of the chocolate bars they always carried for the local children. The little boy's face lit up; he knew what was coming. Gav pulled the bar from his tunic and held it out in front of him for the boy to take.

AS THE BOY reached out for something the soldier was holding Hakim pressed the detonator button. There was a moment's delay before the hillside erupted in a deafening roar, dust, rocks and stones filling the air. As the dust slowly settled the sound of the blast echoing around the valley and loose rocks and stones rolling down the hillside was all that broke the silence. Omar and Hakim's part of the mission was over, the rest of the ambush was down to the others. There were more than enough men in their team to finish the job, they had expected at least three vehicles. They would wait for the other foreign soldiers to go to the aid of their fallen colleague then cut them down. Omar and Hakim disappeared into the hills, ghosts once more.

CROUCHED DOWN and partially shielded by the boy, Gav had avoided the worst of the blast. He lay halfway down the hillside staring up at the cloudless blue sky above. Covered in dust and the remains of the boy's body he could hear or feel nothing.

For a few seconds Mac was stunned. He stood motionless, stopped in his tracks by the huge blast, staring at the dust cloud where Gav had stood seconds earlier hoping he would emerge as the dust settled but knowing he wouldn't. They'd spent countless hours training for situations like this, but this was no exercise, this had never happened before on any of the patrols they'd previously been on. Finally, his training kicked in and he came back to his senses.

"Call in backup," he shouted into his helmet microphone as he made his way to some cover. "Helicopter extraction and air cover if there's any nearby." He looked over to Jock and nodded to a small rocky outcrop over to his right. They'd been on so many patrols together much of what they did was by instinct, or in this case a nod was all that was needed. Jock looked over to the rocky outcrop Mac had indicated, from there he could cover the rest of the team on the hillside below and have cover for himself from any enemy fighters coming down the hill.

"If you see anyone engage them, don't wait for them to fire first. Anyone on this hillside is only here for one thing," Mac said into his helmet mic. Without a word, Jock made his way to the outcrop to take up a covering position.

The rest of his team knew that in these situations the bomb blast was just the start. There would be insurgents in the surrounding hills waiting for them to go to Gav's aid. As soon as anyone came out into the open, they would be cut down in a hail of bullets.

In the personnel carrier, the navigator radioed for support. After a brief exchange with base he gave Mac the news. "American helicopter close by. They're on their way. Should be here in less than one minute."

"Thanks, keep me posted. Gav can you hear me," he shouted, "are you okay?" There was no reply, his own voice echoing around the valley now the only sound breaking the silence. Mac hoped Gav's lack of response was down to temporary deafness caused by the blast, the alternative was something he didn't want to think of. "Chopper here in one minute, keep under cover until it arrives." He needed to keep his team informed there was help on the way. He knew they would be frustrated at not being able to rush to Gav's aid, but they all knew to do so would be suicide.

ON THE HILLSIDE overlooking Mac's team the rest of the ambush team could hear the approaching helicopter echoing around the valley. They would stand no chance if it was one of the American Apache or Warthog helicopter gunships coming towards them. The gun on the front of either of those helicopters could fire hundreds of rounds each minute and could cut a man in half. Better to retreat and fight another day than be target practice for the Americans. They thought they had killed one foreign soldier, a victory even if only a small one. None of them gave the little boy a thought. They picked up their guns and spare ammunition then disappeared into the hills.

AFTER THE ARRIVAL of the helicopter Mac thought it was safe enough to move his team. Not knowing the extent of Gav's injuries, they had to get to his aid as soon as possible. "Smithy, can you get to him?" he shouted.

"On my way guv," Smithy replied. Covered by Taff on the lower slopes and Mac and Jock above Smithy scrambled across the hillside to where Gav lay, his efforts unleashing another small avalanche of rocks and stones down the hillside into the valley below. Breathing hard after the struggle to get to his injured colleague Smithy knelt next to Gav. Placing his fingers on his friend's neck he checked for a pulse. Shouting into his helmet mic over the noise of the helicopter overhead he gave Mac an update on Gav's condition. "He's alive guv, but it's difficult to see how badly injured he is. He's covered in blood and bits of the boy's body."

With the helicopter gunship giving cover overhead Mac and Jock worked their way down the hill to where Gav lay.

Mac took his canteen and gently poured water over Gav's face cleaning it of the worst of the dust and blood the blast had left on him. "Mac, my foot," Gav groaned. He tried to push himself up to see the extent of his injuries, but Mac put a hand on his shoulder stopping him from leaning forward.

"Let us deal with this Gav, just relax and everything will be okay." Mac looked down at Gav's legs, covered in dust and blood any assessment of his injuries was impossible. As gently as he could Mac brushed away as much of the debris the blast had left on him as he could. The right leg of Gav's uniform had been shredded and Mac could see exposed bone and lumps of flesh missing from around his ankle. From his training he knew he needed to reassure his friend and keep him calm. "Don't worry, we'll get you out of here as soon as we can."

"I can't feel my right leg Mac, is my foot still there?" A tear slowly trickled down the side of Gav's face through the dust Mac hadn't washed away.

"Yes, it's still there Gav. The medics will be here soon, they'll look after you." He moved away from his injured friend and spoke into his helmet mic. "We need a Medivac chopper here now. One man down with a badly injured right leg and possibly other multiple blast injuries."

"Already done, they'll be here in two minutes," the navigator in the personnel carrier replied.

While Mac was getting an update on the helicopter Smithy tended to his friend. He took what painkillers they had in the field kit and injected them into Gav's arm. "How bad is it Smithy?" Gav asked.

"Well you won't be running the London Marathon this year mate, but the medics will be here soon, they'll see you right."

"Maybe next year then?"

Smithy gently placed his hand Gav's shoulder. "Yes, maybe next year," he said trying to keep his voice steady. He looked away not wanting his friend to see the tears coursing down his face.

Right on time the helicopter appeared and landed on the road between the personnel carrier and the landslide. The door slid open and two medics jumped out, crouching to avoid the wash from the rotor blades they ran through the swirling dust, carrying a stretcher towards where Gav lay on the hillside. As soon as they were clear the helicopter rose back into the sky in a cloud of dust.

"Where are they going?" Mac shouted to one of the medics over the noise of the helicopter.

"Don't worry he'll be back as soon as we have the casualty stable and ready to go to hospital. The helicopter is too much of a target sitting on the road."

They treated Gav's injuries as best they could in the field, pumped him full of morphine and rigged up a drip to pump fluids into his body. With Smithy and Mac's help, the medics put him on a stretcher and carried him back to the road. Right on cue the medivac helicopter reappeared and landed on the spot from where it had taken off minutes before. The stretcher crew shielded Gav from the blast of dust and stones as it landed, once Gav was loaded aboard the medics jumped in and pulled the door closed. The helicopter rose once more into the clear blue-sky leaving Mac and his team crouched on the slope trying to avoid the dust and stones whipped up by its rotor blades.

Although they'd all trained for and heard about these types of attacks it was still a shock to see one of their colleagues injured like this, not to mention the small boy Gav was handing the chocolate bar to when the bomb was detonated. Mac thought they'd been lucky, his team had been involved in combat situations on many occasions, but they'd never been involved first-hand in roadside bomb explosion, most of the other units back at the camp had. Hard as it was after witnessing their friend being injured Mac needed to take charge and get his team back to the safety of the camp.

"Okay lads, let's go home." Mac watched his team wearily climb into the personnel carrier to begin the ride back to base, desperate to be away from the scene of the nightmare they had just lived through.

It was a sombre return journey, a complete contrast to the outward leg. The high spirits and witty banter they'd exchanged earlier replaced by a stony silence. As the personnel carrier slowly made its way out of the hills each of them stared at the rifle and dust-covered helmet Jock had placed on the seat Gav had occupied on the outward journey, a poignant reminder of their missing colleague. The enormity of what they had just experienced was slowly dawning on each of them. They were all in a state of shock.

Covered by the American gunship overhead the personnel carrier made its way out of the hills then joined the road to the base and medical centre where the thoughts of each man in the back of the vehicle were.

When they arrived at the camp Mac asked Jock to take his kit back to their accommodation then quickly made his way to the medical centre to check on Gav. After finding the surgical ward he was informed that Gav was still in surgery, he would have to wait for the doctor performing the emergency operation before they knew anything. He sat impatiently for an hour in the waiting area going over in his mind how he could have done things differently to avoid this outcome. Eventually, the surgeon emerged from the operating suite still wearing his scrubs. Mac stood and approached him. "How is he doc?"

"Too early to tell at the moment I'm afraid, but it doesn't look good. He's lost a lot of tissue around his lower right leg and there's considerable damage to the bones and nerves around his right ankle. We'll make him as comfortable as possible then get him on a plane home for more surgery, but I must say I think he'll be lucky not to lose his foot. He's a very fortunate young man, being so close to an explosion like that I would expect injuries far worse than he has. Other than the damage to his leg he only has a few minor cuts and bruises. He's temporarily lost some hearing but that should come back in the next few days."

Mac's shoulders dropped. It was the news he feared, but after seeing Gav's injuries for himself thought the surgeon's prognosis inevitable. It was certainly not what he wanted to hear, especially on his last day of active service. "Thanks Doc," he said trying to sound sincere. He closed his eyes for a moment and thought of the poor little boy. The doctor didn't know that it wasn't only luck that had saved Gav's life. The little lad standing in front of him had taken the full force of the blast and it had been him more than anything else that had saved Gav.

As he made his way back to their accommodation Mac wondered how his team would take the news. Like him they probably feared the worst. After years of serving together they were an especially tight knit team and he felt terrible to be leaving them at a time he felt they would need him most, he just hoped they would be able to get over this after he left in the morning.

Self-doubt filled Mac's mind. Would his team have the

same doubts as him? Was it his fault Gav was lying in a hospital bed, possibly maimed for the rest of his life? There would never be a good day for this to happen but why did it have to happen on the last day of his active service? He walked towards the team's accommodation self-doubt continuing to swirl around his mind.

A blast of cool air from the air conditioning greeted him as he opened the door. Sitting on their bunks Mac's team looked at him expectantly as he stepped into the room. Reluctantly he gave them the bad news. "It's not good news I'm afraid lads. They're sending Gav home for more surgery. The Doc thinks he may lose his right foot."

"Bollocks." Smithy threw a towel onto his bed. "The sooner we get home the better. I'm fed up with this bloody country. I don't want to be sent home with bits of me still over here, or what's left of me scraped together and put in a box. These people don't want us here and we don't want to be here. Why don't the politicians just bring us home?"

"He's alive Smithy, that's the main thing. It's a miracle it was only his leg. Think of that poor little boy, his parents will be devastated. You know the medics can do wonders now. Once they get Gav home, he'll be as right as rain." Mac was trying to lift his team's spirits by sounding confident, but it was a confidence he didn't feel.

Jock stepped forward, towering over Mac who was now sitting on his bunk. "Mac, this is your last day here. I know none of us feel like celebrating but I'm sure Gav would want us to take a wee dram with you before you set off home. I think it would do us all good and help take our minds off what happened out there for a little while. And while we're there we can take a dram to wish Gav good luck. We probably won't see him before they fly him out."

Mac looked around the rest of his team. They all looked at him expectantly. "I think you're right. Just give me time to have a shower and get changed then we can head over to the mess." He picked up a towel from his bunk and headed for the showers.

Smithy was already heading for the door, "I'll see you there, I need a drink now," he said as he disappeared through the door.

Mac turned and looked at the others, "Jock, can you go with him please, and keep him out of trouble. You know what he's like when he's had a few. I'll be there as soon as I've cleaned up."

2

The following day Mac woke with a thick head, not ideal for the long journey he faced. Despite the circumstances he'd enjoyed the last night he would spend with his team while serving in the army. He packed his few belongings and looked around the hut. Scattered around the accommodation were a few pictures of the loved ones waiting for them to return, but no real creature comforts. This place may have been their home for the last few months, but he knew he wouldn't miss it.

It was a day Mac didn't think he would ever have looked forward to, the day he would start his journey home to leave the army, but after the previous day's traumatic events, he knew the time was right.

Mac had joined the army as a young man straight out of university, full of enthusiasm and ready to serve his country. For twelve years the army had been his life, almost like family, but now he was disillusioned and tired. Disillusioned by politicians who sent them to fight a war most of them didn't believe in. Tired of fighting for the right equipment to fight those wars. Tired of having to justify what he did to those who believed the politicians were wrong to send the troops abroad to fight. Tired of seeing young men like Gav badly injured, or worse, fighting that war, and tired of seeing innocent people like the young boy on the road killed. He shook hands with each of his team and left to see his commanding officer before heading for the helicopter ride back to the main airport.

Like all the other commanding officers serving at the camp Mac's commander was a man under pressure, and not one for small talk. He wished Mac good luck and shook his hand. Mac turned and headed for the door. "Oh, one last thing Mac," his commander said stopping him in his tracks. "You'll have company on the trip back to base, they're flying Gav home with you, at least as far as Cyprus."

Overnight more doubt had crept into Mac's mind. Had he done the right thing on the road yesterday? Had he put his team in unnecessary danger? Had his team's relaxed mood in the personnel carrier taken his focus off the job? Had he been complacent because it was his last day? Were Gav's injuries his fault? Did his team now look at him as a liability and were glad someone else was taking his place, someone who wouldn't take chances with their lives? Was his team having the same doubts about his leadership abilities as he was? So many questions swirled around his mind, none of which he had answers to. Self-doubt and questions repeatedly ran around his head. Gav's presence would be a painful reminder of yesterday's terrible events during the long hours they would spend together travelling to Cyprus.

Mac left his commander's office and headed for the helicopter. When he arrived at the helipad the medical team were loading Gav aboard. Once they'd made him comfortable one of the nurses turned to Mac. "You'll have to squeeze into the back I'm afraid sir, this one takes priority." As he watched the medical team set up a drip for his injured friend Mac was pleased to see Gav was asleep. Once they were all on board, safely buckled up and the pre-flight checks completed the helicopter rose into the clear blue sky.

CROUCHED in the hills above the base Omar lifted the binoculars to his eyes. Shrouded in a cloud of dust a helicopter slowly rose from the compound, it banked slowly, then turned towards him. He continued to watch as it flew directly overhead and faded into the distance.

HIGH ABOVE THE HILLS, Mac looked out of the helicopter window. Far below he thought he saw a glint of sunlight reflecting off a glass surface below and what looked like a man crouched behind a rocky outcrop. When he reached the airport he would contact his commanding officer to let him know what he thought he'd seen on the hillside overlooking the base. He hoped today would be the last he saw of this godforsaken country. He wanted nothing more to do with it or its people. He made a promise to himself, when he got home, he would keep an eye on Gav's progress and do everything he could to make sure his friend made a smooth transition into civvy street, whichever way his surgery and recuperation went.

AFTER ANOTHER LONG day exposed to the fierce sunlight watching the army base from the hills Omar wearily made his way back to the compound where he and his family now lived. Their house was no more than a hut, constructed from bricks fashioned many years ago from the red clay of the surrounding hills. He pushed open the door to what his family now called home. Two rooms for himself, his wife, and their son. It was far from the relative luxury they'd once enjoyed in their former lives when they lived in Pakistan.

He hid his rifle under the mattress laid on the ground and gave his son a hug. After what he'd seen happen to the little boy on the road the day before, a boy no older than his own son, he wondered if he was doing the right thing fighting this war. Could any cause justify the death of an innocent young child? Hakim had seen the boy walking along the road just as he had, but despite Omar's pleading, he didn't hesitate before pressing the detonator button. He knew there was no chance the boy would survive, but he went ahead regardless. The little boy was invisible to him. Their target, the foreign soldier, was all he could see. Omar held his precious child close for a moment longer than he usually would, the memory of the young boy on the road still fresh in his mind. His thoughts went out to the little boy's family. He'd come back to his homeland to drive the foreign army out not to kill innocent children of his fellow countrymen.

Omar and his family lived in a small community inhabited mostly by other freedom fighters. Its remote location meant it was far enough from the beaten track to be out of range of the foreign soldier's patrols. There were occasional flyovers by jets and helicopters but, because of the distance to the foreign army's base, there had never been a visit by one of their patrols. Among the people living in the village were a few elders who'd fought in the earlier war against the Russians, a couple of goat herders, and one man who grew poppies in the fertile valley fields as well as tending his goats. The remainder of the inhabitants were freedom fighters, most of whom were from abroad.

Having his family with him made Omar unusual in the camp. Most of the men fighting the foreign army were single and much younger than himself, only two other fighters in the compound had their families with them as he did. The men spent most days sitting in the shade talking and drinking tea, plotting ambushes, coordinating the rendezvous to pick up more guns and ammunition, and making the explosive devices such as the one they believed had killed the soldier the previous day.

Each week the camp was paid a visit by a team of men in jeeps who held meetings with the leader of their group. They brought arms, explosives, and money for the camp's living expenses. Omar assumed these visits were to plan strategy and co-ordinate attacks with other groups, but the longer he lived in the camp the more he wondered where the money came from. If these men were funding the groups fighting the foreign army the amounts of money they were handing out each week was staggering. The group he was part of wasn't generating any income and none of the other groups he knew of were either, so where was this money coming from?

Like all the other small communities in the surrounding hills Omar's group had basic needs that could only be satisfied by a visit to a bigger town. To satisfy those needs tasks were delegated on a rota system to all those living in the group, but many of the young men refused to take their allotted turn. They saw it as women's work, not befitting brave men fighting for the freedom of their country. The one chore on the rota Omar hated was the market, but he knew it was the only way to ensure his family was well fed. They would all go hungry if he and the other older members of their community didn't take the younger men's turn.

The market was always hot and crowded, the produce limited compared to what was available from the supermarkets his family was accustomed to in their former life in Karachi, and the walk to and from the market was a long and usually hot one. Once again it was Omar's turn to visit the market and as always, whenever his turn came around, he would take his wife and son with him. With so many hot-headed young men around he didn't want to take a chance leaving them alone in the compound while he was away buying the camps provisions.

As usual, the market and the roads leading to it were crowded, people jostling to reach the stalls oblivious of those around them. As they approached the town Omar sat his son on his shoulders, he felt the safest place for him was above the crowd. In his mind's eye he could still see the small boy reaching out a hand for the chocolate bar being offered by the soldier before Hakim pressed the button taking the boy's life and carrying the soldier down the hillside to what he assumed to be his death. He would do anything to protect his son.

The market square was hot, dusty and chaotic, full of people pushing their way through the crowds trying to reach stalls before the limited produce on offer was gone. Traders shouted above the noise of the crowd trying to attract customers, frightened animals added to the cacophony. A group of fighters moved amongst the crowd trying to recruit more men to their cause. Carrying guns and with spare ammunition slung across their shoulders they were easily identified amongst the crowd. Omar did his best to avoid them, steering his family away from men he considered dangerous not only to the enemy but also to the very people they were supposed to be fighting for. Some were fanatics, willing to pick a fight with anyone and everyone, even those already fighting for the same cause as themselves.

Omar and his family moved around the market as quickly as the crowds would allow and, after buying the provisions the camp needed for the next few days, they set off on the long journey back to the compound.

The roads out of the market were more crowded than when they'd arrived earlier that morning, latecomers streaming in as those who'd arrived early were trying to leave. Men pushing handcarts bringing produce late to their stalls and donkeys carrying heavier loads adding to the congestion. The chaos was worsened by jeeps crowded with fighters occasionally firing guns into the air, causing more bottlenecks on the already congested streets.

Feeling a sense of growing panic beginning to overwhelm him Omar was desperate to get his family away from the chaos. Although he was around death and destruction each time he went out as part of the ambush team he never wanted to place his wife and son in any kind of danger. He needed to get his family away from this crowd and particularly the young men in their jeeps. He was certain these men would eventually bring trouble to everyone in the market, and on the roads that led to it.

With his son still on his shoulders safely above the crowds, and laden down with provisions, it was hard to make any kind of progress but Omar, followed by his wife holding on to his belt, gradually fought his way through the crowds towards the exit from the market. Soon they were outside the town on the road leading home. Surrounded by a small group of people headed along the same stretch of road Omar felt a sense of relief, his family were away from the crowds and more importantly away from the hot-headed young men in jeeps. They would soon be back at the compound, safe in the humble building they called home.

They walked on in the blazing sun carrying the provisions the compound needed. Through the heat haze Omar could see two jeeps parked across the road ahead, young men standing with rifles casually held at the ready. Another militia checkpoint he thought, not unusual in these parts. As they approached a helicopter flew overhead, some of the young men raised their rifles firing wildly into the air. Omar watched as the helicopter banked steeply and flew into the distance. The men in the jeeps continued firing into the air, shouting in triumph, although what that triumph was Omar wasn't quite sure.

After watching the helicopter disappear the group returned their gaze to the road and continued to approach the roadblock. As they neared the jeeps two of the young men stepped forward raising their guns to stop the group approaching any further. Overhead Omar heard the screech of a jet engine, out of nowhere a huge explosion engulfed everyone on the road.

3

Blinding sunlight streamed through the window silhouetting a man standing next to the hospital bed. Omar slowly opened his eyes, blinking rapidly as he became accustomed to the bright sunlight and his unfamiliar surroundings. As his sight gradually returned, he could see the man standing beside him was dressed in a dirty white gown with a stethoscope hung around his neck.

The doctor looked up from his notes, realising Omar was finally coming out of the coma he'd been in for the last two days. "Hello, my friend," he said, "can you hear me?"

"Yes, I can hear you" Omar croaked, barely audible. "Where am I?"

"You are in the Kandahar field hospital awaiting transfer back to your home, wherever that may be." The doctor gently lifted Omar's head and held a bottle of water to his lips. "Please drink, it will help you."

After quenching his thirst Omar looked around the makeshift hospital ward. "Where is my family?" he asked. The beds he could see were fully occupied, some of the less fortunate patients were laid on thin mattresses scattered around the floor, some had blankets, many did not. Omar could see no sign of his wife and son.

"I'm sorry to have to tell you this my friend, but you were the only survivor of the attack."

Omar stared at the doctor in disbelief, unable to take in what he was being told, stunned to hear such devastating news. He turned his head away to hide his grief from the doctor standing beside his bed. He was supposed to be a fearless warrior, to show no emotion, but if what the doctor said was correct his beloved wife and son were both dead. What kind of man could show no emotion when his loved ones had been taken from him? Their deaths were as much his fault as the men flying the plane that had dropped the bomb. If only the young hotheads manning the roadblock hadn't fired at the passing helicopter none of this would have happened. It had achieved nothing other than the deaths of innocent people on their way home from the market.

Omar's wife had never wanted to leave Pakistan. She had pleaded with him to reconsider when he'd told her of his decision to leave his job at the bank and head for Afghanistan, but he would not be moved. As a young boy, he'd made a promise to return to the land of his birth if it ever needed him, a now he was fulfilling that promise.

Omar could still remember his father ruffling his hair when he'd told him of his promise. "By the time you are old enough to fight the Russians will be gone Omar," his father had said. "Over the centuries many foreign armies have invaded our land, eventually they all tire of the fight and return to their own countries."

His father had been proved correct; the Russians had left only to be replaced by another foreign army years later. Omar had ignored his wife's pleas and honoured his promise to return and fight. The good life his family had once enjoyed in Karachi, the promising career Omar had at the bank, the small house they owned were all gone. And now the people he held most dear, his wife and his son, were also gone, all because of his stubbornness.

MANY YEARS BEFORE, Omar's father had stood beside his patient's bed just as this man was standing next to his. As a doctor his father had worked in the main hospital in the capital Kabul. He made no distinction between who he treated. The sick and injured all needed his help and he was happy to give it, no matter what their political allegiance or religious beliefs. As a young boy Omar was fascinated by medicine. His father often took him to the hospital where he would sit silently at the side of the ward watching him work. But when the Russian invaders arrived everything changed. Soon after the tanks rumbled into the city a Russian officer arrived at the hospital and accused his father of treating the child of a suspected Mujahideen fighter. His father protested his innocence, he told the Russian that he made no distinction between who he treated, he didn't know or care if his patient was the Russian's friend or foe, the child was his patient and needed medical treatment therefore he would tend to her needs. Omar watched in horror as the Russian officer stepped forward and slapped his father across the face, humiliating him in front of his staff and onlooking son. His father pleaded that his patient was an innocent child who was not involved in the war, but the Russian officer would not listen.

"You will only treat comrades who are fighting to rid your country of this scum. If I find that you have been treating the enemy or any of their families, I will see to it that you never work in medicine again." He picked the young girl from her bed and headed for the door.

In the room outside the ward a young man sat anxiously waiting to hear from the doctor how his daughter's treatment was progressing. He was startled when a Russian officer burst through the doors carrying what he thought may be his daughter. Stunned by the sudden appearance of the Russian carrying a child the young man hesitated a moment before jumping from his chair to follow the officer. That hesitation would prove to be a defining moment in the young man's life. Before he could react the Russian carried the young girl through the main doors, he stopped at the top of the steps for a moment before letting the girl fall from his arms and down the steps in front of the hospital.

The young man rushed past the officer to comfort the young girl. Taking his distraught child in his arms he slowly climbed the steps to confront the Russian.

"How dare you treat my child like this," he said. "What kind of man treats an innocent child so brutally? Have you no compassion? She's being treated in this hospital for an unknown sickness. You are nothing but an animal."

The Russian officer fixed the young man with an icy stare for a moment, a stare full of contempt. "Don't ever speak to me again. Take your child and leave while you still can. If I ever see you here again, I will have you and the rest of your family arrested. You are an enemy of the state, a terrorist, fighting against your own people. You should be ashamed of yourself." He waited for the young man to follow his orders to take his child and leave, but he remained staring at him, a stare full of hatred. After waiting for a few seconds, the Russian stepped forward and shoved the young man in the chest pushing him back down the hospital steps.

Cradling his sick and injured child at the roadside the young man looked up to see the Russian staring at him, a grin on his face. After a moment he turned and disappeared through the hospital doors. The young man vowed that whatever it took, and however long it took, he would avenge the treatment he and his daughter had been subjected to. One day this man would pay for the pain he'd inflicted on his daughter and the humiliation on himself.

Each day for the next week the Russian returned to the hospital determined to find enemy fighters or their families among the doctor's patients. Each day he found nothing. Omar's father was becoming increasingly desperate and frustrated. He pleaded with the hospital authorities to consult the Russian officer's commanders. He needed to treat the sick and injured, whether they were involved in the war or not and regardless of which side of the struggle they may be fighting on. But his superiors told him to follow the Russian's orders, orders that were from much higher in the Russian army, ones they had no influence over. Short of drugs and modern equipment, much needed investment from the Russian government was dependent on the hospital not treating patients that were viewed as the enemy. The officer in question had the final say on who could and could not be treated.

But Omar's father would not stop. Secretly he treated anyone who needed him, sometimes in a quiet area of the hospital, sometimes smuggling drugs from the pharmacy to treat patients at their homes. Suspecting Omar's father was secretly treating enemy patients the Russian had him followed. Each time he was caught the officer would beat him and humiliate him in front of the nurses before throwing his patient out of the hospital. Eventually the beatings and humiliation became too much, his father could take no more. A beaten and broken man, he decided he must take his family and leave the land they called home, he had to distance himself from these men who had no compassion. Omar and his family joined the other four million refugees fleeing the land of their birth looking for refuge in neighbouring countries. For his family it would be the long and dangerous trek to Pakistan.

THE DOCTOR STANDING at his bedside gently shook Omar by the shoulder. "Are you all right?" he asked. Still drowsy from whatever drugs he'd been given Omar slowly came around. He felt a sudden pain shoot up his right arm as he tried to pull himself up. He lifted it from under the filthy single sheet to reveal a bloody bandaged stump. His arm had been amputated just below the elbow. Omar stared in horror. How could this be happening to him? First his family and now this. Piece by piece his world was slowly falling apart.

"There was nothing we could do to save your arm I'm afraid. I'm sorry but we did everything we could. We'll continue to give you what medicine we have but you will need to be moved soon. There's been a major offensive and we are expecting more casualties, what beds we have will be badly needed." The doctor made a note on the clipboard he was holding, returned it to the end of Omar's bed then walked away to treat his next patient.

Omar dragged himself up. His memory was hazy, but he

could remember walking along the side of a dusty road with his wife and son on the way home from the local market with food for the compound. Overhead he'd heard the roar of a jet engine before everything went black. There must have been at least twenty people on that stretch of road as they'd approached the roadblock. Surely, they can't all have been killed, he thought. Someone must know more than the doctor. He couldn't leave without being sure of the fate of his beloved wife and son.

For the next two days, Omar sat in the hospital grounds watching the constant stream of vehicles bringing new casualties to the hospital. The dilapidated building was already full to capacity and he knew he would soon be moved on, but he had to confirm what the doctor had told him about his family before he was forced to leave. He asked questions about the fate of those who'd been with him on the road that day to anyone who would talk to him. Eventually he came to the crushing conclusion, the doctor was correct, everyone on the road that day had been killed. Everyone except him.

Five days after arriving at the hospital, devastated by the realisation that his family was gone, Omar climbed onto the back of a flatbed truck to begin the long journey back to Pakistan. The same painful journey he'd made as a boy was beginning again, but this time he would be travelling without his family. As the truck slowly made its way out of the hospital grounds memories of the journey he'd made with his mother, father and brother all those years ago came flooding back. Chased out of their own country by invaders from the West, his father a broken man, his mother and brother Salman crying for what seemed like most of the journey. Though still only a boy he vowed that one day, when he was a man, if his country ever needed him, he would return and fight. He had answered that call and now he, like his father before him, was fleeing his homeland a broken man.

Three other casualties accompanied Omar in the back of the truck for the journey home, all of whom had injuries much worse than his. They made slow progress over the bumpy, dusty terrain, often stopping to remove obstacles in their path and to negotiate progress at the numerous impromptu checkpoints set up by the various local militias. Money and goods often changed hands to ensure their safe passage. The days were scorching, spent on the hard floor of the truck in the full glare of the fierce sun, the wounded men groaned in agony as they were jolted around while they made their way along the bumpy roads. The nights were freezing, the thin hospital blankets they'd been given were no match for the biting cold.

Looking around his travelling companions Omar knew they wouldn't all survive. Two of his fellow passengers were far too badly injured to make such an arduous journey and two days after leaving the hospital his fears were confirmed, one of the casualties succumbed to his wounds. The driver and guard dumped his lifeless body at the side of the road. There was no ceremony, no words to their god for the man who'd given his life fighting for the freedom of their country. Their passengers were nothing more than cargo, something to be delivered, after which they could return to the hospital where their next cargo would be waiting.

Progress was slow and the days dragged on, each seemingly the same as the day before. With so much time on his hands, Omar began to reflect on his life and wondered, if he survived the journey, what the future would hold for a man with only one arm? Before being recruited to the cause he'd worked in Karachi's business district in international banking and finance and had lived in a good neighbourhood not far from his brother and his family. He had no option but to ask for their help and support once he reached the city. He was sure they would help him just as he had when they'd asked for his help.

SIX YEARS earlier Omar's brother had asked to meet him outside the local mosque after Friday prayers. His daughter Hadia was the brightest pupil in the local school but was finding it difficult to secure a place at one of the city's many Universities. The country had come a long way, but most institutions were still run by men who clung to the old ways, one where women were seen as second class citizens and should be grateful for the small amount of education they were now grudgingly given. Hadia desperately wanted to go to university to study business and computer sciences, but if she couldn't find a place in one of Karachi's universities, her only option seemed to be a university abroad, and she longed to study in either America or Britain where she could experience a culture different to her own. Salman couldn't afford the fees but knew his brother Omar could, he was Hadia's last hope of a university education. Salman explained Hadia's dilemma and after five minutes consideration, Omar agreed to fund her study abroad. It would not be in the USA, the fees were too high, but in England. Hadia, with due deference, promised that she would study hard, get a good degree and on her return, once a good job her degree would secure was found, would repay her uncle every penny.

The following year having secured a place at the University of Leeds Hadia, her father, mother, uncle, aunt and cousin met in the departure lounge of Karachi International Airport. Emotional farewells were exchanged as she went through to departures for the twelve-hour trip to London's Heathrow airport. She turned to wave a final farewell to her family as she approached the passport control gate. The money her uncle could afford for her education abroad did not stretch to visits home during university breaks. It would be three long years before Hadia would see her family again.

Nothing Hadia had seen or experienced at home prepared her for the sights she would see over the next three years in a city so alien to her. Scantily clad women drunkenly staggering around the city, even in the depths of winter. Men in a similar state but wearing a few more clothes, although most of the younger ones seemed to wear shorts all year round even in the biting cold of winter. Fighting on the streets. Men leering at her and telling her to go back to where she had come from. Behaviour totally alien to her which would never be tolerated back in her homeland. It was behaviour that shocked and sickened her. In Hadia's culture strangers were welcomed and respected. She kept her head down, kept to a small group of friends, mainly from a similar background as herself, studied hard and achieved a first in her chosen subject. Relieved that her long ordeal overseas was over she boarded the train to London at the start of her journey home. As she took her seat on the plane at Heathrow, she vowed she would never return to this godforsaken country.

Hadia arrived home to an emotional welcome to match that of her departure. Everyone who was present to wish her good luck when she left was there to greet her on her return. Now she set about the not inconsiderable task of finding a job. Like students all over the world, she applied for everything she thought she was suitable for, but she got little or no response to her applications. It seemed that nothing had changed since she'd left. Despite having qualifications far better than most of her male counterparts the old guard still held a tight grip on who was recruited to what they perceived to be the most influential jobs. Inevitably the best jobs were always given to men.

Reluctantly Hadia accepted a job as a junior computer analyst in a local bank, a job she was vastly overqualified for. She thought that if she accepted the job offer and worked hard to impress her new employers maybe they would see her potential and promote her to a role more suited to her qualifications and abilities. But she was wrong. After two months she knew everything there was to know about the job and was keen to progress, but despite her pleading, she was told by her manager that she should be grateful for having this job. There was no point in promoting her as she was *only a woman* and soon she would be married and leaving to have a family. She realised there was no chance to advance her career in her current job but there seemed to be no other employers out there willing to give her a chance. Frustrated that her capabilities and knowledge were not being fully utilised, and with no prospect of promotion Hadia continued to apply for other positions she felt qualified for, but for the foreseeable future, she was stuck in a dead-end job.

4

Omar's long journey home in the back of the truck dragged on. Hot days followed by freezing nights, barely any food or water, each day a repeat of the last. As they climbed into the mountains another of the wounded passengers succumbed to his injuries. The men from the cab carried his body to the side of the road then threw it into the raging river in the valley below. Once again there was no ceremony. It was one more piece of cargo they wouldn't have to deliver.

As the men climbed back into the cab Omar looked across the bed of the truck to his last remaining travelling companion. He realised how little they'd spoken to each other during the journey, something he put down to the shock caused by each of their injuries. He didn't even know the man's name.

"It looks like just the two of us now," he said. "My name is Omar. I'm returning to Karachi hoping my brother will help me after I was injured during the war," he lifted the stump of his right arm. "What's your name, my friend?"

The man looked at Omar with what he thought to be contempt in his eyes. "My name is Khalid. As you can see, I too have been injured in the holy war. I will return to Karachi to recuperate, but once I've recovered, I will return and continue the fight. I want nothing more than to feel a gun in my hands and to watch our bombs kill the foreign invaders. Seeing their comrades suffering saps the will of the other soldiers to stay and fight. We will drive them out and take back our lands."

The man became more animated as he spoke of the war. Omar recognised the type of man he was travelling with; he'd met his type before in Afghanistan. He was a fanatic, just like the men in the jeeps at the market and those at the roadblock where his family had been killed. A fanatic like Hakim with his cold dead eyes, the same eyes that were now staring at him from the other side of the truck. After their brief exchange it was clear that this man did not want to talk, his only interest was returning to the war and killing foreign soldiers. Omar sat back against the hard side of the truck, without a companion to talk with and pass the time it was going to be a long and lonely journey.

After days on the road they had fallen into a routine at each overnight stop. Khalid would start a fire, Omar collected wood and the driver and guard would prepare the meal. Early one evening as he returned to the camp with some more wood Omar overheard the driver and the guard talking.

"What use will they be to anyone? A couple of cripples, neither of them will ever work again and they'll be nothing but a burden to their families. I think we should do it tonight."

"I agree," the other said. "But we'll do it at first light, that way they can clear up and keep the fire going," they both laughed. "Then in the morning, once we've done it, we can set off for Kandahar. We can ditch their bodies in the river and share what's left of the money, no one will ever know. We'll be doing their families a favour."

After putting the wood he'd collected next to the fire Omar walked to the rear of the truck to tell Khalid what he'd overheard. Despite what he felt to be animosity and contempt towards him Omar couldn't leave this man to the fate their escorts had planned for them, and he thought their chances of survival were better together rather than alone. If they were to survive, they needed to escape before morning. "As soon as they're asleep we must leave," he said. "We need to get as far away from them as we can before they wake tomorrow."

Khalid looked at him doubtfully. "Are you sure that's what they said?" he asked looking back to where the driver and guard were preparing the meal. "We'll never get far enough away if we leave. It will be easy for them to find a couple of injured men like us on the roads in these hills. Look at us, a man with one arm and a man with one leg wandering the countryside. We won't last long out there without food and water," he pointed into the gathering gloom.

"Then I suggest we eat well tonight my friend. It may be the last good meal we have for some time."

They ate unusually well that night. A hearty meal for a condemned man, Omar thought while eating as much as he could. After the meal the driver returned to the truck's cab, re-appearing seconds later carrying a bottle of the Afghan spirit Zarbali. A potent drink made from fermented green raisins, highly illegal and dangerous if you were caught with it in your possession. They had used a couple of bottles as *baksheesh*, or bribe, at roadblocks on the journey but still had a few remaining in the cab. He called Omar over. "We'll be sleeping in the back of the truck tonight, we're fed up sleeping in the cab, it's too cramped and too uncomfortable. You two can sleep where you like, in the cab or on the ground, it's up to you." Omar thought their easiest way to escape would be to sleep outside, not that he had any intention of sleeping. They would slip away into the darkness as soon as their escorts were asleep. Hopefully, they would never see them again.

Omar joined his companion to talk over his plan. They kept themselves busy cleaning the cooking pots, searching for firewood and keeping the roaring fire well stocked. Wary that their escorts may change their minds and carry out their plan that night, they kept a distance between themselves the driver and the guard who had already finished one bottle of the potent spirit and were about to open another. Before long both driver and guard were feeling the effects of the strong alcohol and decided it was time for them to sleep. Warmed by the fire and alcohol they gathered their blankets from the cab and climbed unsteadily into the back of the truck.

Despite the driver and guard paying them no attention, Omar and Khalid went through the façade of laying their blankets on the ground and pretending to settle down for the night close to the roaring fire. It wasn't long before Omar could hear the two men in the back of the truck snoring loudly, both dead to the world.

Omar shook his companion by the shoulder. "Gather up the blankets," he whispered, "we'll need them in the hills. I'll get the rest of the things we need." He grabbed Khalid's hand and hauled him upright, handed him his crutch, then headed for the cab. If there was anything that might help them survive in the hills, he thought it would be in the front of the truck. Silently he opened the door and pulled himself onto the driver's seat. He searched the spartan interior but there seemed to be nothing that would be of any use to them. There was no food, they bought what they needed each day from roadside villages on the route. The only thing he thought that may be of use was the gun laying on the passenger's seat. He took the Kalashnikov and spare ammunition then slowly eased himself out of the truck. Leaving the door ajar he hoped with the interior light on all night the truck's battery would be drained and the engine wouldn't start in the morning. Omar unclipped the magazine from the gun, put it with the spare ammunition in his pocket and checked there was no round in the chamber. Satisfied the gun was unloaded, he walked towards the rear of the truck where Khalid was busy rolling up their blankets.

Omar looked into the flatbed of the truck where he could see the guard lying flat on his back snoring loudly. The fat roll of money he'd been using to buy food and pay for their safe passage was poking out of his pocket. He set the Kalashnikov down and pulled himself up onehanded on the side of the truck. Balancing himself carefully he gently removed the wad of cash from the sleeping man's pocket then silently lowered himself to the ground. The guard continued to snore loudly, oblivious of the fact he'd just been relieved of the money he intended to share with the driver once they'd dispatched the remaining cargo they were carrying. Omar stuffed the cash into his pocket, picked up the Kalashnikov and joined his companion.

"Why do we need the gun?" Khalid whispered, "it's just one more thing to carry and will slow us down. And where's the ammunition? The gun's no good without it. Did you leave it in the cab?"

"I'm not sure we do need it," Omar whispered, "I just don't want them to have it. I have the ammunition in my pockets. At least with this we can defend ourselves if they manage to find us."

"We need to get out of here as soon as possible," his companion said. "The more distance we put between us before they wake the better."

"One moment," Omar said. "I think there may be a way we can slow them down. Give me one of the blankets." He handed Khalid the gun and returned to the front of the truck. Kneeling beside the huge front wheel Omar pushed a twig into the valve of the front tyre. Covering the valve with the blanket to muffle the sound of escaping air he waited until the wheel rested on the ground, the tyre completely deflated. Encouraged by his success Omar moved to the other side of the truck and repeated the task. A few minutes later he returned to his companion. "That should slow them down a little," he whispered. "Now let's go."

The unlikely pair stumbled into the darkness, away from the two men asleep in the back of the truck and the fate they had planned for them in the morning.

Avoiding the road in the hope of evading the truck and it's occupants Omar and his companion walked slowly through the hills. He knew they wouldn't last long in the scorching heat of the day and freezing cold of the night. Already weakened by their injuries they would need food and water and shelter from the elements if they were to survive.

On the second day of walking through the countryside, just as he began to believe they would never find their way out of the hills Omar spotted a herd of goats in the distance. If there were goats, he thought, there would be someone tending to them. Maybe not with them now but someone who would return before sunset to take them back to wherever they would be safe. Omar and Khalid reached the herd and settled down in the shade of a tree to wait for whoever was tending the herd to arrive.

"You know we should have shot those two while they were asleep in the back of the truck," Khalid said. "If we had we wouldn't be wandering around these hills looking for food and shelter. We would have been doing to them what they planned to do to us in the morning. We could have disposed of their bodies just as they did with those men who died of their injuries, then we could have driven the truck to Karachi ourselves and disappeared once we arrived."

Omar's suspicions were confirmed. He'd recognized Khalid as a fanatic the first time he'd spoken to him. He was relieved he hadn't given him any ammunition with the gun while he was deflating the tyres, if he had he would have killed the driver and guard.

"Aren't you tired of all of the killing Khalid?" Omar asked. "I want to get away from that. All the people killed in this war probably have families waiting for them at home, do you ever think of them? While we were in Afghanistan we were fighting for a noble cause, not committing murder. I don't want to be responsible for any more unnecessary deaths." Omar's mind flashed back to the little boy on the road reaching out for what the soldier was offering before their bomb was detonated. Not for the first time he felt the guilt of the boy's death wash over him.

Khalid looked at Omar with the same stone cold, dead eyes as the group's bomb maker. Omar knew he'd made no impression on him. As far as Khalid was concerned there was no unnecessary killing in their war.

They sat under a tree in the late afternoon sun.

Exhausted and hungry after their long walk through the hills Khalid dozed off. Much as Omar would have liked to join him, he knew this could be their last chance to find shelter before the elements did to them what the truck driver and guard had intended. He had to be awake when the herd's keeper arrived.

As the sun began to sink below the hills in the west an old man came into view. Carrying a shepherd's crook he could be nobody but the herd's owner. Omar stood and approached the shepherd. "Salam my friend, I hope I haven't startled you." He pointed to his companion asleep under the tree. "We are two wounded men returning from the war in need of food and shelter, would you be willing to help us?"

Surprised to see anyone in the hills the shepherd looked Omar up and down then glanced over to the man asleep under the tree. "Salam my friend," he finally said. "You must be a long way from home, no one ever passes through these hills. Of course, I will help you. I too fought the invaders but that was many years ago, it was the Russians then, but foreign invaders are all the same. Will they never learn? Our country is not like their own and will never be ruled by foreigners. Will they ever understand that trying to impose their ways on us will never work.

"Follow me and I'll take you back to my home. It's humble but warm, a shelter from the elements out here in the hills. We will eat well tonight, you both look like you need it." He pointed his shepherds crook to Khalid still sleeping under the tree. "You may want to wake your friend, or he may be there all night. I need to get my goats back home before it gets too dark to see the trail." He turned to gather his herd then started back down the track he'd emerged from.

Omar ran back to Khalid and shook him awake. He

pulled him upright before he could come to his senses. "Quick," he said handing him his crutch, "we have food and shelter for the night, follow me."

When they arrived at the shepherd's home, he opened the door gesturing Omar and Khalid inside. "While I make sure my goats are safe for the night make yourself at home. If you could light a fire, you'll find tea on the shelf. I'll be back soon and will cook us a meal."

Two hours later they were sat on the floor of the shepherd's home eating the hearty meal he'd prepared. "Thank you for taking us in, giving us shelter and feeding us," Omar said. "I don't think we could have survived much longer in these hills if we hadn't found you. We were travelling from Afghanistan with two other men in a truck. They may be looking for us and if they find us, they'll kill us. If you see them, please tell them you haven't seen us."

"Don't worry, you'll be safe here. They'll never know you're here if you stay inside." After eating and clearing away the cooking pots they sat around the fire, Omar and the shepherd recounted their experiences in the wars, experiences that struck Omar to be similar despite the time difference between them. Omar tried to include Khalid in the conversation, but he didn't seem interested, only muttering a few one-word answers. As the evening grew late the shepherd said he would be making an early start in the morning, he needed to take his goats to new pastures on the other side of the valley, so it was time he got some sleep.

When Omar woke the next morning, the shepherd was gone. Khalid continued to sleep while he wrestled with the problem of how they would get to Karachi. There was no way they could walk such a distance, and they couldn't stay with the shepherd indefinitely. As he sat wondering the sound of a truck approaching disturbed the quiet of the hills. Omar shifted the corner of what looked like an old sack used as a curtain and looked out of the dirty window. The truck they'd been travelling in was lumbering up the hill towards them. His plan to drain the battery had failed and they'd obviously managed to inflate the tyres. He picked up the gun he'd taken from the truck and clicked one of the ammunition magazines into place.

The sound of Omar racking a round into the chamber woke Khalid. "What's going on?" he asked.

"The truck's coming up the road towards us," Omar replied.

"Give me the gun." Khalid held out a hand expecting Omar to hand it over. "You can't handle it with only one arm."

Fearing what Khalid would do after telling him what he would have done while he was deflating the tyres Omar was reluctant to hand the gun over. "Let's wait and see what happens, maybe they'll leave without us having to use it."

Seeing the truck coming up the hill the shepherd led his goats across the road deliberately bringing it to a halt before it reached his home and the men the occupants were looking for. The passenger door opened, and the guard climbed out.

Omar could see the shepherd shake his head, he waved his arms around then pointed to the hills as he spoke. He couldn't hear what was being said but the shepherd pointed down another dusty road with his crook. The guard appeared to thank him, climbed back into the cab and in a cloud of dust and exhaust fumes the truck slowly disappeared down the track.

While the shepherd was out tending his herd Khalid and Omar spent the day resting and preparing an evening meal. As the sun was setting over the hills the shepherd returned, delighted his visitors had prepared the meal. The conversation once again started on the topic they all had in common, the wars to rid their country of foreign armies, but late in the evening turned to the problem Omar and Khalid now faced, how they would continue their journey to Karachi? The shepherd sat in silence for a moment. "I've been thinking about this all day, there may be a way for you to reach the city without a long walk. You could travel to Karachi with my friend. The local farmers in these hills pay him to take their animals to market in his truck, he goes there once a month. I could go and ask if he will take you after I've taken my goats to their new pastures tomorrow, it's the only way I can think of without you walking through the hills again."

"I don't think we have any option. Our injuries mean we're not fit enough to make the journey on foot. Please tell your friend we don't have much money, but what we have we are willing to use to pay for our passage."

The following evening the shepherd returned to his hut. "I have good news. My friend says he will drop you on the outskirts of Karachi, not at the market. He thinks it's too dangerous for him to take you all the way there. He's worried the men looking for you may see you in his truck in the busier parts of the city. I'm sure you understand, he doesn't want these men following him and visiting his home one night. He will take you both there for an agreed fee."

"How much?" Omar asked, afraid it would be more than he had in his pocket.

The shepherd told Omar the amount his friend had asked for. It was more than Omar expected to pay, almost all the money he'd taken from the sleeping guard just days before. But without walking all the way he could see no alternative.

"Thank you, and we must pay you for your generosity,"

Omar said not knowing how they could pay for the hospitality and shelter the shepherd had given them with what little would be left after paying for their ride to the city. As he reached for the money in his pocket the shepherd held up his hand.

"I don't want your money my friend, but you will have no use for this in the city," he pointed to the gun Omar had taken from the truck which was now leaning against the wall in the corner of the room. "That will be of more use to me here in these hills."

"Then it's yours." Omar picked up the gun and spare ammunition and handed it to the shepherd.

The next day Omar and Khalid thanked the shepherd for his hospitality and bade him farewell. They climbed into the cab of another truck for what they hoped would be the final, easiest and most comfortable leg of their journey. It would be a welcome change after travelling for so long in the hard unforgiving back of the last truck.

Three weeks after setting off from the hospital Omar and his travelling companion arrived in the outskirts of Karachi. The truck pulled up beside a bus stop and their driver switched off the engine.

"I must leave you here my friends. I'm sure you understand if I were to take you any further it may put myself and my family in danger should we be seen together." Omar thanked him and handed over the money they'd agreed on before setting off.

Omar and Khalid stood in the road staring at the truck as it disappeared around the corner at the far end of the street. "Where will we go now?" Khalid asked.

During their journey together Omar had become increasingly frustrated with Khalid. He'd done nothing to help their escape from the men in the truck, he'd complained constantly about the lack of food and water while they were in the hills and had done little to help during their stay with the shepherd, his focus totally on recovering from his injuries and returning to the war. "You told me Karachi was your home, you must know someone here who can look after you. This is where we part company. I will go to my brother's. You must find your own way now."

"I'll need some money. You took money from the guard in the truck, we should share what's left."

Omar looked at Khalid in disbelief. There was barely enough money in his pocket to cover the bus fare, but he was tired of Khalid's complaining, he just wanted to be rid of this man and get to the sanctuary of his brother's house. He took what little money they had left from his pocket and counted out half for himself and half for his ungrateful travelling companion. "It's not much but it should be enough to get you to family or friends who can look after you."

"It's a poor return for lost limbs," Khalid said leaning on his crutches and staring at the money in his hand. "Maybe you should have haggled over the price of our ride here. Now what do we do?"

Omar crouched down at the side of the road. "We wait, this is a bus stop and now you have some money for the fare to wherever you need to go in the city. There should be a bus along soon. We will travel into the city then we go our separate ways."

Crouched at the side of the road they waited in silence. Twenty minutes later a bus pulled up at the stop. After the passengers filed off the two weary men climbed the steps of the bus, Omar asked if the bus stopped anywhere near his brother's address. The driver told him the last stop was the main terminus in the city from which he could catch another bus to his brother's neighbourhood. As Omar took a seat he wondered if he would have enough money for the onward fare.

One hour later he arrived at his brother's street, his journey finally at an end. He realised what a dishevelled state he was in as he made his way along the dark road. He hadn't washed since leaving the hospital weeks ago and his clothes were in tatters, almost falling off him due to the amount of weight he'd lost, something that hadn't been important when he'd been fleeing the men in the truck. He looked himself over, disgusted that he'd let himself get into this state. The last time he'd seen his brother was the day he'd left his job at the bank, he'd called to tell him he was leaving to join the fight in their homeland. On that occasion he'd arrived wearing a suit and tie, not the dirty rags he was now clothed in, but there was nothing he could do to change his appearance now. Wearily he climbed the steps and knocked on the door. A familiar voice called out, "go away, we don't give money to beggars".

"Salman, it's your brother, Omar."

Moments later Salman opened the door. He stared at the wretched creature before him, hardly believing what he saw standing on his doorstep could possibly be his brother.

"But where are..."

"Gone," Omar said before his brother could finish his question. "Killed by the Americans, and they are responsible for this too," he raised the filthy bandaged stump of his right arm.

Salman stared at his brother, shocked at the news of his family and his terrible injury. "Come in my brother, come in." He ushered Omar into his home, tears welling up in his eyes.

He called his wife and daughter to come and greet his brother, although he knew they would struggle to recognise him just as he had.

Omar sat in front of his brother's family and recounted his journey from recruitment to the cause, the many skirmishes he'd been involved in, the attack that had taken his beloved wife and son to the long and painful journey in the truck, his escape from the driver and guard, his wandering in the hills and finally, with the help of the shepherd, his journey back to Karachi.

Salman and his family listened to Omar's story in disbelief. "You must stay with us and recover," his brother said. "You showed great generosity when you paid for Hadia's education abroad, now it's our turn to help you. You must stay with us and rest after your long journey and recuperate from your terrible injuries."

Salman's wife and daughter busied themselves preparing an evening meal and a bed for Omar. The house was small, Hadia would be sleeping on the floor in the main living room while her uncle stayed with them. While they were busy Omar recounted parts of his story to his brother, parts he thought Salman's wife and daughter should not hear. Some of the things he'd witnessed, things some of his comrades had done, he was not proud to be a part of. He believed a fight for freedom from oppression was a noble cause, but kidnapping, rape, torture and beheading were the actions of a barbarian, the very reason he'd made his vow to return if needed all those years ago.

Omar excused himself for a few minutes while he washed and changed, the clothes Salman had given him hanging loosely from his emaciated frame. As they ate Salman and his family continued to bombard him with questions. Where had he been, for how long, what fighting had he been involved in, what had he seen of the enemy, what were they like? Omar tried to be as vague as he could with some of his answers. He ate little of the meal they'd prepared, thanked them for taking him in, then excused himself late in the evening and wearily dragged himself up the stairs to bed.

Alone in the darkness, Omar thought of his wife and son, a tear slowly ran down his cheek. Although it was the enemy who'd killed his family, he felt responsible for their deaths. He'd put them in harm's way against their wishes. They never wanted to travel to Afghanistan to join the fight. Once more he went over how his wife had pleaded with him not to go. He had a job with prospects, their life in Pakistan was good, why throw it all away? But he was insistent. They must all go and join the war against the foreign invaders. If his people did not take a stand they would forever be under the yoke of western oppression. They had paid the ultimate price and here he was, the one who deserved to die for dragging them into a war they never wanted to be part of. A man who would be living off the charity of his brother and his family for the foreseeable future.

And what would he do once he'd recovered from his journey? A one-armed man who used to work in the banking sector. Someone who would never get a respectable job if his past was discovered. He was no use to anyone, the truck driver had been right, he would only be a drain on his brother's meagre income. Maybe he should have insisted on staying in Afghanistan. Perhaps he should return and learn to make bombs as Hakim did. It would be difficult with only one hand, but he was sure he could do it. Unlike Hakim he would show mercy, he would never knowingly take the life of an innocent child. The memory of the small boy on the road still haunted Omar. He didn't want sympathy in a country where there were as many as 27 million disabled people, he wanted to be useful. He wanted a job and to be independent, and the more he thought of it he wanted some kind of revenge for the killing of his family, however small that revenge may be.

As the weeks passed Omar grew stronger, he regained the weight he'd lost on the long journey home, but the one thing he was struggling to regain was his self-respect. He had been reduced to completing domestic chores around his brother's house. Shopping and cleaning were not jobs for a proud man who'd fought for the freedom of his country, one who'd been injured and lost his family for the cause. With each passing day he was slowly sinking further and further into a depressed rage.

5

————

Not since his brother had knocked on Salman's door six weeks earlier had anyone called late in the evening. Suspicious of who could be calling at such a late hour he pulled the curtain across slightly and looked out of the window. He turned to look at his brother, terror written across his face.

"Omar it's for you. *Do not* let these men into my home. You have led them here, now please see what they want then get rid of them."

"How do you know they are here for me?" Omar asked. "Who is it?"

"I don't know their names, but I know who they are and what they represent," Salman replied, "they must be here to speak to you. They've got no reason to talk to anyone else in this house, it must be you they want. They're trouble Omar, trouble of the worst kind. Please do not let these men into my home."

Whoever the callers were Omar could see the terror they instilled in his brother. "Don't worry." Omar rose from his chair and headed for the door, "I'll see what they want then ask them to leave." He opened the door and swiftly stepped outside to greet the visitors, quickly closing the door behind him. Three men stood outside. With a long white beard, wearing an intricately decorated karakul, the traditional Afghan hat, and flowing robes of what looked to be expensive cloth, the oldest man was obviously the most senior in rank of the three. In comparison to him, the two youngest of the visitors were scruffily dressed, they looked like the old man's bodyguards and seemed uninterested in whatever business their older colleague was there to discuss.

"Greetings brothers, how can I help?" Omar asked.

"Welcome home brother. I trust you are recovered from your injuries and your tiresome journey home from the war," the old man said.

"Thanks be to Allah, yes thank you." Omar was immediately suspicious. How did this man know he'd been injured in the war and of his journey home?

"And you are settled here?" the old man asked.

"Yes, for now," Omar replied.

"For now," the old man repeated slowly nodding his head. After a moment's silence, he looked at Omar with piercing eyes. Realising he was not going to be invited into the house he decided to come straight to the point of his visit. "The organisation I represent would like to put a proposition to you, one that would help you find some worth and help us continue the struggle in our homeland. Should you accept our proposal it would be financially beneficial for both parties," he said.

After weeks of searching for a fulfilling job and some independence Omar was taken aback by the unexpected offer. "I'm afraid my brother's family have pressing matters, otherwise I would welcome you inside to discuss your kind proposal, but alas as you know this is not my house and I cannot offend my brother's family after the generosity they've shown me since my return."

"I understand," the old man said, obviously irritated that he would not be invited inside to discuss his proposal. "Perhaps we could meet tomorrow at the coffee shop near the market to discuss our offer. Shall we say after morning prayer?"

"Yes, I know the one," Omar said, "I'll see you there."

Omar watched as the old man and his two bodyguards turned, descended the steps and disappeared into the gloom. He stood alone in the darkness for a few moments intrigued by what the old man could possibly offer a one-armed man that would be beneficial to both himself and whatever organisation he represented and how much they seemed to know about him, and concerned by his brothers fear of these men.

When he returned to the kitchen Salman was waiting, eager to hear the reason for Omar's visitors call. "What did they want? You must have nothing to do with them, they will cause you nothing but pain and trouble."

"Don't you think I've suffered enough pain already?" Omar said raising his voice. "I've lost my family and until now I've had no prospect of ever getting a job. Somebody wants me Salman, somebody thinks I can be useful. Somebody thinks I can do more than shop and clean and perform meaningless tasks around the house. Maybe he will give me a job where this doesn't matter," he lifted the stump of his right arm. "Tomorrow I'm going to hear what this man has to say and what he has to offer. What harm can it do?"

"Please Omar, look at what happened to your family because of them," Salman pleaded.

"Enough," Omar raised his hand to stop his brother from continuing. "Be careful Salman, you are treading on dangerous ground. My family didn't die because of them, they died because of me. Against their wishes I selfishly took them back to the land of our birth to fight a war they wanted nothing to do with. I'm as much responsible for their deaths as the men who dropped the bomb from that American plane, possibly more. I'm going to meet this man tomorrow to hear what he has to offer. I need a job Salman, I need to feel useful to someone, I need to get my self-respect back. I can't spend the rest of my life being a domestic help around your house. I need to build a new life for myself, one where I have my own money and can be independent despite this," he said, raising the stump of his right arm again. "If that means you want me to leave then so be it."

"You'll be endangering all of us if you work for these people. Everyone around here knows who they are and what they're capable of. Please don't take their job, whatever it is," Salman pleaded again. "Give us some more time, we'll find you something else, something befitting a war hero."

Omar laughed. "A war hero, I certainly don't feel like one. I've come home after losing my family and now all I do is housework. You know I've been looking for a job for weeks, but nobody's interested in employing an invalid like me. I don't want to endanger anyone, least of all you and your family after all you've done for me. Look at what happened to my wife and son because of my stubbornness. I can't have anything more like that on my conscience. I think your fears are unfounded but if I take this job, I'll find a place of my own and keep you and your family out of it."

"If I'm right about these people that won't be possible. If anything goes wrong and they lose money while you're working for them, they'll treat all of us as if we're part of their organisation. It's the way they operate, they instil fear into their employees to ensure their honesty and loyalty. If anything goes wrong and they think you're guilty the whole family is included in any punishment."

"Don't worry, nothing will go wrong." In an effort to allay his fears Omar placed his hand on his brother's shoulder, but he could see his words and gesture were in vain. The anger in Salman's eyes convinced Omar that he would need to find a home of his own if he accepted the job.

The next day, sitting at one of the outside tables in the shade of a palm tree Omar waited for the old man to arrive. At exactly eleven the old man appeared along with the same two bodyguards who'd accompanied him the previous evening. Just as the night before when they'd first met the old man was dressed in traditional Afghan attire, the same ornate karakul and loose-fitting robes. Once again Omar thought that the old man's clothes appeared to be expensive, unlike the scruffy bodyguards who walked away to smoke a cigarette as soon as the old man was sat at the table. This man has money Omar thought, was his wealth generated by the business he was about to offer Omar a job with?

Omar stood to greet the old man.

"Salam," the old man said placing his hand over his heart.

Omar returned the traditional greeting but was unable to reciprocate the act of respect with his missing right hand, instead he bowed awkwardly.

"Please, shall we?" The old man gestured to the seats around the table Omar had been sitting at before his arrival. Once they were seated a waiter appeared and took their order. The old man waited until he was out of earshot before continuing.

"Before we discuss the job tell me a little about yourself, about your family, how you came to be fighting in the war and how you got back here," the old man said.

Omar told of his family's life in Afghanistan, about his father's work in the hospital and how he'd been beaten and humiliated by the Russian officer, and his family's flight from their homeland to Pakistan. He spoke of his education and work in the banking sector before fulfilling his promise to return to Afghanistan after the foreign invasion. He glossed over his part in the war, something he was still troubled by after seeing the young boy killed by a bomb he'd been part of setting, and finally death of his family, his journey back to Pakistan and escape from the truck driver and navigator.

The old man nodded, surprised at how much of Omar's story seemed connected to his own. Finally, he was ready to discuss the issue that had brought them to the coffee shop. "I expect you've been wondering why I asked you here," the old man said as the waiter returned and placed their coffees on the table.

"Yes, all kinds of possibilities have been going through my mind during the night," Omar replied.

"Then let me enlighten you. The Russians invaded Afghanistan on 24th December 1979. They said it was to support our government, but it was no government that I, nor many of my countrymen, recognised. Like you, I took up arms and joined the fight against these invaders. We were no match for such a formidable army in the early days of the war. We were short of men and poorly equipped, the only weapons we had were the few old guns we'd had in our homes for years and anything we could steal from the Russians. None of it was a match for their tanks and heli-copters. We needed more sophisticated and powerful weapons. Eventually, these were supplied by the West, mainly the Americans. We fought the Russians for nine long bloody and years before they left with their tails between their legs like the cowards they are. Now we are using what's left of those weapons to fight the very people who supplied them. But these arms are old, our resources are diminishing, and we need money to buy more weapons."

"But I thought the finance came from the poppy harvest and our Arab cousins?" Omar interrupted.

The old man shook his head. "Unfortunately, that's no longer the case. When the invaders find the poppy fields, they burn the crop. They pay the farmer what his crop would be worth at the market and he's paid to grow an alternative crop in the future, usually wheat or rice. The amount they pay is nothing to them but a fortune for the farmer. Our Arab cousins have come under pressure from the west, been threatened with sanctions and have tired of financing us.

"I'm part of a group responsible for recruiting brave men such as yourself to replace our lost income and to finance the continuing struggle to free our country. Men who have shown that they are willing to fight to free our homeland. As a man who has given so much for the struggle, and one who formerly worked in the banking sector, you are an ideal candidate. If you agree to work for the organisation I represent you will be continuing the struggle, in some small way avenging the loss of your wife and son and regaining your self-respect as a man."

Once again Omar wondered how this man knew so much about him. "Where would this job be based?" he asked after a short pause.

"Here in Karachi. There's a small team responsible for the international financing of our struggle," the old man smiled.

"How do you get this international financing?" Omar asked. "Surely no legitimate bank would fund what they believe to be money laundering or terrorism, especially with no return for themselves?"

"We are not terrorists," the old man said, a touch of irritation in his voice, "we are freedom fighters. We have teams based in Western Europe, America, Canada, Australia and a few other rich Western countries who persuade people to part with their money. This money is transferred here from those countries then onward to other banks to finance the war. The citizens of these countries pay taxes to their own governments to finance the war against us, it's only fair we redress the balance in some small way by taking some of their money to finance our side of the struggle." To Omar it sounded like part of a presentation, a speech the old man had used before. "Unlike some organisations operating similar schemes we do not profit personally from our venture. We cover our operational costs here and abroad, everything else is sent to fund the war."

It was a scam, Omar thought. No matter how the old man might embellish it they were operating nothing more than a scam. Admittedly it was probably a sophisticated scam on an international scale and likely to be reaping rich rewards if it was financing the war, but it was still a scam.

Despite his misgivings, Omar was intrigued. Perhaps this was the opportunity he was looking for, a way of being useful again, a way out from being the domestic help he'd become at his brother's house. After weeks of trying he could see no other way of getting a legitimate job, if this could be called a legitimate job. It may be his only chance, and from what the old man had told him earlier it was well-paid, and in some small way would be a way to avenge the deaths of his wife and son and continue the fight to free his country of invading foreign armies.

"Of course, all of what I've told you must remain secret," the old man said. "You must not breathe a word of what we've spoken about to anyone, not even your brother. Should you do so, and we are found out by the authorities, the consequences could be dire, for all of us, including you, your brother and his family. But I don't suppose that will be a problem, will it Omar?" The old man smiled, but once again Omar thought there was a hint of menace in his voice.

"Don't worry, your secret's safe with me," Omar replied.

"Good. If you are interested, I would like to show you our finance facility."

Omar sat quietly for a moment thinking, wary of committing himself after his brother's warnings. Was his brother right about these men? The old man's insistence that he should tell no one about what they'd discussed and the veiled threat to himself and his brother's family if they were discovered certainly fitted with what his brother had said. But what did he have to lose? He needed a job, and this was the only offer he'd received since returning home. He reasoned that these people had sought him out therefore they must be keen to employ him. "Yes," he finally said, "I am interested."

"Good, wait here a moment and I'll arrange transport." The old man placed some money on the table for the coffees then walked to where his bodyguards were waiting. After a short conversation, one of the bodyguards disappeared. Minutes later a black Mercedes pulled up at the kerbside beside their table. The old man gestured towards the car. "Shall we?"

Thirty minutes later they were standing in a small unit on an industrial park, not the City's finance district that Omar had previously worked in and where he'd expected to be taken.

"As you can see," the old man began, "this is a small operation, but it yields a vast amount of money. We have one man who oversees the operation. He is the senior man reporting directly to me. His main responsibility is to check that the amount of money coming into what we call our transit account is what we expect from each of our overseas operations. Money from the West is transferred into this account all day and all night in small and large amounts and in various currencies. At the end of each day the balance in this account is transferred to another secure account which can be drawn on by those leading the struggle. We have one person who logs amounts coming in from around the world and who is responsible for the transfer of funds at the end of each day," he pointed to a young man sitting at a computer terminal. "We also have two men who act as guards, just to make sure the office is secure, although we've never had any trouble in the past. Your role would be the overseer, making sure our money is safe and that every opportunity is being maximised by our field operations in the West. You will investigate how other operations such as ours are generating their income. If there's an opportunity you think we may have missed bring it to my attention. We may decide that we too need to introduce such money-generating schemes. We must do everything we can to maximise our income. The struggle to rid our lands of foreign invaders depends on us."

"What happened to the last senior man?" Omar asked.

"Regrettably he got greedy, we had to terminate his," the old man paused for a moment, he smiled apparently enjoying the drama, "employment. You will be rewarded handsomely for this job, and you will be helping our men in the field to continue the struggle. This is an important job Omar, we can't continue the struggle without the money operations such as this generate, and it could be important to you too, as it would give you back your pride. So, are you still interested my friend?"

"Yes, I am interested but this is totally unexpected. I would like a little time to think about it now I know what's on offer. Can I give you my answer tomorrow?" Omar asked.

The old man hesitated, obviously irritated by Omar's delayed decision. "Very well," he said, "but I must have your answer when we meet tomorrow. I need to find someone else quickly if you don't want this job. And please remember, do not breathe a word of this to anyone."

"I understand," said Omar. "I will tell no one."

After discussing what he would be paid for the job the old man told Omar to meet him at the same coffee shop the following morning when he would expect his decision. As he turned to leave, he stopped and fixed Omar with his piercing eyes. "Remember my friend, not a word to anyone. I will see you tomorrow." The old man got into the waiting car and left.

Omar stood outside the unit he'd just been shown around and watched the car leave the industrial park. Standing alone in the car park he wondered where in the city he was and, with no money in his pockets, how he would find his way back to his brother's house.

The evening meal with his brother's family was eaten in an awkward atmosphere. Salman hoped after returning from his meeting Omar would tell him he'd rejected any job offer, but instead, he told him he was still considering it. Salman made no more effort to dissuade Omar, he'd made his position clear, there was nothing more he could do.

After the meal Omar returned to his room to consider the

old man's proposal. He had no doubt it came with a veiled threat to both himself and possibly his brother's family. But the old man was correct, the job would give him back his pride. He could not live a life looked upon with pity, a life feeling all he was good for was domestic chores and helping around the house. With the money he would earn he would be able to afford a house of his own, a little independence. He would no longer be financially reliant on his brother's family, and perhaps if he moved to a house of his own it would keep his brother's family safe should anything go wrong. In the back of his mind he believed that in some small way he would be helping those fighting the forces that had killed his family. Late that night he came to the conclusion that this was probably the only job offer he would receive. His decision was made, he would accept the old man's offer.

After prayers the next morning Omar headed for the coffee shop. When he turned the corner into the square, he saw the old man waiting for him at the table they'd occupied the day before. Once again, his two bodyguards were standing a few yards away each smoking a cigarette. The old man greeted Omar as he had the previous day, "Salam," he said placing his hand over his heart, "please take a seat." He didn't wait for Omar to return his greeting before sitting. "I've taken the liberty of ordering for you," he said.

"Salam," Omar said dispensing with the awkward bow from the day before as he sat, "thank you."

"Well my friend, have you come to a decision?" The old man asked.

"Yes. I would like to accept your generous offer."

"Good." The old man slipped a piece of paper across the table. "This is the address of the office I showed you yester-day. You start there tomorrow at eight. They will be expecting you." The old man rose, placed some money on the table and left. As he walked away with his bodyguards the waiter appeared and placed two cups of coffee on the table in front of Omar.

As Omar watched the old man climb into the waiting Mercedes he thought back to his time in Afghanistan when the men would visit each community distributing money for living expenses and arms. He was now convinced this was where that money had come from.

FOR THE NEXT SIX MONTHS, Omar fine-tuned the finance operation, changing some practices and doing away with others he thought unnecessary. Eventually he had everything running like clockwork, he could sit back and watch the money flow in from around the world. He was astounded at the sums being transferred into the transit account each day. On most days the total ran into millions, sometimes tens of millions of US Dollars. He couldn't believe the citizens in the West could be so gullible, and stupid enough to be so easily parted from their money.

6

Once more Omar glanced at the clock on the office wall, something he'd been doing for the last thirty minutes. Eight thirty, and still the last member of his staff, the man responsible for transferring the money at the end of each day, was yet to arrive. His senior man had been working with Omar for just over a year and it was unlike him to be late for work, and he never took time off sick. Initially Omar thought he must have been delayed, but as time passed and with no call to explain he began to worry.

Had this man fallen foul to greed like his predecessor? Had Omar missed something this man was doing, something that would bring the wrath of the old man down on him? Although he was innocent of any wrongdoing Omar could only guess at the consequences for himself should the old man believe he was party to anything that lost the organisation money. Would the old man blame him and exact the same terrible retribution he had on his predecessor? Although no one knew for sure what had happened to him the rumours around the office left Omar in no doubt that whatever his fate it wasn't something he or anyone else wanted to go through. Reluctantly he decided it was time to contact the old man and let him know the most important member of his team had not arrived for work. He picked up his phone and dialled the old man's number.

After two rings the call was answered. "Good morning Omar," the old man said. The cheerful note in his voice suggested to Omar that he was unaware of the reason for his call.

"I'm afraid I have some potentially terrible news," Omar said.

"Yes, I know," the old man replied. "Your senior man didn't arrive for work this morning. Unfortunately, he died last night. Natural causes, so my contacts at the hospital tell me."

Omar was astounded, the old man seemed to have contacts everywhere.

"You know you should have phoned me earlier. Never try to keep anything from me, eventually I will find out and I won't look favourably on you if I think you are deliberately withholding information from me. You hold a trusted position in our organisation Omar, I expect you to be open and honest with me at all times, and to notify me of any problems as soon as you become aware of them. Being a man short gives us a problem," the old man continued, the death of one of his employees seemingly a mere inconvenience, "he needs to be replaced, and quickly. I'm attending a conference in Kabul for a week which means I won't be able to recruit his replacement. You've proved yourself to be an honest and conscientious employee, if you know of any suitable candidates, perhaps among your former banking colleagues, contact them and ask if they would consider working for us.

If any show an interest let me know and I'll consider their application. You know the role your unfortunate colleague performed and all the passwords, you'll have to fill his role until we can find a suitable replacement. Call me tomorrow night if you think of anyone," the old man rang off.

Omar stared at his phone. Was the old man playing games with him? He'd known his senior man had died in hospital the night before. Omar wouldn't have been put through the worry of wondering if his colleague had been stealing if he'd contacted him first thing in the morning. Instead he'd chosen to wait for Omar to call. He wondered if the old man was testing him in some way.

That night he returned to the small home the money from the job had allowed him to purchase. As hard as he tried Omar couldn't think of a suitable candidate from his former life in the banking world to fill the vacancy. Since returning from the war he'd kept himself to himself and only had contact with his work colleagues, his brother Salman and his family. He had no idea where he might find a suitable replacement.

The next day Omar assumed the role of his dead colleague. With the use of only his left hand he found using the computer keyboard cumbersome and slow. He toiled all day doing both his own job and the one he was now forced to take on, knowing he couldn't do both for any length of time. His main priority now was to try to think of someone who could fill the vacant role. He'd lost contact with his old banking colleagues, and despite the money on offer he doubted any of them would be willing to give up the security and comfortable life they'd forged for the uncertainty that this job could offer, and, if his brother was correct, the threat to both themselves and their families.

On his walk home that night it suddenly occurred to him. The perfect candidate for the job was his niece Hadia. She had all the right experience in banking and computers the job required, but would she be prepared to work for such an organisation? She was a headstrong and determined young woman, proud of her Afghan heritage and the struggle her country had made with its many oppressors over the centuries. She felt her talents were wasted in her current job and from what she said there was no prospect of promotion. The only way to find out was to ask, but he was worried about what his brother's reaction would be. Salman had been opposed to Omar taking a job with what he always referred to as "*those people.*" He knew his brother would be even stronger in his opposition to any more family involvement with the organisation Omar worked for, especially his beloved daughter. But he knew if Hadia made up her mind to join him there would be nothing his brother could do or say that would persuade her otherwise.

After eating his evening meal Omar walked the short distance to his brother's house, still unsure whether he should involve Hadia and his brother's family any further in the organisation. Still undecided as he the climbed the steps to Salman's front door he thought the decision should be Hadia's. He took a moment to compose himself before knocking on the door.

Salman was surprised to see his brother at such a late hour. "It's good to see you, please come in."

"Thank you. I need to speak with you and Hadia."

"Is anything wrong?" Salman asked, worried his fears about his brother's job were being proved correct.

"No nothing's wrong," Omar said, "I just have something I need to ask Hadia, and I think you should be present".

Salman stared at his brother; the atmosphere had changed in an instant. There was a moment of awkward silence between them. "This had better not be what I think it is. I've told you before I want nothing to do with these people, and that includes Hadia. It's bad enough having one member of the family working for them, I don't want any more, especially my daughter. You know my feelings on this and the fear I have of any punishment should anything go wrong. Please don't involve my family any more than you already have."

"Don't you think it's a decision Hadia should make for herself?" Omar asked. "She's stuck in a dead-end job looking for something more suited to her qualifications. If this is the opportunity she's been waiting for and she finds out you've denied her the chance of taking it she will never forgive you."

"I won't let you speak to her about this, so she'll never know," Salman said, his voice raised. "I will not let you come here and dictate to me what I can and cannot do in my own home." Salman closed his eyes and took a deep breath trying to calm himself. "I think you should leave Omar, and don't mention this to Hadia," his words were now almost a whisper Omar could barely hear, the short confrontation appearing to have sapped his energy.

Omar stared at his brother. This was the first argument they'd had in many years. He could see the anger in his brother's eyes. Maybe it was for the best if Omar left and told the old man he couldn't think of a suitable candidate for the job.

Resigned to the fact he wouldn't be offering the job to Hadia, and that he would be filling two roles for the foreseeable future, Omar turned to leave. As he approached the door Hadia and her mother entered the room.

"What's all the shouting about?" Hadia asked.

"It's nothing, a misunderstanding," Salman looked at his brother. "Your uncle is just leaving."

"No Salman, it's not nothing. I've come here to offer Hadia an opportunity that will give her a chance to leave her dead-end job and become an important member of my team, and be paid handsomely for doing it."

"No Omar, I've told you we will not discuss this. I've asked you to leave, now please go."

Hadia was intrigued. What did she have to lose by hearing what her uncle had to say? She agreed with Omar, the decision should be hers. She could always say no. "Father please let Uncle Omar speak, I'd like to know what this opportunity is."

Before Salman could respond Omar took the chance to tell Hadia what he'd come to say. "There's a vacancy where I work that I believe you would be suited for. It involves computers and banking both of which you have experience in. The pay is vastly more than I believe you are paid now, and who knows what the future may bring. There can be no less chance of promotion than where you work now. Would you be interested?"

"No," Salman interrupted before Hadia could answer. "I will not allow it. I've told you I will not endanger my family any further by letting my daughter work for these people. Now please leave Omar."

"It's too late for that," Omar said. "You said yourself now I'm working for them if anything should go wrong, we will all be implicated. But I'll make sure nothing ever does go wrong. You have nothing to fear."

His brother slumped into a seat, his head in his hands. "Omar why have you put us in this position? From the moment they knocked at the door I told you to have nothing to do with these people. Eventually, they bring nothing but pain and suffering to everyone they meet. Once you are part of their organisation you can never leave. And what happened to the person doing this job before? Did they do something to annoy the people you work for and now they've mysteriously disappeared?" Salman turned and looked at his daughter. "Hadia, you must not work for these people, I forbid you to take this job."

Hadia glared at her father, for a moment there was silence. "Father I've told you I must speak for myself," she said finally breaking the tension.

"No Hadia I will not allow it," Salman said, his voice raised once more. "While you live under my roof you will do as I say. You will not work for these people."

"Father, I'm not a little girl any more I'm a grown woman, I should be allowed to give my opinion and make my own decisions. I'm ambitious and want to buy a house of my own, maybe a car, and I want to travel abroad. I will never be given the opportunity to further my career where I'm working now simply because I am a woman. Whenever there's a chance of promotion I'm overlooked for men who have fewer qualifications and are inferior at the job. I'm tired of applying for better jobs and constantly being turned down. I want to work somewhere where I will be appreciated for what I can do rather than for what I am. And look at what the West has done to our family. Uncle Omar has lost his family and suffered a terrible injury, you and your parents were forced to flee years ago. It's time we stood up and took our country back to rule as we see fit. This may be the only opportunity I get to help rid our country of the foreigners and to make a difference to my life, and possibly yours."

Omar was surprised at the passion Hadia demonstrated towards a country she'd never been to.

"No Hadia, I'm sorry, but I will not allow it," Salman repeated.

"Father can't you see what you are doing. It's exactly what the people that I work for now do. You are not allowing me the chance to prove myself and make a better life for myself. I should be allowed to decide my own future, even if it means I'm making a mistake. If you forbid me to take this job, I will leave home and take whatever job I wish, and you will never know. Is that what you want?"

"It could be a mistake that loses you your life, loses all of us our lives." Salman knew this was an argument he would not win. Years before Hadia had told him that she would never agree to an arranged marriage, she would choose a husband when she was ready, if she ever was ready. She was a headstrong young woman who, once she'd made up her mind, would not be moved. If he continued to deny her this opportunity Salman feared his daughter would do as she'd threatened and leave with Omar and he may never see her again.

"This may all be academic," Omar said trying to defuse the situation. "I need to let my boss know of anyone I can think of for the job, he may not accept you as he has no knowledge of you, but I will vouch for you as being trustworthy and a hard worker. I don't know of any other women working for him so he may consider that to be a problem, I don't know him well enough to know his attitude towards women. If you're sure this is what you want, I'll call him later and let you know you're interested. I'll let you know as soon as I know his decision."

"Thank you for giving me this chance uncle," Hadia said glaring at her father. "Yes, I'm sure."

As he walked home in the dark Omar wondered if Hadia was genuinely interested in the job or simply taking it to defy her father's wishes. He hoped not. If Salman was right about the people he was working for Omar was placing Hadia and her family in even more danger should anything go wrong.

Salman spent the evening trying in vain to persuade Hadia to change her mind. His only hope now was Omar's boss would not want a woman working for him and offer the job to someone else.

Later that night Omar telephoned the old man with the details of the only candidate he could think of. He told the old man of Hadia's banking experience, her education abroad and her fierce pride in her Afghan heritage.

"How do you know this young woman?" The old man asked.

"She's the daughter of a friend." By hiding the family connection Omar hoped it may protect her and his brother in the future should he be suspected of any wrongdoing. "She wants to progress in her career but feels her current job will never give her the opportunity of promotion simply because she is a woman."

There was a moment's silence on the line, "I will consider it overnight, but if you think of anyone else in the meantime let me know," the old man said. "We have another problem, the meeting I'm attending has been extended by a further week. We need this replacement in place as soon as possible, the operation must not be disrupted. We are currently planning a major offensive and need all the finance we can generate. Do you trust this woman Omar?"

"Yes," Omar replied without hesitation.

"And do you think she will accept the job if we offer it to her?"

"Yes."

"Very well, I'll think about it overnight and call you with my decision tomorrow." Once the call was disconnected the old man dialled the number of one of his many contacts in Karachi. "I need you to find everything you can on someone," he said. He gave the details of the woman Omar had put forward for the job then disconnected the call.

Two hours later his call was returned. The old man was supplied with the information he'd asked for. "One last thing," the caller said. "The woman in question is his niece." The old man smiled. It was useful information he could use against Omar in the future should the need arise. What worried him most was that Omar had withheld this information. Why would he do that? Suspicious of everyone the old man wondered what other secrets he might be withholding.

7

The following day Omar struggled filling both his own role and that of his dead colleague. He tentatively tapped away at the keyboard with his left hand but couldn't concentrate on the work. The anticipation of the old man's impending decision proving too much of a distraction. To his relief his mobile phone eventually rang, the old man's number displayed on the screen.

"My friend," the old man began, "I'm afraid there have been no other candidates for the vacancy. We have no alternative but to offer the job to the woman you suggested. It will be on a trial basis for two weeks. I want you to keep a close eye on her during that time. I want to know that she's capable of the job and if there are any problems."

"Thank you," Omar said, relieved he would soon be relieved of the responsibility of two jobs, "there will be no problems. I'll contact her today with the good news."

And I will have my people in your office keep an eye on both of you, the old man thought as he disconnected the call. He couldn't afford to lose two people from the office but if

Omar had kept the fact that this woman was his niece a secret what else was he keeping from him? Was this woman part of a plan to steal money just as his predecessor had? But until now Omar had proved to be a trusted member of the team. He'd fought and been wounded in the war. The old man had no doubt about his loyalty when he'd first recruited him but had the influence of the vast sums of money flowing into the account turned his head? He would need his security guards at the unit to keep a close eye on both Omar and the new recruit.

On his way home from work Omar called at his brother's house to give Hadia the news. After hearing of the job offer, Salman desperately tried one last time to persuade his daughter not to accept. "Please reconsider Hadia," he pleaded. "You're putting all of us in great danger, you know these men are killers. If anything goes wrong, they won't limit their wrath to you and Omar, they'll kill all of us." Hadia listened to her father's argument but she would not be persuaded. She accepted the job offer, took the office address from Omar and said she could start in two days.

As he turned to leave Omar thought of one last thing, something he hoped would protect Hadia and the one thing he hadn't told the old man about his latest recruit. "Remember," he said, "nobody knows you are my niece. When you talk to me at work it's important you call me Omar and do not speak of your family. Tell anyone who asks that your name is Hadia Bukhari and that I'm a friend of the family."

"Doesn't this tell you something Hadia?" Salman seized on what he thought would be his last chance to persuade his daughter. "Your uncle tells you to use a false name and not to speak of your family. Doesn't that show you the kind of people you'll be working for and the danger you'll be putting all of us in?"

"Father please, you're being overdramatic. I've made up my mind. I'm taking this job." Hadia's decision was final. There was nothing more to say. Omar headed for the door.

"I hope you know what you're doing Omar, otherwise you may be condemning all of us to death."

Omar could hear the emotion in his brother's voice. "Salman you have nothing to worry about. I've worked for the organisation for over a year now and nothing's gone wrong. I'm a trusted member of the team and I'm sure after a short while in the job Hadia will be too."

"I hope you're right, but I have a terrible feeling about this." Salman opened the door for his brother to leave. "You know my feelings about these people. Look after her Omar, and don't put her, or any of us, in any danger."

When Hadia arrived on her first morning Omar showed her around the small office and introduced her to the rest of the team. Once the introductions were complete, he began the task of showing her the process of logging each receipt from their operations in the West, and at the end of the day showed her how to transfer the total to the main account. She asked where the main account was, but it was information he didn't have access to. She picked the job up quickly and after a few days needed no supervision. Hadia, like Omar before her, was astonished at the sums of money flowing in from the West.

Two weeks later, after returning from his conference in Kabul, the old man paid the office an unexpected visit. After speaking to Omar he slowly walked around the unit, a deathly silence fell over the office. Finally, he came to a halt behind Hadia's desk. For a few moments he stood looking over her shoulder watching her work. She had no idea who this man was, but it was clear from the way he was dressed and the way the others in the team reacted to him that he was a man of some importance, someone who instilled both a sense of respect and fear into everyone in the unit.

As he silently watched her working Hadia looked down, her hands were shaking. She could feel a strange aura of menace emanating from this man. She breathed in deeply trying to compose herself, concentrating hard to complete tasks she normally wouldn't need to think twice about.

After a few minutes spent watching his latest recruit, the old man asked Omar to join him in his office. Sitting in Omar's chair the old man gestured for him to take a seat on the opposite side of the desk.

"You appear to have chosen well, my friend. She appears to have picked the job up quickly and have all the skills we require. The question is do we really trust her? And does she have the dedication we need? Monitor her progress and let me know of any problems." The old man smiled, knowing the family connection he knew it was something Omar couldn't do, but he didn't want Omar to know he was aware of his relationship to the woman he'd recruited. His security guards would be keeping a close eye on both her and Omar, they would alert him if they had any suspicions. The old man stood and left the office along with his bodyguards.

Omar called Hadia into his office to inform her the job was hers. He relayed the old man's concerns and reminded her of the need to be careful and the importance of not telling anyone where she worked or what she did, and most of all that she was his niece.

Six months after starting, Hadia was comfortable in her role. Omar could leave her alone safe in the knowledge that she was more than capable of doing the job unsupervised. The old man's concerns about her trust and dedication had been proved unfounded, and Omar was sure he was happy with the results they were achieving.

The extra money Hadia was bringing into the household was certainly welcome. Her father's fears appeared to be unfounded and for the moment she was happy in her role, which had become something she could do almost without thinking, until one day when she noticed what she thought might be a problem. The funds being transferred from the UK were diminishing each day. Initially, she put it down to the usual fluctuations in amounts that were transferred, but each day the takings were decreasing, something that had never happened during the time she'd been working for the organisation. After monitoring the transfers for a few days Hadia decided it was time Omar knew of her concerns. She left her desk and entered his office closing the door behind her.

"Omar," she said awkwardly still uncomfortable addressing her uncle by name, "I think there may be a problem with the money coming from the UK. The funds transferred this week are almost ten per cent down on last week. I know the amounts vary but this is a big drop and the amounts being transferred have been going down every day. Do you know if there's a problem over there?"

"Not that I know of, maybe there's an explanation. Keep an eye on it over the next week and let me know how much they transfer each day. In the meantime, I'll contact them to find out if they have a problem and why there's been a drop in the amounts they're transferring."

During a brief conversation with the UK office, Omar was told one of the team operating the phones was sick and had been away from work for two weeks which would account for the reduction in money coming into the account. He was told the man in question had returned and was assured that funds would soon return to their former level.

For the next few days Omar and Hadia monitored the transfers, but instead of returning to former levels the money transferred continued to reduce each day. At the end of the week funds were down a further five per cent.

Omar had no alternative but to call the old man. Feeling nervous about bringing such bad news he dialled his number. In hindsight he thought he should have called him sooner. Delaying the call for an additional week had allowed their takings to reduce even further. He knew the old man would not be pleased and would ask why he hadn't alerted him to the problem sooner. He could only hope the news he was bringing wouldn't be a surprise and that the old man was already aware of the problem, just as he had when his colleague had died.

"We appear to have a problem with the UK operation," Omar said when the old man answered. "Funds are down significantly. We've monitored the amounts being transferred over the last week and they appear to be going down each day. Last week I spoke to the man responsible for transferring the money, he told me one of his team had been off work sick, but he's back now and the transfers should return to their former levels, but they haven't, they've continued to decrease. Do you know if they've got any problems that would reduce what they're transferring?"

There was a short silence. While he waited for the old man's response Omar wondered if the call had been disconnected. "Why didn't you let me know of this sooner?" the old man finally said, the tone of his voice conveying the annoyance he felt on receiving such bad news. "How much are we talking about?"

Omar told him the weekly amounts they were receiving before Hadia had brought the problem to his attention, and the amounts they'd received in the previous two weeks.

"I don't know of any reason why the funds should be going down each day," the old man said. "We can't tolerate such a loss in revenue. Monitor the income closely over the next week and report to me each day how much they transfer. I'll make some enquiries of my own during that time to establish why the transfers are down so much, who is responsible and what we need to do to rectify the situation."

The following two days saw funds transferred from the UK down a further two per cent. Each day Omar made his call to the old man with the news.

"We've completed our own investigations and need to take immediate action to stop this loss of income," the old man said. "I'll call you tomorrow to let you know what we actions we will be taking."

The next day the old man called. "It appears that the person responsible for transferring the funds was foolish enough to believe that we wouldn't notice if some of the transfers were being directed to his own bank account. Once he'd successfully transferred a small amount without being discovered he got greedy and thought that if he could steal enough over a short period of time he could disappear. Fortunately, we managed to stop him before he completed his plan and have," the old man paused, "*persuaded* him to transfer the money back to our account in the UK. You should see extra being transferred into our account later today which should cover everything he's stolen.

"I'm sure I don't have to tell you that this person no longer works for us, which leaves us with another problem. We need to replace this thief, but there's nobody available in the UK. The operation there is vital, it's one of our most lucrative. We have security watching over the proceedings, but we need somebody in that office we trust to make the transfers to the main account here. You know any delay leaves the money vulnerable to being reclaimed by those who've "*donated*" it to us. I want you to send the woman working in your office to the UK to take over this position. She studied there, she speaks the language and knows the country so she should have no trouble settling in, and she's proved herself trustworthy during the time she has been working with us here. I'll send someone to the office with money for expenses, a visa and ticket to London and any other paperwork she will need, including a passport. I realise that this will leave you without the most important member of your team, so I'll arrange for a replacement to be with you tomorrow morning". Before Omar could argue the phone went dead. The old man had made his decision, there would be no discussion on the matter.

While they'd been working for him the old man never had any cause to doubt either Omar or Hadia's were trustworthy. But because Omar had concealed the fact that Hadia was his niece there was always a nagging doubt at the back of his mind of what they could possibly be planning. The problem in the UK office had given him an opportunity to separate them just in case there was such a plan. They hadn't been responsible for the organisation losing any money during the time they'd been working together but he was glad of an excuse to put some distance between them.

Omar called Hadia into his office to explain the situation. "When you finish tonight go home and pack enough for a couple of weeks away. We're sending you to the UK to take over responsibility for transferring money here. Tell your parents you'll be working abroad for a short period, hopefully you should be home soon. Some money, a visa and a passport will be provided."

Hadia sat in silence for a moment, shocked at the news. "I have my own passport. Why would I need a false one?" she asked.

Omar rose from his desk and closed the office door. "The name on your passport is your real one. I didn't tell the old man you were my niece when you were recruited, and I gave him a false name. The old man thinks your name is Hadia Bukhari, that's the name that will be on the passport one of his men is bringing. And we don't want the authorities to be able to trace you. You know what you're going there to do is illegal. We need to make sure you can't be traced back to us if you are caught."

"But what if I don't want to go?" Hadia protested finally grasping what was happening. "How long are you sending me there for? A couple of weeks isn't a definite amount of time, do you actually know when I'll be coming home? You know I hated living in the UK while I was at university and I said I would never go back. Why can't they send the person they're sending to replace me here to the UK instead? There must be someone else they could send."

"I'm sorry Hadia but you have no choice. The people responsible for transferring money to our account here have always previously worked in this office receiving the funds. It's a matter of trust. When you work for this organisation you do as you're told, they pay us well and expect us to do as they wish. I'm afraid there's no negotiation. Go to the UK and put things right over there and I'll do everything I can to find a replacement and get you home as soon as possible."

Hadia returned to her desk, desperately unhappy and annoyed she had no say in this decision. She was being sent back to a country she hated and had vowed never to return to. She wondered if she'd done the right thing accepting this job, it had proved to be no more fulfilling than her last dead-end role at the bank. Her only consolation was that the pay was much better and the thought that she was helping in the fight against the foreign armies in her homeland. She had a horrible feeling her father had been correct when he'd told her not to accept Omar's job offer. Now she was working for this organisation she could see no way out.

At the end of the day, she transferred the balance in the account and shut down her computer. She picked up her bag and went to Omar's office to wait for her money and travel documents. Ten minutes later one of the old man's bodyguards arrived with money, visa, passport and ticket as promised along with the address she would be staying at in the UK. He handed everything to Omar and left without saying a word.

The next morning Hadia made the same journey to Karachi International Airport she'd made years earlier, but this time she travelled alone. Although she was annoyed and disappointed to be returning to the UK, she was more upset that her mother and father had not come to wish her goodbye and good luck. Whatever they felt about the people she was working for she was still their daughter. In stark contrast to her last journey to the UK this one would be made with a heavy heart and the hope she would soon be returning home. She took one last look at the name on the passport to remind herself of her false identity then approached passport control.

Later that day Hadia landed at a cold and grey Heathrow Airport. She collected her bags and proceeded through passport control and customs without a problem. She caught a train into central London then another north to the house rented for the people working for the organisation. When she arrived, she was shown to a bedroom much smaller than the one she had left at home. Hadia returned to the kitchen after unpacking her bags to be told that her new workmates had already eaten. If she wanted to eat, she would have to cook for herself or order a takeaway. Worried the unfriendly welcome was a sign of things to come Hadia told them she wasn't hungry but was tired after the long journey, she would return to her room to rest and prepare for the new job the following day.

Hadia woke late the next morning to find her new work colleagues had already left for work. She quickly ate breakfast then set off for the office address she'd been given. Once again she hoped the attitude shown the previous evening by the men she would be working with was not a sign of things to come. They had been far from welcoming and seemed to resent her arrival. She hoped they didn't have the same attitude to women she'd experienced while working at the bank in Pakistan.

When she arrived at the address, a small unit on an industrial estate not unlike the one she was working in two days ago in Pakistan, she realised she hadn't been given the entry code for the keypad. She knocked on the door, after a few seconds it was opened, and she was beckoned inside. There were five men in the room. Amir and Imran worked the phones, Hassan sat at a computer plucking at the keyboard with one finger as if it were about to bite him. The other two members of the team, Nasir and Tariq, were security and performed any other tasks the team required. Playing on a loop over speakers mounted on the walls was the sound of a large office or call centre, telephones ringing, background voices and the sound of typing on computer keyboards.

Tariq pointed to the computer station. "This is where you will be working," he said. Hassan jumped out of the chair, the relief that someone had come to replace him written all over his face. He showed Hadia the role she would be performing, gave her the bank login details and the account details to which she would be transferring money to then left her to it.

Within days funds being transferred from the UK returned to their previous levels.

8

The sound of his mobile phone ringing and vibrating on the desk of his student accommodation woke Sam at ten-thirty. He stretched out an arm but couldn't quite reach the phone. Whoever was calling could wait, he thought. It couldn't be anything important this early in the morning. Thirty seconds later the noise from the phone stopped followed by an alert that the caller had left a message. With a little more sleep, a coffee and a shower he hoped his hangover would wear off. He rolled over, pulled the quilt back over his exposed shoulders and tried to go back to sleep.

Sam's student loan had arrived in his bank account the day before and he'd spent the evening celebrating being solvent again with his mates at the student union. Despite being the son of a multi-millionaire businessman Sam was in the same financial position as most of his student friends. Each month his father sent the same amount of money to his bank account that he believed most of the other parents sent their undergraduate children. He didn't want Sam to stand out or to be everybody else's banker. After all, as Sam recalled his father saying before he left home for his first year at university, he wanted Sam *"to have the real uni experience,"* whatever that was. Despite what his father said Sam knew he would send extra money if needed, all he had to do was call and it would be sent without question.

Sam understood his father's reluctance to give his son unlimited funds. He didn't want him to stand out from his fellow students because of his money. He'd seen students from wealthy families throwing their money around, it attracted the kind of shallow friends only interested in their apparent wealth. He didn't want to be treated any differently to the other students, he wanted to be regarded as an ordinary student from an ordinary background. Most of his friends knew of his father's wealth but none of them mentioned it, and none of them expected him to subsidise them. He wanted true friends, not those who were only interested in him because of his father's wealth and position.

An hour later, after a shower and a coffee but still with a nagging hangover, Sam picked up his phone and listened to the recorded message he'd missed earlier.

"This is a call from The National Crime Agency. Your name has been passed to us by HM Revenue and Customs in connection with an investigation into serious criminal activities. There are outstanding legal proceedings against your name. Do not ignore this call, legal action will be taken and you may be prosecuted. Please call 01928 628376 to discuss this case."

The message immediately grabbed Sam's attention and seemed to cure his hangover instantly. He didn't know whether to be worried or blasé. He thought it must be a case of mistaken identity, or possibly a wrong number. Just to be sure he listened to the message again. Now convinced he was not the person the call was intended for he was certain a quick call would clear the misunderstanding up.

Using the call back function on his mobile phone Sam called the number. His call was answered immediately. "Hello this is Samuel Hills," he said, "someone from your office phoned me earlier regarding some legal proceedings outstanding against my name." In the background, Sam could hear what sounded like the noise of a busy office or call centre, the constant clatter of keyboards, the ringing of phones and chatter of people on other calls.

At the other end of the line, Imran noted the caller's name and the callers number displayed on his phone. "Thank you for calling back Mr. Hills, can you confirm your postcode and date of birth please."

Convinced he was talking to the police Sam gave his post-code and date of birth without question.

Imran noted the information and typed the postcode into the search bar of his laptop. "That's Woodhouse Lane, Leeds. Can you confirm the house number please?"

Sam explained that he was living in student accommodation and gave his flat number.

Imran noted the address. From previous experience, he knew students were invariably not worth pursuing. For a moment he contemplated telling the caller it was a case of mistaken identity, but he had no other calls waiting so decided to continue.

"Thank you for returning our call Mr. Hills. My name is Ken Martin, I am part of an investigation by the National Crime Agency into suspected money laundering. My officer number is 36369. We've called you today in connection with case number DC7010. A car hired in Manchester under your name and using your postcode has been found by police, inside of which was found a large amount of money and drugs. There were also weapons and blood found in the car. Have you ever hired a car in Manchester, Mr. Hills?"

Sam hesitated. "No, I can't drive, and I've never been to Manchester. Look, this is obviously a case of someone else using my name to hire this car."

SAM'S MIND flashed back to the one time he *had* been to Manchester, and the incident that had taken place almost a year earlier. Something that happened while he was on a stag weekend that he'd never spoken about. After a pub crawl, he found himself in a club with no money for a taxi home and no bank card to withdraw cash. Two of the stag party, lads Sam didn't know, offered him a ride. In his drunken state, Sam thought nothing of it, just relief that he had some way of getting home. It wasn't until he was sitting in the back of the car that he realised there were no keys in the ignition and wires were hanging from the dashboard. Even though he was a little drunk Sam knew he was in a stolen car with two people he didn't know.

"Cheaper than a taxi mate," the driver said. "How come you didn't have enough cash for a taxi?"

"The club was more expensive to get in than I thought it would be, and I never bring my wallet or bank card with me on nights out like this, just in case I have too much to drink and lose them."

The driver looked at him in the rear-view mirror. "Strange considering who your old man is,"

"Really, and who might he be?" Sam asked.

"Don't play games with us mate, we know who you are, and who your old man is."

"It makes no difference," Sam said. "I'm in the same boat as all the other students."

"You don't really believe that, do you?" the driver asked.

There was an awkward silence for a moment. Sam knew he had to get out of this situation as soon as possible. "Is this your car?" He asked trying to change the subject.

"It is for the moment." Both the driver and his front-seat passenger burst out laughing.

"Look, I don't want to be involved in this. Just drop me here and I'll find my own way home, thanks."

The front passenger reached out towards Sam. "Chill out man. Here try some of this, it's good stuff, it will calm you down." In his outstretched hand was a small clear plastic bag containing a white powder.

Although he'd never encountered it before Sam was sure he was being offered cocaine. The situation was getting worse by the second and he knew he had to get out of this car as soon as he could.

"Go on mate, try it. You'll feel better for it."

"No thanks. Look, drop me here and I'll call a cab."

"You told us you don't have enough money for a cab, that's why we offered you a ride home."

"I don't, but I'd rather take my chances than be caught in a stolen car with drugs in it."

"Please yourself, rich boy." The driver pulled over and Sam got out as quickly as he could. The car pulled away with a screech of tyres before he could close the door.

As Sam watched the car disappear around a corner at the end of the road rain started to fall. He turned to retrace his journey back towards the city centre, hoping to find somewhere he could shelter from the weather until morning when he could phone his father and arrange some way of getting home.

As he trudged along the road in the pouring rain a police car pulled up alongside him. Slowly the window powered down, the officer inside looked at him. "Not really dressed for the weather are you, sir?"

"No, but I wasn't expecting to be walking in the rain." Being stopped by the police so soon after being in a stolen car and being offered drugs Sam was struggling to keep his nerves under control and to appear calm to the officers.

"Can't you call a taxi?"

"No, I've only got about a fiver on me, not enough for a taxi home," Sam replied.

"Do you intend to walk home then?" the officer asked.

"No, it's too far to walk, I live in Leeds. I thought I'd go into the city centre and find somewhere I can keep dry and maybe get a coffee. Then I can call my Dad in the morning."

"Good old Dad eh?" The officer looked at his colleague then turned back to Sam. "Jump in son, before you get soaked. Our shift has finished and there's a place we can drop you on the way back to the station. It's nice and warm, open all night and has decent coffee. A fiver should get you a couple of cups while you wait."

After what had just happened Sam thought it ironic that he would now be retracing his steps in a police car.

"MR. HILLS, ARE YOU STILL THERE?" Imran asked.

"Oh, sorry." Sam was brought back to the present moment.

"The case against you involves drug trafficking and money laundering. These are very serious allegations. Do you have a bank account Mr. Hills?"

"Yes." Confused by the quick change in direction of the conversation, Sam wondered what his bank account had to do with a police investigation into drugs and weapons in a car.

"And do you have a regular income paid into this account, sir?" Imran asked. The initial questions were deliberately short to keep a fast pace to the conversation, and with quick changes of subject designed to confuse their intended victim and stop them from having time to think.

"No, I'm a student, I only have my student loan and what my father sends me each month paid into my account."

"And nobody else pays money into your account?" Imran read from his script.

"No, just my student loan and money from my father," Sam repeated.

"How much is in your account now, sir?"

Sam thought for a moment trying to calculate how much was in his account. The rent on his student accommodation was due to be paid that day and then there was what he'd spent the night before in the bar and the money he'd spent on the train fare returning to uni. He made a quick calculation then told the officer the amount he believed to be in his account.

Based solely on what the person at the other end of the call told him was in their bank account, it was at this point Imran made the decision whether to continue the scam or end the call and move on to the next victim. Anything over five hundred pounds was usually worth pursuing and based on what the young man had told him Imran thought this one fell firmly in that category. "From what you've said Mr. Hills I assume you deny these charges?" he asked.

"Yes of course, I told you I can't drive and...."

Before Sam could go any further Imran interrupted, "Sir, I'm going to pass you over to the senior officer investigating this case. Please hold the line while I transfer you."

Sam could hear his heart pounding while he waited for a minute in silence, he felt totally disorientated. This whole thing was careering out of control. He was climbing out of bed to have a shower thirty minutes ago, now he was entangled in a police investigation involving drugs. He'd already told them he couldn't drive and had lied about never being in Manchester, why wouldn't the people on the other end of the line just listen to him? They would realise that this was a case of identity theft if only they would stop and listen. Eventually, a new voice came on the line.

"Hello, my name is James Douglas officer number KRM469238. I should make you aware that this call is being recorded and that we are on a three-way call with the legal team and prosecutors dealing with this case. Do you understand sir?" Amir asked.

"Yes."

"I understand that you have a bank account sir, do you have any other investments?"

"No," said Sam.

"And how much is in your account Mr. Hills?"

"I told the other officer, I don't know exactly, probably around four and a half thousand pounds."

"As my colleague explained we are investigating a case of drug trafficking and money laundering, and in cases such as this we need to freeze the bank account of the suspect for up to ninety days while the investigation takes place. We want to prevent whoever is committing these crimes access to bank accounts, to stop them moving drug money in and out of the country, possibly using your account, and from taking your money, sir," Amir said.

"But it's not me. I've already told you the only money going into my account is from my father and my student loan, and I've never been to Manchester." Sam was becoming increasingly frustrated; these people weren't listening to anything he was telling them.

"I understand that sir, but whoever has committed these crimes has used your identity to hire a car in Manchester. We must assume they also have access to all your other personal details, which will include your bank account. You must understand that this is a very serious matter, one that carries a custodial sentence. We need to convince the prosecutor and legal team who are listening to our conversation that you are not the person committing these crimes. At present you are liable for prosecution for some very serious crimes and could face jail time if found guilty. Do you understand?"

"Yes but...."

"Sir," Amir interrupted, "let me put you on hold while I speak to the prosecutors. Please don't hang up, if you do, we will assume you are using the time to move money and cover your tracks. We'll take it as an admission of guilt." Amir pressed the hold button on the phone, cutting Sam off before he could protest any further.

Leaving the caller on hold was one of the scammers usual tactics. While there was silence on the line the person at the other end of the call would be thinking of all sorts of scenarios, worried that they were implicated in a serious crime, facing prosecution and possible time in jail, unable to think of a way out. The victims, such as the young man currently on hold, were unaware that in a few moments Amir would be offering just that, but at the price of his bank balance.

On the other end of the phone Sam was beginning to panic. How could this be happening to him? He'd never been in trouble with the police before. Did this have something to do with the stag night in Manchester the year before? Why had he lied to the policeman about never being in Manchester? Surely what had happened that night couldn't have anything to do with this case. Why would anyone target him for this, and how had they got his details? And why wouldn't these people listen to him? They would realise that he was innocent if he could just make them stop and listen.

Amir disconnected the call from their latest victim, someone they had scammed out of six thousand pounds. He took a sip of his coffee and checked his mobile phone for any messages. The other man had been on hold for a couple of minutes, time to continue this call. He checked the name at the top of his list and reconnected the call.

"Mr. Hills, thank you for holding. I've talked to the legal team and we don't believe that it's you who has committed these crimes, but we need your co-operation while we investigate this case and try to catch the criminals who have. Are you willing to help us, sir?"

"Yes." At last Sam thought, relieved the people at the other end of the line finally realised they were pursuing the wrong man.

"Good, then this is how we need to proceed. As I previously said your bank account will be frozen preventing both you and anyone else from accessing it. Before we freeze your account, we need you to transfer the balance to a government treasury escrow account which will keep your money safe while the investigation proceeds. Do you know what an escrow account is sir?"

"No." Being the son of a multi-millionaire businessman Sam felt that maybe he should.

"Sir, do you have internet access?" Amir asked.

"Yes."

Good, another piece of the puzzle in place Amir thought. "Could you log on to the internet, and once you've done that let me know and I'll give you a website that will explain what an escrow account is and how it works."

"Okay, hold on a moment while I log in to my laptop." Sam put his phone on the desk and turned on the speaker-phone so that he could listen and type at the same time. "Okay, I'm logged in."

"Type into the search bar dot gov," Amir said, "then choose the second option on the list, IEIM401860 – Financial Accounts, then please read the explanation."

Sam did as the officer asked, "Okay," he said when he'd finished reading the explanation.

"Did you understand it, sir?" Amir asked.

"No, not really," Sam replied.

"Basically, it means that the balance of your account will be held in an account by a third party, in this case HM Treasury. We'll send two officers to your house tomorrow with statements detailing everything we've spoken about today and various other documents for you to sign. They will give you a cashier's cheque equal to the four thousand five hundred pounds you will be transferring. What time would it be convenient for our offices to call?" Amir asked.

Despite his initial relief that these people now believed him to be innocent the situation was once again spiralling out of Sam's control. Events were moving at a pace he felt he couldn't control. He was becoming more and more disorientated, confused and panicked by what was happening. "Err... around 10.30 tomorrow morning would be fine," he said. With what had happened over the last few minutes going around his head he couldn't remember if he had lectures to attend the following morning or not but at the moment that seemed irrelevant. He needed to concentrate and resolve this situation before he could think of anything else.

"Good, when the officers call tomorrow they'll show you their ID badges and officer numbers as proof of identity. They'll ask you to sign a statement confirming everything we've talked about today and documents confirming the balance transferred to the escrow account. Are you ready to transfer the money now sir?" Amir asked.

"Yes," Sam said. Bewildered by what was going on he was almost acting like a puppet whose strings were being pulled by the man at the other end of the phone.

"Okay sir, if you could log into your bank account then I'll give you the sort code, account number and name of the account the transfer needs to be made to. Let me know when you are ready".

Sam logged in to his bank, checked the account balance then navigated to the transfer screen. "Okay," he said, "I'm logged in."

"The account details are, sort code 04-00-75, account number 07931336, the name of the account is William Rieds, I'll repeat that" Amir repeated the sort code and account number, "I'll spell out the name of the public prosecutor's account," he read out the name letter by letter, "it is W-I-L-L-I-A M space R-I-E-D hyphen S."

Sam typed the account details in as Amir read them out, all except the name. A mistake, he thought. Surely it was an apostrophe not a hyphen at the end of the name? He typed the account name in as he thought it should be and completed the transfer amount, three thousand nine hundred and fifty-two pounds seventy pence, then pressed confirm. "Okay," he said, "there wasn't four and a half thousand pounds in the account, but I've transferred the balance." Sam told the officer the amount he'd transferred.

"Sir, you told us you were transferring four thousand five hundred pounds, this will now cause us a problem. We've already instructed the prosecutor to draw a cashier's cheque for that amount. It doesn't look good on you sir, it appears that you haven't been entirely honest with us, it could look like you are trying to hide something." This wasn't an unusual situation for Amir. In his experience, people rarely knew exactly how much was in their bank account, but he had a tactic to take the difference between what Sam had told them was in his account and the amount he'd already transferred.

"No, I wouldn't have transferred *any* money if I was trying to hide anything," Sam said. "I gave you the balance of what I thought was in my account. Surely you can't expect me to know exactly what's in my account at any one moment."

"Sir, let me talk to the legal team to discuss this problem. I'm going to put you on hold for a moment."

As the seconds ticked by and with silence on the line, Sam finally had time to think about what had happened over the last whirlwind few minutes, and the more he thought the more concerned he became. How had this happened? Drug trafficking, money laundering, weapons, blood in a car in Manchester. This was the stuff of nightmares. His heart was racing, his head spinning, he couldn't think straight. If only he could talk to his father, he would know what to do.

Amir came back on the line. "Mr. Hills, the only solution to the problem you've caused is for you to transfer the difference between what you said was in your account and what you've transferred to the Treasury escrow account. The difference is five hundred and forty-seven pounds and thirty pence. This problem will be solved if you transfer this amount to the same account I gave you earlier."

"But I can't transfer money I don't have. Surely it would be easier for you to cancel the cheque and write another for the correct amount?"

"Sir, you've caused this problem by not being honest with us in the first place. You need to transfer the difference to the account I gave you earlier."

"But I have been honest. You asked me if I would help in this case and I have. I've transferred everything that was in my account, I can't transfer any-more." Sam was becoming annoyed and frustrated with this man, he wasn't listening to anything he said. Everything that had happened since he'd called this number was going around his head and he was beginning to question everything he'd been told. Two men with broad Asian accents named Ken Martin and James Douglas. The use of an apostrophe instead of a hyphen in the account name. The insistence of transferring money he didn't have to the type of account he'd never heard of. But he was still unsure. "Look, I'm uncomfortable transferring any more money, I've transferred everything that was in my account. That's all I have. I'm a student and I don't have an overdraft. If I go overdrawn the charges will be astronomical which I can't afford, and I don't think the bank would let me make the transfer anyway."

"Sir, we are only trying to protect you and your hard-earned money and to catch the real culprits committing these crimes," Amir was now trying to prolong the conversation for as long as possible.

"I'm trying to protect my money too. I've done everything you asked. I transferred the balance in my account, I can't transfer money I don't have." There was a long pause. In the silence, Sam plucked up the courage to say what had been on his mind for the last few minutes. "How do I know this isn't a scam?" Finally, he'd said it. He knew the man at the other end of the phone wouldn't admit it was a scam, but he wanted to hear how he would react.

"Sir, we are trying to protect you and your money, please don't insult me by accusing me of being a thief. It's you who's caused this problem by not being honest with us. You told me you were transferring four and a half thousand pounds, but you've transferred less than that. It's caused trouble for me and I'm trying to help you. You need to transfer the rest to the account I gave you earlier. Are you ready to transfer the rest?"

From the tone of his voice Sam thought the man at the other end of the phone was becoming more and more aggressive. "No, I'm not prepared to transfer any more money. I've already told you I've transferred everything that was in my account, I don't have any more. I'm not sure I should have transferred any money at all." There was a moment's silence before Sam continued. "I think I'm going to phone my bank and stop the transfer I've just made. If this is genuine you can come and arrest me. If this ever gets to court, which I doubt it ever will, you'll see that I'm innocent."

"Sir if you do that you will be making a very big mistake. We'll send officers to your house to arrest you for the crimes we've detailed if you disconnect this call. You wouldn't want that would you sir?" Amir was doing his best to delay any call Sam might make to his bank. The longer he kept him on the line the less chance Sam would have to stop the transfer. Sat opposite him, Hadia was waiting to transfer the money to Karachi as soon as it arrived in their account. Once the transfer was made there would be nothing in the account for Sam's bank to recover.

Sam picked up his mobile phone and turned the speaker-phone off. Still a little unsure he was doing the right thing he decided not to end the call. Although he was now convinced this was a scam at the back of his mind there was still a nagging doubt, what if he was wrong? What if this was legitimate and it really was the police on the other end of the line? He slipped the phone into his pocket, careful not to end the call, and stepped out of his flat. He left the student accommodation and ran down the road looking for the nearest public phone. Ten minutes later he entered the student union and eventually found the phones he'd walked passed on numerous occasions but had never noticed. He looked up the number for his bank and dialled. The wait while the automated voice went through his options and informing him that all calls were recorded for training purposes seemed to last forever. He knew time was critical in this type of transaction. His money would be gone if he didn't stop the transfer he'd just made quickly enough. Finally, he got the option number he needed. "Hello," he said, "I think I've been the victim of a scam. I need to stop a transfer I've just made." He looked at the screen of his mobile phone again, the call to the National Crime Agency had been ended, but not by him.

"One moment please, I'll put you through to someone who can help you," the voice at the other end of the line said.

A moment later another voice came onto the phone, "Hello, I understand you believe you've been the victim of a scam?"

"Yes," said Sam.

"And when did this happen?"

"About thirty minutes ago."

"And how did this scam happen?"

"I transferred the balance of my account to someone who said they were from the police."

"Did you make the transfer online or was it done at one of our branches? The lady asked.

"I did it online."

"Okay, can I take your name and date of birth please?"

Sam gave the information.

"And the first line of your address and your postcode."

Again, Sam gave the information.

"And I assume you would like me to stop the latest transfer you made today?"

"Yes please," a note of desperation had crept into Sam's voice, he needed this to be done quicker. To him, there seemed no urgency from the lady at the other end of the phone.

"One moment while I log in to your account. Can I take your account number please?"

Sam's mobile phone rang as he reached for the wallet in his back pocket, he looked at the screen. It was not a number he recognised. He declined the call.

"Mr Hills, your account number please," the voice asked again.

"Sorry, one moment." Fumbling for the bank card in his wallet Sam pulled the card out and dropped both his wallet and card. As he leant down to pick them up he noticed his hands were shaking. He took a moment to compose himself then picked up the card and wallet. He was about to give his account details when his mobile phone rang again. The same unrecognised number displayed on the screen as the last call. He declined the call again. Trying to compose himself once more he read his account details to the lady from the bank.

"Okay, Mr. Hills, I can see you have made a transfer of three thousand nine hundred and seventy-two pounds seventy pence just over half an hour ago. Is this the transfer you would like me to try to stop?"

"Yes please." Hurry please, he thought, I really don't want to lose this money. Any doubt he previously had was gone, now convinced the money he'd transferred was to a scam.

"Okay, please give me the account details of the beneficiary, the account where the money has been sent to."

Sam gave the details. He could hear the clatter of the keyboard as she entered the information he'd given her.

"Mr Hills, all I can do is apply to the beneficiary's bank and try to recover this transfer as fraudulent. If they are happy that it is fraudulent the transfer will not go through and the money will appear back in your account sometime tomorrow."

Sam's phone rang again, the same unrecognised number. He declined the call for a third time.

"I have to tell you Mr. Hills, these transactions are time sensitive and these types of transfers are seldom recovered. With faster online payments the money would appear in the beneficiary's account almost immediately. If this is a scam the money you transferred will be forwarded to another bank account, probably abroad, as soon as it arrives and will be impossible to recover."

Sam's heart sank, "Okay," he said.

"One last thing Mr. Hills, and probably the most important thing. You didn't give these people your account details, did you?"

"No."

"I've done as much as I can at the moment Mr. Hills, I'm going to put you through to our fraud department, they will take the details of what's happened to you. If there's any official investigation or prosecution, they will assist the police." Sam was transferred to the fraud department and went through the whole sorry episode again. When he'd taken all the information he needed, the man in the fraud department thanked Sam for his time and repeated the fact that he was unlikely to get his money back then ended the call. Sam though it would probably be to take a call from another mug who'd just been scammed.

Sam's phone rang again, the same unrecognised number. He declined the call again. Only forty-five minutes had passed since Sam had called what he'd believed to be the National Crime Agency. During that short space of time, he felt that he'd lost control of his own fate and his world had fallen apart.

IN A SMALL INDUSTRIAL unit sixty miles away Hadia stared at her computer screen as three thousand nine hundred and fifty-two pound and seventy pence arrived in the account from a Mr. S Hills. She confirmed the receipt to Hassan then transferred the money on to the account in Karachi. Amir listened with relief. It was one transfer the victim had been too late to recover. He moved on to their next victim.

SAM FELT DRAINED, exhausted, a physical and emotional wreck. Slowly he made his way out of the student union and headed for his accommodation hoping he wouldn't meet anyone he knew. The way he was feeling he wasn't sure he could face anyone without breaking down. In his head, he went through what had happened over and over again. As he sat alone in his room the whole episode overwhelmed him and tears began to course down his cheeks. How could he have been so stupid? How had he not realised what the people who'd called were doing? He'd heard of so many different types of scam but never believed he would be caught out and fall victim to one. He always believed the victims of crimes like this were old and gullible, not young and savvy like he believed himself to be. But the stark reality was that he was sitting alone in his room, heart still pounding, tears streaming down his face and nearly four thousand pounds worse off. He now knew anyone could be caught out. People would do almost anything to clear their name if these people scared them enough.

Twenty minutes later when he'd calmed down Sam remembered the unrecognised calls he'd declined while talking to his bank. He typed the number into the search bar on his phone and stared in horror at screen. The number was recognised as West Yorkshire Police. Suddenly his earlier doubts returned, Sam started to panic again. What if it hadn't been a scam? What if the whole thing was real? Would the police be calling at any minute to arrest him for a crime he hadn't committed? He decided not to use the call back function but dial the number he'd just looked up.

"Hello West Yorkshire police," the voice at the other end of the line said. "How may I direct your call?"

"Hello," Sam said, "I think I've been the victim of a scam. I've had had four calls from your number."

"One moment sir and I'll direct your call to the correct department."

Once he'd been put through and explained what had happened the officer checked the call records. "There's no record of calls made to your number, sir. I think the calls were made by whoever was scamming you. It's called mirroring or caller ID spoofing. Your phone displays a number the scammers want you to believe is a legitimate organisation, they hope you'll use the call back facility on your phone which will direct the call back to the scammers' number. It's used to convince victims that the people they are calling are who they say they are, in your case the National Crime Agency, then they continue their scam."

Sam felt a huge sense of relief, at least he'd done something right, he thought. He would have believed he was talking to the National Crime Agency if he'd used the call back facility when the first call came through, and if the bank had allowed him, he may have transferred a further five hundred pounds.

The police officer gave Sam a case log number and advised him to contact Action Fraud who would investigate his case and try to prevent others from falling victim to the same scam.

Sam sat on his bed and looked down at his hands, they were still shaking. The whole experience had left him feeling exhausted, both physically and emotionally drained, constantly on the verge of tears. He looked at his phone lying on the bed beside him. Now for the most difficult call, he thought to himself, the call to his father.

9

The old man looked around the other assembled delegates sat at the conference table. Like him, many of them were old, veterans of wars fought in years long gone. Some of the younger ones around the table came from countries he'd never heard of, countries that didn't exist when he was their age, part of the former Soviet Union. Whatever their countries were called now, he hated all Russians.

His hatred stemmed from an incident many years before. Sitting outside a hospital ward awaiting news of his daughter, he was startled when a Russian officer burst through the doors carrying a young girl. He hesitated before chasing after the man carrying what he thought was his daughter. That moment of hesitation had proved to be a defining moment in his life. When he emerged through the doors, he saw the Russian drop his daughter at the top of the hospital steps. Unable to stop herself, the young girl tumbled down the steps and lay on the pavement crying and bleeding. He rushed past the Russian and took his daughter in his arms, trying to comfort her. After taking a few moments to calm his daughter, he gathered her in his arms and retraced his steps to confront the man who continued to stare down at him.

"How dare you treat my child like this," he said. "What kind of man treats an innocent child so brutally? Have you no compassion? She's being treated in this hospital for an unknown sickness. You are nothing but an animal."

The Russian looked at the young man standing before him and smiled. "Don't ever speak to me again. Take your child and leave while you still can. If I ever see you here again, I will have you and the rest of your family arrested. You are an enemy of the state, a terrorist, fighting against your own people. You should be ashamed of yourself." He stepped forward and shoved the young man in the chest. Off balance, he took a step backwards and tumbled down the hospital steps, all the while trying to prevent further injury to his daughter. Lying bruised and dazed on the pavement, he looked up to see the Russian officer grinning at him before he turned and disappeared through the hospital doors.

With his daughter still in his arms and surrounded by a crowd of onlookers who'd witnessed his humiliation, the young man dragged himself to his feet. With his head hung in shame, he slowly made his way home.

Consumed by anger, he vowed he would avenge his daughter's treatment and his own humiliation at the hands of this monster. Determined this man would pay dearly for the way they had both been treated, he returned to the hospital each day to wait for the Russian to appear. He watched his movements, his arrogant manner and assumed superiority over the people his army now subjugated. The more he saw of this man, the more determined he became that he should pay for the pain he'd inflicted on his daughter, himself and his people.

Each day he watched the Russian, following his every move. Over the next few weeks, he became familiar with his routine, which days he came to the hospital, what time he arrived, what time he left, where he ate in the city and where he was stationed.

He watched the Russian beat the doctor responsible for his daughter's treatment as he stood in the shade of the trees outside the hospital waiting for the him to leave. It wasn't the first time he'd seen the doctor subjected to such merciless treatment. His anger and resolve deepened. This man felt no shame in throwing an innocent child down steps or beating a defenceless doctor treating the sick and injured.

He believed that if he could rid the world of this arrogant man everyone would benefit. The hospital would be allowed to treat everyone, not only those the Russian agreed to, the doctor's beatings and humiliation would stop, and he would never again treat an innocent child the way he'd treated his daughter. A plan began to formulate in his head, one he hoped he would soon be able to put into action.

Waiting in the shadows late one night he watched the Russian leave a bar opened in the city after the invasion. The bar catered solely for army officers, no other ranks or civilians were allowed entry. As he walked back to his barracks it was obvious the Russian had consumed more than was good for him. A little unsteady on his feet and unaware of what was going on around him, he began staggering back to his officer's quarters.

This was the opportunity the young man had been waiting for. Keeping to the shadows, he silently followed the Russian as he made his unsteady way back towards his barracks through the deserted streets. Suddenly the Russian stopped in the middle of the road and looked all around him. He needed the toilet but nowhere was open at such a late hour. His only option would be to use one of the many alleyways. He walked unsteadily along the first dark alleyway he saw, unzipped his trousers and stretched out an arm to steady himself against the wall.

Seizing his opportunity, the young man took out his knife and silently crept up behind the Russian. Still unaware of the man's presence, the Russian officer felt the cold steel of a knife at his throat.

"This is for my daughter and for my people," the young man whispered, the last words the Russian officer would ever hear.

He wiped the blood from his knife on the Russian's uniform and glanced towards both ends of the alleyway. There was no one around, no one to witness the killing. The young man's honour had been satisfied and revenge was complete. He left his victim slumped on the filthy alley floor in a pool of his own urine and blood in amongst the household rubbish and scurrying rats. The young man quickly disappeared into the city's labyrinth of alleyways, content that the Russian would hurt no more innocent children or humiliate doctors treating the sick and injured. He arrived home late that night. His family collected their meagre belongings and prepared to leave the city. He would join his fellow countrymen in the hills fighting the Russian invaders. It would be many years before he returned to the city, and when he did it would be as a very different man.

.   .   .

THE OLD MAN returned his attention to the delegates around the table. They were attending the conference for one reason, how to finance the wars to rid their countries of foreign invaders and those they deemed to be undesirable citizens. Some of the more radicals around the table wanted to establish a caliphate in the region but the old man was sceptical. The Western powers would never allow them to attain their goal. A country established based on strict sharia law would be a step too far for the West. He was here to talk money, and how to get more, not some dream that would never happen and a state that would be too strict for the lifestyle he wanted after retirement.

His particular group ran the finance operation in Karachi, a small operation compared to those some of the others around the table ran, but it generated enough to finance their part of the war, fund his expensive tastes and contribute to his retirement fund.

He'd been running the operation for many years, and each month he took a little of what money was generated from the West to add to his retirement fund. Although he despised the West, there were certain parts of their culture he enjoyed and embraced. At the rate the current operation was generating income, he would have enough money saved in five years to fund the lifestyle he wanted, a lifestyle he looked forward to away from the wars, food shortages, the threat of air strikes and the seemingly endless conferences he was now tired of.

He glanced around the table again. Many of the others who were a similar age to himself also took a share of the money their operations generated, some more than others. It was understood among themselves that it was a benefit of doing the job, remuneration for their services, provided they did it in moderation. The younger fanatics fighting the wars back in their homelands would be horrified if they discovered what the older delegates were doing and how much money they were taking for themselves. But who would tell them? It certainly wouldn't be any of those around the table personally benefitting from the fundraising. Most of the delegates were looking forward to retiring with the money they'd taken from their own individual scam operations just as he was.

The old man prided himself as much for the intelligence network he was operating as the finance operation. He knew the best way to stay ahead of his rivals was to know everything about them. His network had gathered a huge amount of information about all the delegates sat around this conference table, information he could use against them should ever it be needed.

He took the same approach with the people who worked for him. Know everything about them and their families, keep a watchful eye on them and listen to what they say. It was surprising what information could be picked up by simply listening to what his employees believed to be an innocent conversation, at some point it may prove to be an advantage.

When he'd first recruited Omar, the old man had asked him to tell him about himself, something he did whenever he recruited a new senior member to his organisation. He was fascinated to hear of Omar's time in Kabul, the same time he himself had lived in the city, and both seemingly experiencing the cruelty of what appeared to be the same Russian officer. If only Omar's father had delayed his family's flight from Afghanistan his troubles would have disappeared, ended in a filthy alleyway in the depths of the city.

After hearing Omar's account of his journey home from the war, he had also taken action to ensure the same fate didn't befall other men returning home after being injured in the fighting. The driver and guard of the truck had been interrogated by the old man's team who discovered that this was a common practice of theirs. They would travel far enough from the hospital to make it appear that they had travelled to their destination. Once far enough away from the hospital they would kill any passengers who'd survived at that point and pocket the remaining money. Both driver and guard would no longer subject their passengers to such a fate. Their bodies now rested in the same river valley they'd used to disposed of one of Omar's fellow passengers.

His intelligence network had also discovered that the woman they'd sent to the UK was Omar's niece. Why had Omar kept that from him? Was he foolish enough to believe that his secret wouldn't be discovered? The old man respected anyone who'd fought against the invading armies in Afghanistan, especially those who'd been wounded as Omar had, but if he thought he wouldn't discover the woman was his niece Omar was badly mistaken.

The old man's network reached everywhere in Karachi and much further beyond. He had people reporting to him in every country they operated in around the world. He was suspicious of everyone and by trying to keep such a secret Omar had raised his suspicions even further. Was he plotting something that also involved his niece? Had he recruited her to implement a plan to steal the organisation's money? Now Omar had a possible accomplice, the old man would have his people keep an even closer eye on them both.

The problem with the man in the UK had arisen at exactly the right time. He had the opportunity to send Omar's niece abroad and have his man in the UK keep watch over everything she did. He would speak to Nasir the next day to see if she'd been in contact with Omar. He needed to put a stop to any plan they may have before any money was lost.

The old man brought his attention back to the conference. One of the Russians was talking about another invasion, a subject the old man was not interested in. He wanted nothing to do with any plan that would be a drain on their income before he retired, or more importantly a drain on his retirement fund.

Another of the delegates sat across the table from him held a special interest for the old man. Someone who ran a finance operation similar to his own, one that generated more income but with twice the number of staff, three of whom were his sons. His intelligence network had discovered that this man was taking far more money for himself than was normal, not only to fund his own future retirement but also his three son's lavish lifestyles. The old man had been cultivating this man's superiors for many months and at the last conference had let slip in conversation just how much money they were losing and, should they wish, that he would be willing to run their finance operation for a fee vastly less than what this man was stealing. It wouldn't be long before the man across the table, along with his three sons, were no longer part of the organisation. The old man would replace the staff running their scam and would take the modest fee each month they'd agreed on. After a few months he would gradually increase what he took. This combined with the income he already enjoyed from the existing finance operation would hopefully bring his own retirement forward.

10

S am's father, Sir Duncan Hills, widower and self-made millionaire, sat in his London office reading an article in the Financial Times about an African charity protecting elephants from ivory poachers. After visiting a game reserve in Africa and witnessing the carnage poachers wrought it was a charity his business and he personally was glad to make generous donations to. The phone on his desk interrupted his reading.

Sir Duncan put the newspaper on his desk and picked up the phone, "Sir, it's your son," his secretary said.

"Thanks, Emma. Put him through please."

"Hi Dad," Sam said once his call was connected.

As soon as his son spoke Sir Duncan knew something was wrong. "Hi Sam, is everything okay?" Not only was it unusual for his son to call during office hours but it was also unusual for Sir Duncan to be available.

"No Dad, it's not I'm afraid. I've been scammed." Sam went through the story again, and as he recounted what had happened thought how stupid he'd been to be taken in by these people. He struggled to keep his emotions in check as he told his father the story, tears began running down his cheeks once more. He felt embarrassed and a sense of shame telling his father what had happened.

Sir Duncan was a man who, in his younger days, had grafted night and day to establish his fledgling business, often foregoing a monthly salary to invest money back into his business. Now his son was explaining how he'd given away all the money in his bank account so easily.

Despite his embarrassment at being so naïve, Sam felt a sense of relief after telling the story to his father. When he'd finished recounting his story there was silence on the line, Sir Duncan shocked at his son's news. "You didn't give them your account number did you Sam?" he eventually asked.

"No, Dad." Despite feeling embarrassed at being scammed Sam felt relieved he hadn't given his account details. He knew how much worse things could have been if he had.

"How much did they take?" his father asked.

He'd already told his father how much he'd lost but Sam told him again. "Three thousand nine hundred and fifty-two pounds."

"Thank heavens you didn't transfer the rest they asked for. Are you sure you're all right Sam? Do you want to come home? I'll cancel my appointments and drive up to get you if you want to come back for a few days." Sir Duncan's first reaction was to protect his son, but he knew Sam would be reluctant to come home so soon after returning to university.

"No Dad, I'll be okay thanks. I need to be here at uni, my lectures start tomorrow, besides I've only just come back after the summer break. I need to put this behind me as soon as I can and try to get back to normal."

"Okay, if you're sure. I'll transfer the money you've lost to your account after our call. I don't think anyone will call on you tomorrow but if anyone does *do not* let them in. And have someone else there with you just in case, maybe the rest of the rugby team," Sir Duncan said, trying to add a little humour to lift his son's mood. "Are you sure you're ok Sam?" he asked again.

"Yes Dad, I'm just a bit shaken, and feeling a bit stupid about the whole thing to be honest, but I'll be ok. Thanks for understanding, and for replacing the money."

"No problem. The money's not important, as long as you're all right. Call me again tomorrow for a catch-up, any time, and to let me know you're okay." Sir Duncan scribbled a note in his diary to remind himself that his son would call again tomorrow, and if he didn't, he would call Sam in the evening.

"There's one other thing Dad, something I've never told anyone, it's probably totally unrelated to this but...." Sam told his father about the ride in a stolen car in Manchester, and the offer of drugs from two young men who said they knew who both Sam and his father were. "I'm sure it has nothing to do with the scam. I know it was a stupid thing to do but I didn't want the police to know I'd been to Manchester before, just in case. I'm sure it's just a coincidence."

For a moment there was silence. Sam could feel his father's disapproval down the telephone line.

"You should have told me about this when it happened. You had nothing to hide, it wasn't you who'd stolen the car and had drugs on them. It doesn't matter anyway, I'm certain the people you were speaking to were not the police, and I'm sure these two incidents aren't connected."

"I know Dad, sorry."

"If you're ever in a situation like that again, call me. It doesn't matter what time it is. I'll speak to you again tomorrow. Love you son."

"Love you too Dad, and thanks again for replacing the money."

Sir Duncan ended the call and sat for a while, any thoughts of his business or the article he'd been reading before Sam's call now completely erased from his mind. Ideally, he would like Sam to come home for a few days, but he knew he had to let his son make his own way in the world, however difficult. He wondered if it was more a case of him needing Sam home to feel he was protecting him, rather than Sam needing his protection.

He opened his laptop and transferred the money to his son's account, replacing what the scammers had stolen. Three thousand nine hundred and fifty-two pounds the scum had stolen. In his mind, he went over Sam's story again and again, each time he came back to the amount they had stolen. These people were nothing but a leech on society. They contributed nothing and stole from vulnerable people, most of whom couldn't afford to lose their money. He was in the lucky position where the loss of nearly four thousand pounds wouldn't affect him or his son financially, but he knew that wasn't the case for most people who were victims of scammers. So long as his son was all right that was the main thing. Sam was obviously shaken but he was young and with the distraction of a new university year starting he would be over the upset in a few days, although he probably wouldn't forget it in a hurry.

Sir Duncan's mantra in life had always been "*don't get mad, get even,*" it was how he'd built his business. He thought that if ever there was ever a time he wanted to get even this was it.

Sitting at his desk almost in a state of meditation, Sir Duncan continued to go over Sam's story. As much as he was relieved his son was all right, he couldn't get away from the amount of money the scammers had stolen. Three thousand nine hundred and fifty- two pounds. It wasn't a huge amount in the context of his business, but it was the principle. It was theft and he doubted the police could do anything to recover the money or catch the scum who'd done this to his son, and thousands of others too, no doubt.

Sir Duncan had built his business from nothing and could remember when such an amount would have seemed like a fortune. Now he was wealthy and wouldn't think twice about spending a few thousand pounds on something friv- olous he didn't really need. But this was theft, neither he nor his son had anything to show for the money lost from Sam's bank account, and who knew what these people would do with the money they'd stolen. He felt sure that Sam's revela- tion about the stolen car and drugs had nothing to do with the scam but there was a nagging doubt in his mind. Could the two young men who'd stolen the car be connected to the scam in some way? They'd told Sam that they knew who both he and his father were. If they were involved in the scam had they deliberately targeted Sam knowing he had a wealthy father in the hope of getting even more money? He had no way of knowing but if the press got hold of the story about Sam's experience in a stolen car and drugs it would be splashed across front pages of the tabloids which would make both of their lives a misery for a short period.

Apart from his concern for Sam, his overwhelming feeling was that the people who'd done this needed to be taught a lesson. But how? And would it really be worth the effort and expense? Finding the people who'd stolen Sam's money would probably cost a lot more than the amount they'd stolen, that was assuming they could be found. He slammed his clenched fist onto his desk in frustration shattering the silence of his office. "There's got to be a way to find these bastards," he said aloud.

Sir Duncan stood and walked to his office window overlooking Saint Paul's Cathedral. *"Don't get mad, get even,"* he said to himself again. It was the mantra he'd followed all of his business life, but his son meant more to him than anything in the world and he knew if he didn't follow his lifetime mantra on this occasion he never would again, and all the occasions he'd followed it in the past would mean nothing.

After a few minutes staring out of the window, he returned to his desk, picked up the phone and pressed the number for his secretary, "Emma no calls until I say otherwise please."

"But Sir Duncan you have a meeting at the Bank of England scheduled for two o'clock."

"Cancel it please. No calls and no interruptions unless Sam calls again."

For the next hour, Sir Duncan sat at his desk, Sam's story and the amount he'd lost repeatedly going around and around in his mind. Finally, he came to a decision. Needing to stretch his legs and take a break he walked from his office to his secretary's desk. "Emma, ask Mac to come and see me right away please."

"Yes sir. I haven't seen him today, but I'll find out where he is and ask him to come to your office immediately."

Sir Duncan returned to his office to await Mac's arrival.

While he did so he couldn't help worrying about his son. He knew Sam was physically tough, but since his mother's death his emotions were always on a knife-edge, something he knew that would change with the passage of time. Although Sam said he was okay, Sir Duncan knew that this kind of incident could have a delayed reaction. Some of the emotion was coming out now while his feelings were still raw so soon after the scam, but it would take a few days, possibly weeks before Sam would be fully over this.

It had been a long time since he'd seen his son cry. Sam had bottled his emotions up after his mother's death and still changed the subject whenever he tried to talk to him about her. The very thought of Sam in tears brought a lump to Sir Duncan's throat. He knew he had to let Sam forge his own way in the world and make his own mistakes, but this was different. These people had deliberately set out to frighten and confuse him then steal his money. As he had the time and resources, he felt justified in taking matters into his own hands to try to take revenge, and if possible, recover the stolen money. He could feel the anger in him rising as he sat thinking about what had happened to his son. He took a deep breath, "*don't get mad, get even,*" he repeated once more.

His son was a sensible young man, how could he have been caught out by such a scam? With scams on the rise, his Head of Security had persuaded Sir Duncan to accompany him to a business security seminar where he learned how scammers first tried to scare their victim, then offer a way out which would include the transfer of money in some form. The victim was usually so relieved they would follow instructions just to make the situation go away. In almost every case once the facts were looked at in the cold light of day it was obviously a scam, but at the time when the victim was afraid and disoriented, they would happily transfer their life savings. They thought they were helping the authorities and at the same time keeping themselves out of trouble. Sam must have been really scared to fall for this, he thought, and if his son could be so easily fooled, he was certain almost anyone could be caught out.

As he sat thinking of his son Emma knocked on the door and entered. "Sorry, Sir Duncan, but Mac's on a week's leave. I'm not sure if he's gone away, would you like me to try his mobile or home number?"

"Yes, and please tell him it's urgent."

11

Alistair MacDonald was now in his late thirties. Since leaving the army he'd been Head of Security for Sir Duncan's business. Everyone knew him as Mac, most people didn't know his real name and that was the way he liked it. The very small circle of friends he had were the only ones who really knew him. Being a bit of a loner was a personal trait he'd had all his life, one which he believed had led him to apply for service in the SAS. As part of a small team, you worked alone or in pairs for much of the time, often going days without seeing or speaking to another soul. Standing at just over six feet he'd kept himself in shape after leaving the army in the small gym he'd installed in the cellar of his farmhouse.

As with all senior appointments, Sir Duncan liked to get to know the person before offering them a position in his company. After two interviews and dinner at a top London restaurant, he felt a certain empathy with Mac. Although not technically a widow like himself, Mac had lost the love of his life at a young age not long after leaving the army. At the time

Sir Duncan recruited him, Mac was looking for something to throw himself into to take his mind off the loss of his fiancé. He knew Mac had served with special forces during his time in the army and had tours to Iraq and Afghanistan among others under his belt, but he seldom spoke about his time in the forces. What he'd seen on those tours sickened him and he wanted to put the experience behind him. He told Sir Duncan that all wars were a waste of good young men and women's lives. He'd seen friends and colleagues die for a cause many of them didn't believe in, fighting against men whose only aim was to rid their country of invading foreigners, not the terrorists politicians wanted the public to believe they were fighting. Over the centuries the same thing had happened time and time again in Afghanistan and it never ended well for the invading armies, but as Mac said, orders were orders. After leaving the army he thought a job in security would be a bit of a cliché, but Sir Duncan had pursued him through a mutual friend and made him an offer he couldn't refuse. Since accepting the job, he'd completely transformed the security of the business and forged a strong working relationship with his boss.

Before leaving the army, Mac had bought a ramshackle farmhouse in the remote countryside with his fiancée Lucy. It was to be their forever home, but fate had intervened. Soon after moving in together, Lucy began to feel unwell, the feeling continued for another week before Mac finally persuaded her to see a doctor. After almost a month of hospital visits, tests and scans they received the devastating news that Lucy had terminal cancer. She had just a few months to live. The house renovations came to an abrupt halt as Mac nursed Lucy through the final days at home until she could bear the pain no more. She spent her last week in a hospice before succumbing to the terrible disease, Mac at her bedside each day and each night.

After the joy of their first house purchase together, and the memories of the time he'd spent with Lucy making plans for their future, Mac wasn't sure he could continue living at the farmhouse. Despite the short time they'd spent renovating their new home there would always be something in the farmhouse that would be a reminder of her. But in his grief, he had no inclination to move and gradually time began to diminish the raw emotion. After six months, Mac made the decision to stay at the farmhouse and resume the renovations. It was something he could throw himself into to take his mind off his loss, something he was sure Lucy would approve of. The renovations were now almost complete.

Mac sat on the farmhouse roof finishing the netting that would hold the thatched top ridge in place. He'd had professional help with most of the thatch, but after some tuition, he felt confident that he could complete this finishing touch on his own. He sat shirtless in the afternoon sunshine astride the ridge, covered in dust, sweat and reeds from the thatch. After being exposed to the sun all day he was looking forward to a hot shower and a cold beer as soon as the job was finished.

He heard the faint sound of his mobile phone ringing as he pulled the netting tight. He knew there was no point rushing to answer, by the time he'd reached the bottom of the ladder the caller would have hung up. He would check his missed calls once he'd finished the roof. He carried on pulling the netting tight and pushing pegs in to hold it in place. Five minutes later his phone rang again. If it was the same person calling, he thought they were certainly persistent, but he was determined to finish the job before doing anything else. He was on holiday and needed to finish the thatch while the weather was good.

An hour later, after finishing the ridge and packing his tools away in the barn, Mac walked into his kitchen and took a bottle from the fridge. After working in the sun for most of the day he thought he deserved the reward of a cold beer. He opened the bottle and took a long pull on the refreshing drink, then remembered the missed calls. He put the drink down and picked up his mobile phone from the kitchen table. There were three missed calls, all from work. Typical, he thought, a security alert while he was on leave. They hadn't had one for over a year then as soon as he was away from the business one comes along, or so he assumed. He pressed the number for the office, after a couple of rings Emma answered.

"Hi Mac, thanks for calling back. Sir Duncan would like to talk to you urgently, I'll put you through."

"Good afternoon Mac," Sir Duncan said once the call was transferred, "sorry to interrupt your holiday but something urgent has come up. I know it's asking a lot but is there any chance you could come into the office this afternoon?"

Mac looked at his watch. Whatever the crisis was, he thought it must be urgent. Sir Duncan knew where he lived, it would take at least an hour and a half to get to the office, by which time most people would be heading in the opposite direction out of the city. And whatever Sir Duncan was calling about was something he obviously didn't want to discuss over the phone.

"I'll need to shower and change. Provided the trains are running on time I should be with you around five o'clock if that's okay?"

"As soon as you can Mac, and don't worry about the time,

I'll stay here until you arrive," Sir Duncan said. "And sorry again for interrupting your holiday."

Mac finished his beer then quickly showered and changed. He headed for the train station hoping to arrive in time to catch the four o'clock fast train. He made it just in time and took one of the many empty seats, seats he knew that would be full travelling in the opposite direction in a short while. As the train pulled out of the station he wondered what was so urgent and why Sir Duncan hadn't told him what the problem was over the phone. He had remote access to the company's security systems so unless it was a personnel matter there was no reason for Sir Duncan to ask him to make the journey to the office.

At five twenty Mac knocked on Sir Duncan's open door and walked in closing it behind him. Sir Duncan stood and shook Mac's hand then gestured for him to take a seat. He picked up his phone and pressed the number for his secretary. "Emma, no calls or interruptions please, and please leave at the usual time. There's no need to wait, we may be some time. I'll see you tomorrow morning."

"Mac, sorry again for dragging you into the office when you're supposed to be on holiday, but I have something of a delicate and personal nature I want to run by you. Something I would like to act on as quickly as possible which is why I wanted to see you in person at such short notice. Once I've told the reason I've asked you to come in I want you to take some time to think over what I'm about to ask before you give me your decision. And please feel free to say no, I won't be offended. This isn't part of your job role with the company, and I'll respect your decision, and whatever you decide it will have no bearing on your future here. What I'm about to tell you is private, the less people who know about this the better, so I would appreciate your discretion."

Mac nodded. "I understand," he said intrigued.

"The story is very simple," Sir Duncan began. "Earlier today my son was called by someone claiming to be from the National Crime Agency. They told Sam his name and address had been used to hire a car in Manchester, this car had been discovered by the police and contained a large amount of money and some weapons. There were also traces of blood in the car. This was supposedly part of a money-laundering operation and as part of their investigation they needed to freeze Sam's bank account, but before doing so they needed him to transfer the balance of his account to what they told him was a government escrow account. As we both know these people use scare tactics and Sam did as they asked. As soon as he realised it was a scam, he contacted his bank to try to stop the transfer. We probably won't find out until tomorrow if he was successful but given the time that had elapsed between the transfer and Sam contacting the bank, I think it very unlikely the money will be recovered. So, there you have it, that's the reason I've asked you to come into the office today."

Mac sat back in his chair, slightly bewildered by what Sir Duncan had just told him, and still none the wiser why he'd called him into the office. To anyone in his line of work, it was a depressingly familiar story. "I'm sorry to hear your son's been scammed, but I'm not quite sure what do you want me to do," he said.

"I know this may be asking a lot Mac but, if possible, I want you to find the people who did this and teach them a lesson. You know what I always say, don't get mad, get even, and if there was ever a time I wanted to get even this is it. I realise it won't be easy, but I would like to try nonetheless."

Mac took a moment to take in what his boss was asking of him. "Sir Duncan, you do realise that many of these types of scam are carried out from abroad and involve people of many countries? Whoever's doing this could be operating from anywhere in the world, and if they are, we have no hope of finding them."

"I know that, but if there's even the smallest of chances we could find these people I'd like to give it a try. Would you be willing to investigate and try to catch the bastards, and if they are based here in the UK, try to get the money back? I realise you won't be able to do this alone and I don't want you using the security team here, so if you have any colleagues from your old regiment who may be willing to help I'll pay them well for their time spent on this, whether you succeed or not. It must be a small team, the fewer people that know about this the better. And don't worry about the security here, your team will cope. You've done a good job since you joined us so I can't see that we'll have any problems while you're doing this. That's if you decide to take it on, of course."

Mac sat in silence for a moment, Sir Duncan knew him well enough not to interrupt his thoughts. "Let me go back to my office and think about it. I'll come and see you once I've made a decision," Mac eventually said. "While we're on the subject, I think you should be aware that security here is now at full stretch. The rest of the business has expanded but the security hasn't increased with it, we need at least one more person, probably two. Without me here, even for a few days, it leaves us badly exposed."

"Yes, I'm aware we're light on that side of the business. I'll think about an additional person for your team and let you know tomorrow, but for now I'd like you to concentrate on what we've just spoken about. Look Mac it's late and I know you've got a long journey home, why don't you think about it on the way home, or overnight. You can call me with your decision any time tonight or first thing tomorrow. I wanted to explain what had happened while it was still fresh in my mind and I didn't want to do it over the phone. You don't need to be here to make a decision, it can wait until tomorrow."

Mac sat back in his chair still mulling over what Sir Duncan had asked of him. "No, I'd rather think it over and give you my decision before I leave. If I go home to think about this I won't sleep. And besides, if I decide to go ahead, I'll need to contact my old team tonight. As you said, we need to act quickly, or we may miss any opportunity we have."

"Okay, but take your time please. I want you to be sure about this, whichever way you decide. I'll see you as soon as you've reached a decision."

Mac returned to his own office and ran through the story in his head. If the police couldn't catch these people how was he expected to? But the police had so many cases to investigate they probably couldn't put the time and resources into this case that he could, especially if it was the only thing he was working on. He had the security of Sir Duncan's business running like clockwork, even though they were a man short, and it wouldn't miss him for a couple of days.

The thought that kept coming into Mac's head was that it would be a challenge, some excitement and hopefully a bit of fun, especially if he could get his old team from the regiment back together. They hadn't met up for a couple of years, it would be good to have a catch up to find out how they were all getting on. For those reasons alone he thought it would be worth accepting the job.

An hour after being told of Sam's story, his decision made, Mac knocked on Sir Duncan's open door again.

"Come in Mac," Sir Duncan said. He knew it would be Mac, apart from his secretary everyone else had gone home, she wouldn't leave until he did despite being told she should go.

Mac entered, closed the door and sat in the chair he'd vacated an hour earlier. "I'll take the job, but I'm sure you realise our chances of getting Sam's money back are slim, to say the least. It won't be easy, and it's nothing like my team has ever done before but if they're willing, I'd like to give it a try. I think I can get some of the lads from my old team to help but it's late and they may already have other commitments." Mac paused before asking what was really on his mind. "Before we put anything into motion are you sure you really want to do this Sir? It will cost a lot more than Sam lost."

"Yes Mac, I'm positive. The longer I've had to think about this the more determined I am about doing something to teach these people a lesson. When I was younger, and building my business, I did a lot of ducking and diving, sailing close to the wind, but I never resorted to cheating people out of their money. I want these bastards to have a taste of their own medicine, I don't care how much it costs. I want them to feel the same way they made my son feel. I'll be paying the team you put together handsomely from my own pocket, not from the company. Don't worry about time-keeping while you're doing this, I know this type of thing doesn't run by normal office hours, come and go as you please. All I ask is that you keep me updated."

Mac was still sceptical. Had his boss really thought this through and considered all the risks? He could only assume he had and was prepared to lose money if he and his team were unsuccessful.

"Okay, if the lads from my old regiment are willing to hear what I have to say we'll meet close by. I don't want them coming here unless they agree to come on board. I know what office gossip is like, tongues will start wagging as soon as they enter the building. I don't want to start the rumour mill going unnecessarily if they decide not to sign up. Then if they're up for it, I'll introduce them to you and set up base in a spare office here if that's okay. I'll start straight away but I can't promise anything, they may not be available or may not want to be part of it." Mac knew this wouldn't be the case. If they were anything like he remembered they would jump at the chance of a reunion and a little excitement, however mild that may be compared to what they were used to while serving in the regiment.

Sir Duncan nodded. "Thanks, Mac. I'll let you get started."

Mac returned to his own office, he wanted to get everything Sir Duncan had told him down on paper while the story was still fresh in his mind. Once he'd finished making notes it was time to make a few calls.

As he reached for his phone Mac stopped himself. He sat back in his chair and thought of the last disastrous day his old team had worked together. The memory of Gav and the little boy came to mind once again. Luckily it was an image that came to mind less frequently with the passing of time, but it was one he would never fully forget. Although he'd met his team on numerous occasions since leaving the regiment he wondered if they would have reservations about working with him again after what happened on their last day serving together. All the old doubts came flooding back. Did they still blame him for what happened that day? Had it been profes-sional pride or a misplaced belief in his own abilities to lead his men that had put Gav in danger? He'd analysed it himself on numerous occasions and still found it no easier to answer the questions. There was only one way to find out. He searched through his contact list and an hour later had arranged to meet four of his old team the following day in The Black Friar, a pub on Queen Victoria Street.

It was late, time to go home and do some research on scams, he thought, and some planning with what little infor-mation he had, something he hadn't done for a few years. He relished the prospect even though he knew it would mean he had a long night ahead of him.

THE SAME EVENING Mac was contacting his old team, Sam waited in his student accommodation. With six friends from the university rugby team in his small flat they could hardly move. As expected, their wait was in vain. No police officers called with papers to sign or a cashier's cheque, and three thousand nine hundred and fifty-two pounds and seventy pence did not come back into his account from William Ried's, public prosecutor.

12

———

A few minutes after 11 o'clock the following morning, Mac walked past the copper statue of a monk at the doorway of The Black Friar, a grade one listed building and London's only true art deco pub, and one of his favourites in London. He liked places like this, not one of the main tourist sites, but a place that had a bit of character as well as history. Built on the site of an old Dominican friary, Henry VIII's court had apparently met at the site of the Black Friar to discuss the dissolution of his marriage to Catherine of Aragon. He thought it fitting that he was about to discuss another type of dissolution here with his team. He was always fascinated by the art-nouveau reliefs on the walls depicting monks getting up to all sorts of no good. Appropriate again, he thought, knowing the sort of mischief his team used to get up to, and he had no doubt that some of them, if not all, still did.

The main attraction today though was not the history and decoration of where they were meeting, but the fact that it was close to the office and had some very private alcoves where they wouldn't be overheard or interrupted. It also helped that they were meeting before the lunchtime rush when tourists visiting nearby attractions such as Saint Paul's Cathedral, the Tate Modern, The Globe Theatre and The London Dungeons amongst others would descend on the pub for a traditional English pub lunch. He just hoped it wasn't too early for his old team, some of whom had quite a distance to travel.

Mac stood at the bar where he could see anyone entering through either of the pub's two doors. He ordered a pint and leaned against the bar to wait for his old team to arrive.

First to arrive was Stephen Jones, a proud Welshman. As the only member of the team from the principality he was inevitably known as Taff. His short red hair went with his short fiery temper. He fancied himself as a lady's man and despite the passing years still had a twinkle in his eye.

"Good to see you Taff. Usual?" Mac asked as they shook hands.

"Please," Taff replied.

"A pint of Guinness please," Mac asked the young lady behind the bar. "How are you, Taff? You look like you've kept yourself in shape."

"I'm good thanks sarge, got to keep in shape if you want to be popular with the ladies," Taff said in his lyrical Welsh accent. "Cheers," he winked at the woman behind the bar as he sipped his beer. "Quite fit some of the East European birds."

Mac shook his head. Same old Taff, he thought. "If you could keep it in your trousers you wouldn't be divorced," he said.

"Divorced twice, but it's not my fault sarge, the ladies just can't keep their hands off me, can they? It's them that's taking it out of my trousers not me!" There was silence for a moment while they both took a drink of their beer. "This a big job is it?" Taff asked.

"Could be," Mac replied.

"Much money in it for us?" Taff asked again.

"Could be," Mac repeated.

"Good, I could do with some extra cash. Got a bit behind with the child support payments, haven't I? Sandra's on my case all the bloody time."

Same old Taff, Mac thought again. "Look Taff I'll explain why I've asked you all here when the others arrive. See that table over there," Mac pointed to the alcove in the corner, "that's the most secluded spot in the pub, could you go and grab it while I wait here for the others. Once the tourists arrive this place will be heaving, and I don't want what I have to say to the team being overheard."

"All the other's coming are they?"

"They said they would," Mac replied. "Jock, Scrump and Smithy. Now go grab that table before someone else gets it." Taff sauntered over to the alcove, as he took a seat the second member of the team arrived.

William "Billy" Bryant, known as Scrumpy, or Scrump, to the team on account of his liking of cider. Originally from Bristol, Billy had a hard time adjusting to civilian life after leaving the regiment. Like many ex-servicemen and women returning from a war zone, what he'd experienced remained with him and still haunted him. The nervous tension caused by the thought of someone waiting to shoot or blow you up each time the safety of the camp was left and what he'd seen on operations in Afghanistan and Iraq had left him deeply troubled. Seeing some of your mates blown up and shot had a different effect on each of the men serving on the front line, even the hardest of them.

Billy's life had spiralled downwards when he arrived home, he looked for solace in alcohol and soon became addicted. Things got worse and, although his wife wanted to help, he couldn't inflict any more of the nightmares or drink induced comas he was having on her and their children. He ended up living on the street. Eventually, he could take no more and started to attend the counselling offered by the Army for his post-traumatic stress disorder and Alcoholics Anonymous for his addiction. He'd been dry now for two years and still attended sessions for the PTSD. Gradually he turned his life around and now had a job with the charity Help for Heroes that had helped him get his life back on track.

"Usual Scrump?" Mac asked as they shook hands.

"No, coke for me please sarge. I had a bit of trouble with the booze after I left the regiment. I'm teetotal now. Two years and counting."

Mac caught the attention of one of the bar staff and ordered the drink. "Sorry Scrump, I didn't know. You okay now though? Wife and kids okay?"

"Yes, we're getting by thanks. I'm working for the Heroes charity in Salisbury, doing my bit to help some of the lads in the same state I was in. Unfortunately, there are a lot of guys out there in the same boat as me. I know how they feel so I think I'm in the right place to help get them back on their feet again."

"Good man. Taff's in that alcove in the corner." Mac pointed to the table Taff was sitting at. "I'll wait here for the others, why don't you join Taff and have a quick catch up."

"What's this all about then sarge?" Scrump asked.

"I'd rather tell you when we're all together, that way I only have to say it once."

"Okay sarge," Scrump picked up his drink and walked over to the alcove, shook hands with Taff and sat down deep in conversation. Speculating what this is all about no doubt, Mac thought.

Five minutes later Hamish McKenzie, known as Jock to the team, walked through the door. Jock was a former amateur heavyweight boxing champion and a bit of a loner. Originally from the highlands of Scotland, he now lived alone in a flat in Glasgow, taking odd jobs if and when he fancied it, usually as security outside of pubs and clubs. He was an intimidating presence, one look from Jock was enough to deter most people from causing any trouble. He was a mountain of a man and a man of few words.

Mac shook his hand and asked Jock what he'd like to drink, he didn't want to be caught out again after what Scrump had told him. Who knew, maybe the rest of the team had suffered in the same way and he wondered if putting them in potentially dangerous circumstances again was a good idea. He knew plenty of others who'd suffered the same way Scrump had and any stress could set his recovery back. Adjusting to civilian life wasn't easy after years in the army. It had taken Mac some time, especially after the traumatic last day he'd spent with his team in Afghanistan. The distraction of being able to throw himself into the renovation of the farmhouse with Lucy had certainly helped him, even if it was only for a short time before she was taken ill.

"Usual please sarge," Jock said.

Mac caught the barmaid's attention and ordered Jock a pint of Doom Bar. While they waited for Jock's drink Mac asked him how he was. Knowing Jock was a man of few words and not one for small talk he knew he wouldn't get much from him.

"I'm still in the city taking jobs when I fancy it but I'm getting too old for that game now. I want to go back to the Highlands, buy a small croft and live a quiet life but I don't have the money," Jock said.

"Well maybe what I have to tell you will help." Mac pointed to the table where Taff and Scrump were waiting. "The others are sitting at that table in the corner if you'd like to join them. I'll give you all the details in a few minutes."

"Are we all here now?" Jock asked.

"No, we're just waiting for Smithy."

"Aye, that figures," Jock said, "he hasn't changed. Same annoying little bastard he always was. I've travelled all the way here from Glasgow at short notice and I still managed to get here before that lazy little bastard. He only has a few miles to come if he's still living in London." Jock shook his head, he picked up his drink and took his huge frame over to the table in the alcove where the others were waiting. As he approached Taff and Scrump stood and shook his hand, after greeting each other they sat down and continued to speculate why Mac was getting his old team back together and how much money they might earn.

Typical Jock, Mac thought, no questions about why they were meeting up or what may be in it for him. He knew he would find out once the team were all together.

As always James Smith, inevitably known as Smithy, an East End lad who had the shortest journey was last to arrive. He was usually late for most appointments, that hadn't changed since leaving the army, Mac thought. As a youngster Smithy was always in trouble with the law and Mac believed joining the army was the only thing that had kept him out of prison. He was pleased to discover Smithy wasn't living at Her Majesty's pleasure when he'd phoned the previous evening. Joining the regiment had been the making of Smithy, he was proud to serve with special forces, and while he was in the army he liked what he did and was good at it, and he didn't mind telling anyone who would listen.

Five minutes later Smithy walked through the door, the usual cheeky grin on his face. He walked over to Mac and shook his hand. "Alright, guv." Mac had spent years trying to get Smithy to address members of the armed forces more senior than himself, and that was most, by their rank, but Smithy ignored him and called everyone guv. He'd once addressed their most senior officer as guv. The Brigadier turned a deep shade of red while Mac quickly moved Smithy away before their commanding officer exploded. "What does he know about real soldiering?" Smithy asked as he was being led away.

"I suspect he knows a lot more than you do. He saw action before you were even born," Mac said as he marched Smithy away from the Brigadier. "And besides, he's in charge and he makes the rules."

"Well as we all know the rules are only there in an advisory capacity. When you're out in the field you can't follow a rule book, you have to go with the flow, make it up as you go along," Smithy said with his usual cheeky grin.

After the Brigadier incident Smithy was kept away from the most senior ranks, which suited him, he thought most senior ranks were a bunch of Hooray Henrys who knew nothing about real soldiering.

"Drink?" Mac asked.

"Lager please, guv." Mac ordered Smithy's drink, some crisps and peanuts, passed Smithy his drink and led him to the table where the others sat waiting. They all stood, shook Smithy's hand and took their seats again.

Mac threw the snacks down in front of his team and sat at the end of the table facing the others, his back to the rest of the pub. "Well lads, thanks for coming. It's good to see you all again. It's been a long time. Too long. No doubt you're all wondering why I asked you to meet me here so let me put you out of your misery. Yesterday the son of the man I work for was scammed to the tune of nearly four thousand pounds. My boss believes the police have neither the manpower nor resources to catch the people who did it, so he's asked me to assemble a team of the best men I know to find them and try to get his money back. Unfortunately, they weren't available, so I called you lot instead," Mac said with a big smile on his face. He'd slipped back into the old banter, it felt good. The years they'd spent going their separate ways seemed to melt away.

After a few years working for Sir Duncan, Mac felt he was getting a little stale sitting behind a desk, he needed some action to get his pulse racing again. He hoped his old team felt the same. "He wants us to find the people who did this, recover the money and either turn them over to the law or deal with them as we see fit."

"Too right. The bastards did the same to my gran," Taff said. "Eight thousand quid they stole from her. It was her life's savings, she never got over it. She tried to put on a brave face, but she was never the same after she was scammed. She went downhill fast and died the following year. These people don't realise what impact they have on people's lives."

"Don't care more like," Smithy said, "they deserve what-ever they get."

"Well if I get my hands on the bastards, they'll know all

about it," Taff said. He'd been close to his grandmother and it was clear to all sat around the table that he'd been shaken by what had happened to her.

"I'm sure we've all heard of someone who's been scammed," Mac said, "hopefully in most cases the consequences aren't as dire as for Taff's grandmother, but for many, it ruins lives, takes away money people have been saving for years to see them through their old age or something they've been saving towards. In this case, it's slightly different. The person scammed was young and I think he'll soon be over it. It also helps that his father's a wealthy man who can afford to replace the money he's lost. He's one of the lucky ones, most people don't have that luxury."

"So, there you are lads, that's why I've asked you to meet me here. I know it's not the usual sort of thing we did while we were in the regiment but we've done much harder jobs than this and I believe we have the skills to get it done, if, and it's a big if, we can find the people who did it. The question is do you want in?" Mac looked around the table at each of them.

"When does this job start?" Scrump asked.

"If you're in it starts now," Mac said.

"But what about our jobs and families at home?" Scrump asked.

"Take a holiday. You can call your family and tell them you'll be away for a few days on a special assignment, one that will pay you well," Mac replied.

"How much?" Taff asked.

Enough to pay your child support arrears with a bit left over, Mac thought. "That's something between you and my boss, you can negotiate that with him. He pays well and said he will pay you whether we catch them or not."

"Sounds like a no brainer," Smithy said. "We get paid either way, and handsomely by the sound of it. And it's a chance to have a couple of beers and a catch-up."

"If we're starting now where are we going to stay? I didn't bring anything for an overnight stay let alone a long one," Scrump said.

"It won't be a long stay, probably a few days, a week at the most. Look lads this is a golden opportunity to earn yourself a nice bit of cash. We can relive a few old glories, try to put right a wrong and stop these people from inflicting any more misery on innocent people like Taff's grandmother. You either want in or you don't, it's your decision. The question you have to ask yourself is this, if you go back to what you were doing before I called, if you decide this isn't for you, is what you're going back to so exciting and fulfilling you don't want to be part of this?" Mac looked at each of them in turn, he knew he had them. "So, are you in, or are you out?" he asked. "I need to know now because I need to find replacements if any of you decide this isn't for you."

Mac looked across the table, "Taff?" he asked. After hearing Taff's emotional connection to scams he already knew what his answer would be.

"Count me in," Taff said without hesitation.

"Scrump?"

"Yes, me too."

"Jock?"

"Aye."

"Smithy?"

"Can't let you bastards have all the fun, can I? Besides you lot need someone to look after you."

Mac ordered another round of drinks while the old comrades caught up, reminisced about old times, past adventures, absent friends and lamented lost colleagues. Despite the years that had passed since going their separate ways they seemed to pick up where they'd left off. Mac felt as if the clock had been rewound and they were back in the regiment. His worry that his team would have reservations about working with him again had proved unfounded. After giving them enough time to catch up Mac looked at his watch and called them to order. It was time for his team to meet their new paymaster.

13

Mac and his team left The Black Friar and turned right, heading down Ludgate Hill toward St. Paul's Cathedral. As they neared the landmark towering over them, Mac turned and entered a glass and steel office block. Leading them up the stairs to the fifth floor he opened an office door and told his team to take a seat. He would inform their new boss they were waiting for him.

When he arrived at Emma's desk, Mac asked if she would let Sir Duncan know that there were some gentlemen in the boardroom who would like to meet him. Images of the reliefs of mischievous monks in the pub still fresh in his mind, Mac thought it best not to wait for Sir Duncan but re-join his team. He didn't want them getting up to any mischief while he was out of the room, they needed to make a good first impression on their new boss.

Moments after Mac had taken a seat, Sir Duncan arrived. He could smell alcohol as soon as he entered the room. "Mac, have you guys been drinking?" he asked. Sir Duncan wasn't averse to a drink himself, indeed he enjoyed the occasional single malt or fine brandy, but he would not tolerate drinking while at work. "You know my feelings about drinking during work hours."

"Yes Sir I do, but technically these guys weren't working for you when they were having a drink. In fact, they didn't know why I'd asked them to meet me when I bought it for them. And I'm supposed to be on holiday. All they knew was that I wanted to meet them to talk about something," Mac replied. "I thought the best place to meet to discuss the job was in a pub close to the office. Don't worry, that's the last alcohol this lot will have until this is over, whichever way it goes."

Sir Duncan nodded. "Okay but I want you to take this seriously, it's not an excuse for a regimental reunion or a party. I'll be paying you well and I expect you to conduct yourselves in a professional manner at all times, I hope that's understood. Now that we've got that out of the way, why don't you introduce your team."

Mac went around the table and introduced each of his team to Sir Duncan, explaining what each of their speciality was while they served in the regiment.

Sir Duncan took his place at the head of the boardroom table. "Gentlemen, thank you for coming at such short notice. I'm sure Mac has explained the circumstances which have brought you all here, so I won't go over it again. I don't intend to take any part in this operation apart from paying for it, I will leave that all down to Mac and yourselves. I have no experience in anything like this so it's best if I let you professionals get on with it, even if it's not quite the sort of thing you were used to during your time in the army. From what I've been reading on the internet it's vitally important that we act quickly. The people who commit these crimes do so for a short period of time in one place then move on to start up in a new location to avoid being caught, so we need to move as quickly as we can. I'll be funding the operation but will be in the background. Mac, if there's anything you need just ask."

Mac thought for a second. "We need an office with a couple of laptops, a flip chart and some pens. We may need panel vans if we can find where these people are operating from, probably two but three to be on the safe side. If we manage to recover any money, we'll need a bank account to transfer it to. As none of us has come prepared we need some money to buy clothes and a few other odds and ends. The most pressing requirement at the moment is somewhere for these guys to stay while we plan this operation."

"How long do you need accommodation for?" Sir Duncan asked.

"I think two nights will be enough. Some of them need to phone work to book unexpected holiday, and home to let their families know they're okay and will be away for a short while."

"I'm sure you all have a mobile with you but if you don't you can use the phone in here, just dial nine for an outside line. Give me a few minutes and I'll arrange the rest." Sir Duncan rose from his chair and left the room, heading for his secretary.

When Sir Duncan arrived at her desk, Emma looked up expectantly, intrigued by what was going on in the board-room. She stopped what she was doing and picked up a notepad and pen, awaiting her boss's instructions.

"Emma, ask James to meet me in the boardroom please," Sir Duncan said, "and book five rooms at the hotel over the road for two nights in my name. Pay for them using my personal credit card not the business card." When he returned to the boardroom to wait for his Finance Director the room was filled with the chatter of Mac's team still catching up on old times.

A minute later Sir Duncan's Finance Director entered the boardroom. The look on his face revealed his obvious surprise at the sight of the group of men sitting around the table. Not the usual businessmen accompanied by their senior members of staff he was used to seeing in the board-room. "James," Sir Duncan began, "I'm conducting a private operation, one I don't want anyone else within the company to know about. These gentlemen are assisting me in this venture. It's a private matter and not part of the company's activities. I want you to open two offshore bank accounts in my name, accounts that will be difficult to trace back to me, away from prying eyes, in a country where bank transactions are hard for authorities to track. Panama, the Cayman Islands, or maybe Switzerland, somewhere like that. I'm sure you know the type of place I'm talking about. They will only be needed for the duration of this operation, probably a couple of weeks at most. As soon as it's concluded I want the balance transferred back to my investment account and both accounts closed, is that possible?"

"Yes, Sir Duncan, but...." his Finance Director began.

Sir Duncan held up a hand to stop James before he came up with various reasons why what he was being asked to do wouldn't be possible. "James, just do it please, and quickly. And make sure Mac has full access to both accounts. I'm sure there will be some costs involved and he needs access to the funds immediately."

"These types of accounts can't be opened easily, as I'm sure you know Sir Duncan," James said, "there are proce-dures to go through."

Sir Duncan took a moment to think. "Transfer a million pounds from my investment account and put half in each offshore account, that should speed up any procedures."

As James headed for the door Smithy muttered "fuckin' accountants," just loud enough for James to hear. Mac glared at him.

"Mac," Sir Duncan continued ignoring Smithy's jibe aimed at his accountant, "I'll get you some cash so you'll have money while James opens the accounts. Emma's arranging two night's accommodation for you. Use this room as an office. I'll get laptops, a flip chart and some pens sent in. The boardroom will now be out of bounds to everyone except you and your team. Just ask if you need anything else. One thing I would ask of you all is please don't go wandering around the building. I'm sure there will be plenty of speculation about what's going on in here, so I'd rather not fuel it by your team being seen around the building."

"Fine," Mac said, "we'll confine ourselves to the boardroom. One last thing, intelligence is key to any operation like this. Can you ask Sam to write down everything he can remember about what happened to him in as much detail as possible? Most importantly we need the phone numbers. We'll have a planning meeting first thing tomorrow and it would be helpful if we can have it when we start."

"Consider it done," Sir Duncan replied.

As he moved to leave the boardroom Smithy spoke up, stopping Sir Duncan in his tracks. "Sorry to be the one to bring this up guv, but how much are we being paid for this job?" he asked.

"Sorry, it completely slipped my mind. That's a good question," Sir Duncan stood for a moment deep in thought.

"I don't know, I've never financed anything like this before. How long do you think this is going to take Mac?"

"If we can find them quickly probably four or five days, a week at most."

Sir Duncan stood at the door thinking for a moment. "I realise what we're hoping to achieve is probably not legal and therefore I'm asking you to break the law, so I feel I ought to pay you well for taking such a risk. How does ten thousand pounds each sound? Fair?"

"Sounds good to me," Smithy said with a huge grin on his face.

"More than generous," Scrump said.

"Okay with everyone else?" Sir Duncan asked. The rest of the team nodded, not quite believing the amount they would be paid for one just one week's work.

"One last thing Mac, if you've got a second. A business matter, if you could just step outside for a moment." Once they were in the corridor, Sir Duncan closed the door. "Go ahead with the recruitment of your additional security man. I'll ask HR to get the ball rolling and put an advert online and in the trade press."

"Before you do that, I have someone in mind if it's okay with you, Sir? it will save us the advertising and recruitment fees."

"In that case, I'll leave it with you. I'll let you to get on with it. I need to phone Sam and get the information you want for the morning. Good luck and don't forget, if there's anything you need just let me know." Sir Duncan turned and headed for his office to make the call to his son.

"Should clear the child support arrears with a tidy bit left for me," Taff said with the big grin still on his face as Mac closed the door after returning to the boardroom.

Ten minutes later there was a knock on the door and Emma entered. "Gentlemen, Sir Duncan has booked you into the Premier Inn across the road for two nights. These are the booking confirmations and the cash he asked me to give you." She put an envelope on the boardroom table in front of Mac and headed for the door.

"The Premier Inn," Smithy said indignantly once Emma had closed the door. "With a gaff like this he could afford to put us up at the Savoy, it's only just down the road."

Mac shook his head. "Smithy, you're being paid ten thousand pounds for what will probably be no more than one week's work. When this is finished if you want to stay at the Savoy you can pay for it yourself from the money Sir Duncan's paying you."

"That's if they'll let a scally like you stay there," Taff said grinning at Smithy.

Mac picked up the envelope containing the cash Emma had left and put it in his pocket. "None of us have come prepared for an overnight stay so I think we need to go shopping for a few things we're going to need."

Two hours later the group returned weighed down by numerous shopping bags full of essential items they thought would be needed over the next couple of days, along with a few luxuries Mac had let them get away with. Waiting for them in the boardroom was Sir Duncan's accountant, James, sitting at the head of the huge table. "The account details for the offshore accounts Sir Duncan asked me to open," he passed an envelope to Mac. "There's half a million in each account. Please let me have receipts for all expenditure."

Mac put the envelope in his pocket. "Thank you, but you may have forgotten this has nothing to do with the company, it's a private matter between Sir Duncan, myself and my team.

All receipts will go directly to him. Unless you hear otherwise, the day to day running of this operation does not concern you, your only remaining task will be to transfer any money back to Sir Duncan's investment account once the operation is concluded."

Mac could see the irritation on James's face as he stood and strode towards the boardroom door.

"Fuckin' accountants," Smithy said, as he had done earlier just loud enough that the accountant could hear. James turned to face Mac's team. "You heard him," Smithy said, "it's a private matter, it doesn't concern you, now piss off and let us get on with it." Sir Duncan's accountant slammed the door behind him as he left the boardroom.

"We can't afford to piss anyone off Smithy," Mac said. "We need to get this done as quickly and as quietly as possible, then we can get back to our normal lives. No more jibes at James, okay?"

"Fuckin' accountants," Smithy muttered.

"What's your problem with accountants Smithy?" Taff asked.

"I had a used car business with my brother a few years ago. It turned out the accountant had been nicking our money for at least two years. He got two years when they caught him, and I got a bill for the tax and VAT he was supposed to have paid. The business went bankrupt. If I'd got to him before the law caught up with him it would be me inside not him, and I'd be doing more than two years."

"Fuckin' accountants." Taff said in his best East End accent, grinning at Smithy. "Slippery bastards, all of 'em."

The next few hours were spent setting up laptops and assigning tasks. "Jock, I did a little research on scams last night but nowhere near enough," Mac said. "Can you find out all you can on this type of scam ready to brief the rest of us tomorrow morning at ten? Smithy, we may need three panel vans, no rear windows. You're local so you probably know somewhere close by to get them. Hire three to be delivered here tomorrow afternoon at 3, full tanks, please. Hire them for four days with an option for an extra day," he handed Smithy a wad of cash from the envelope Emma had given him. "If it comes to more than that use your credit card and I'll give you the cash when you get back. If we can't find these bastards, we won't need the vans, but if we do, we need to be ready to move straight away. Best to have them ready."

"Won't he need ID and a driving license to hire vans Mac?" Scrump asked.

Mac looked at Smithy. "Got your licence on you Smithy?"

"No, but don't worry about that guv, I've got a few contacts around here, it won't be a problem."

"Nothing dodgy, we can't afford to attract any attention, especially from the law. And we don't want any old bangers that will let us down."

"No worries guv, old bangers are Taff's area of expertise," he said with a grin.

"Okay enough." Mac needed his team to concentrate on the job at hand, they could exchange banter when they'd each been assigned their tasks for the following day. "Taff, we need all the usual stuff if we take hostages, hessian bags, cable ties, gaffa tape and nitrile gloves. You know the score, enough for ten people should be plenty. And bring the receipts back, Sir Duncan is paying for this out of his own pocket and he's paying us well for the job, so no little extras on the side."

"What about weapons Mac?" Jock asked.

Mac shook his head. "No weapons, I don't think we'll

need them. If we come up against a team that's armed this thing will have gone too far, we'll pull out and admit defeat. And besides, I wouldn't know where to get a weapon."

"That's no problem guv, I know a guy...." Smithy began.

Mac cut him off. "No, Smithy, don't even think about it. No weapons. What we're planning is crossing the line already, if we're tooled up with illegal weapons it puts this in a different league altogether."

"Okay guv, just an idea," Smithy said.

"Scrump, once we get Sam's version of events, I want you to try to think of a way we can find these people," Mac said. "You managed it in Afghanistan so it should be a lot easier here."

"Okay Mac, but I'm not sure it will be easier. What these scammers are doing is probably a lot more sophisticated than what I was up against in Afghanistan, but I'll give it my best shot."

At 6.30 the team left the boardroom laden with shopping bags headed for their hotel. "Fancy a swift half?" Mac asked, "after all, we still have a lot of catching up to do, and once this starts there'll be no chance of getting to the pub."

"But you told Sir Duncan..." Taff began.

"I know what I told him. Just a couple then we hit the sack. We're not on Sir Duncan's time now and what he doesn't know won't hurt him," Mac said. "And besides, all I've eaten today is crisps and a few peanuts. I could do with a decent meal and the food at the pub looked good."

"Sounds good to me," said Smithy. "My new local, The Black Friar?"

"Why not," said Mac.

14

At eight o'clock the next morning Mac and his team were sat around the boardroom table, steam rising from the coffee Emma had placed in front of each of them. They were waiting for Sir Duncan's arrival and his son's account of the scam. Thirty minutes later he walked in with an A4 envelope in hand.

"Good morning all, I hope you had a good night. Sorry I'm late but I've been speaking to Sam again, he remembered a few things he'd forgotten to tell me yesterday. Mac, this is everything he can remember including the telephone number he called and the police number that called him after the original call was ended. I don't think that one will be of any use as it's the real number for West Yorkshire police," he handed Mac the envelope containing Sam's version of events. "If there's anything else you need you know where to find me. If I'm out please leave a message with Emma, and if you need more money just ask. It's down to you now so I'll leave you to get on with it. Good luck gentlemen." Sir Duncan turned and left the boardroom.

Mac opened the envelope and read Sam's account of the scam. After a second reading, he made his way to the door. "I think we should all read this, I'll get some copies." Minutes later he returned and handed each of his team a copy. "Go through it and see if you can come up with a plan."

At nine o'clock, Smithy put his copy of Sam's account on the table. "I've got to see a man about a van," he said as he made his way towards the door. "Three, actually. I'll get them delivered here for three o'clock this afternoon."

Taff stood and followed Smithy heading for the door. "Know any hardware shops local, Smithy?" he asked. "I've got a long shopping list." They left the boardroom while the remaining members of the team read and re-read Sam's account trying to think of a way to get to the scammers before they disappeared.

An hour later Smithy and Taff returned carrying bags with the equipment they would need.

"All done?" Mac asked.

"Yes guv, the vans will be here at three as requested. I've asked for them to be delivered to the car park under the building. I told the guy on the gate to call Sir Duncan's secretary when they arrive."

Taff took the bags Smithy was holding and placed them both on the table. "Everything we need Mac. The receipts are in the bags."

"Good, put it all over there please Taff," Mac pointed behind the flip chart. He looked over to Jock expectantly. "Ready?" He asked.

"Aye," Jock replied.

"Okay take us through what you've got please, Jock."

Although Jock was usually a man of few words Mac knew that when given a task such as this, he would do a thorough job and relay all the facts without embellishment so that the rest of the team wouldn't get bored and lose interest.

Jock stood and walked to the flipchart. "The numbers I'm going to give you are the most up to date I can find but are at least six months out of date so the amount being scammed is almost certainly more now than when this data was collected. Scamming is a lucrative business. In 2018 it's estimated that almost one and a half billion dollars was scammed world-wide from individuals who reported money lost to scams. This figure doesn't include all the other scams out there, just money theft such as this case. It also doesn't include scams against companies which, if successful, are even more lucra-tive. Most companies have sophisticated software to prevent cyber fraud and are usually insured against any money lost to scams, so they aren't affected in the same way individuals are.

"In the UK the number of bank transfer scams rose by 40% from the previous year and is rising every year. In the first six months of 2019 six hundred and sixteen million pounds, *million*," Jock repeated for emphasis as he wrote the number on the flipchart, "was stolen by scammers. That equates to nearly three and a half million pounds every day. That's from all scams. Scams where individuals like Sir Duncan's son were conned into making bank transfers to accounts controlled by criminals accounted for two hundred and seven million, five hundred thousand pounds," again he wrote the amount on the flipchart. "This type of scam is offi-cially known as authorised push payment," he wrote APP on the flipchart next to the figure of two hundred and seven million. "The good news, if there is any, is that of the amount scammed around twenty percent was clawed back and returned to the victim's accounts after being identified as fraudulent. Despite the banks introducing measures such as name checks when money is transferred the scammers always seem to be one step ahead, and with the increase in online banking and the use of banking apps it's made it easier for an individual to transfer money to these people.

"While these scammers can come from anywhere in the world many are from Eastern Europe, West Africa, the Middle East and the Indian subcontinent. Typically, scammers set up a small operation in the host country, in our case the UK, then transfer the money through various accounts to the ultimate host account somewhere abroad where authorities can't touch it. The operations in host countries typically take a short-term lease of an office or small industrial unit, usually for no longer than three months, then disappear only to set up in a new location and start all over again. If they think the authorities are on to them, they move, even if they've only been operating from the rented premises for a couple of days. If things get really hot for the scammers, they close the operation down altogether and lay low for a while before setting up again a couple of months later. If there's enough money in any single country, they set up more than one operation there.

"This is big business, operating worldwide in any country the scammers believe has wealthy citizens who may be gullible enough to be parted from their money. They operate mainly in Western Europe, America, Canada, Australia, South Africa, Mexico and New Zealand. These scams are operated by different organisations and individuals. Nobody knows how many scammers are out there trying to get their hands on your money, but the number increases every year.

"The staff of organisations operating scams from overseas are recruited from both the country the scam is taking place in and wherever their main office is based abroad. The person responsible for transferring the money is usually a trusted member of the team sent from the main office overseas. They typically enter the country on a student visa and will be someone who's worked in the office receiving the transfers from around the world. Although to us it may look like a step backwards to be sent abroad to transfer money back to the office you previously worked in it's considered recognition that the people running the scam trust you to handle their money when they can't see what you are doing.

"Some of the money generated from the scam is used to fund the operation. There's rent to pay on the premises they're using as an office, rent on a house for the people operating the scam to live in, and money for their living expenses. The rents are not a problem. Rent for the type of property they use are for a minimum of six months, but they use a network of fellow countrymen and sympathisers to arrange short term rents at discounted rates.

"These types of scams are usually funding some bigger criminal activity or are used for money laundering. The people at the top of these scams typically skim money off the top for themselves. They need all the money they can get if the scam is funding terrorists in the Middle East. Arms are expensive, especially if you can't buy them from a legitimate source. Funding an army is an expensive business, as we all know.

"You should also be aware," Jock continued, "that where police have completed successful investigations, they found that in some of the more sophisticated operations the scammers had a panic button beside the computer from where the money transfers were made. When pressed this button shuts down the computer on site and deletes everything on the hard drive. It also alerts the people receiving the money that there's a problem, the link to that computer is cut and funds are immediately moved out of the receiving account as a precaution. These panic buttons are typically hidden in the drawer beside the computer to avoid being pressed accidently.

"So, as we all know time is against us. We need to act fast before these people move, disappear or change their phone number, in which case we have no means of contacting them. Remember," he continued as he pointed to the numbers on the flipchart, "the numbers I've shown you are only for six months, not a full year, and they're at least six months old. The actual amount is probably even higher as some of the victims are so embarrassed at being caught out, they don't report the scam to the authorities.

"From Sam's account, it appears that these scammers are not asking for their victim's bank details, but even if they don't give their account details many victims feel it's safest to close the account that's been scammed and open a new one. Some even blame the bank for not recovering their money and open a new account with another bank.

"As I said earlier authorised push payments, the type of scam Sir Duncan's son was caught out by, accounted for six hundred and sixteen million pounds in the first six months of 2019 in the UK alone, and these types of scams are going on all over the western world so you can see the numbers involved are enormous." Jock put the pen back on the flipchart and returned to his seat.

"Jesus, we're in the wrong game," Smithy said staring at the numbers on the flipchart.

"Thanks, Jock," Mac said. "Anyone got any questions?"

"Yes, I've got one. How do we know these people are operating from this country and not from abroad?" Scrump asked.

"That's the problem," Jock replied, "we don't, but judging from the research I've done the scammers usually operate in the country they're scamming the citizens of. They sometimes have a base abroad and operate from that single location, but from everything I've read and from Sam's account I would bet they're running this scam from somewhere here in the UK. The first phone number Sam called was a UK number. The scammers want their victims to believe it's a local UK police force contacting them, so the victim needs to recognise the number as one from the UK. The scammers could operate from abroad and route the call through another number to make it look like it was coming from here but that's complicated and expensive, especially if they're constantly on the move, and the second number that was supposedly the police was also a UK number. That along with the language they used, case numbers, the dot-gov webpage and the request for a postcode, not a zone or zip code, makes me pretty sure they're operating from somewhere here in the UK."

"I hope you're right. If they're operating from abroad our chances of catching them are virtually nil, and I don't think Sir Duncan would want us trekking across the globe spending huge amounts of money chasing four grand. So, if they are here in the UK, we need a way to find them. Anyone got any ideas?" Mac asked looking at his team expectantly. The room was silent. "Okay let's take a break and have a coffee. I know where the machine is, so I'll get them, we don't want you lot wandering around the building scaring the natives."

Mac returned to the boardroom and handed out the coffee. As he took his seat, Scrump picked up his copy of Sam's account of the scam and walked to the head of the boardroom table. "I think I may have a way of finding them," he said. "What's the one thing we have on these people, something everyone who's been scammed has?" He looked around the table, the rest of the team looked back at him blankly. "Jock gave me the idea during his presentation." The others continued to stare at him, still with no idea of how to find the people who'd scammed Sir Duncan's son. Scrump finally put them out of their misery. "It's the phone number."

"What are we going to do Scrump, phone them and invite them around to ask for the money back?" Smithy asked.

"Basically yes," Scrump replied. "Well not exactly ask for the money back, we may need to persuade them a little to part with their ill-gotten gains, but that's the basis for the plan I'm thinking of. I know this is a phone scam, but we've all heard of scammers visiting the homes of vulnerable people, particularly the elderly, to take cash from them or to take them to their bank to withdraw cash or transfer money. If we make it worth their while I'm sure we can get some of them to come to us. Once we have them, we can get the info we need, where they're operating from, how many of them are there, layout of the office, all the usual intelligence we would normally gather before paying them a visit. Then we raid the place and get the money back. They obviously won't have cash on the premises but if we can access their computers maybe we can transfer the money to one of the accounts Sir Duncan asked his accountant to set up."

"But won't they know they haven't called us?" Smithy asked.

Scrump shook his head. "No, they won't. They use an automated call system, it calls random numbers. They don't know who's been called. It's like those annoying calls you get about being in an accident that's not your fault. Look at Sam's account of the scam. The first thing he does when he calls their number is give his name, he does that without being asked. Then he gives them his address. They've got all they need to find out a lot more about the caller once they've got that information."

"Well done Scrump, good work," Mac said. "I'm sure it won't be as simple as it sounds, but with a bit of luck it might just work. As you say it would need to be a big enough amount to entice them to pay a home visit, but if they're greedy enough, and I'm sure they will be, they may just take the bait."

15

They spent the next hour drawing up various plans based on Scrump's idea. Finally, they thought they had one that may work. All that was needed was a vulnerable elderly person living in a remote location away from prying eyes. "None of us can pose as their intended victim," Mac said, "they'll know we're on to them as soon as they see us. If they do this kind of visit, I suspect they'll operate in pairs. If one of the scammers stays in the car while the other knocks at the door and one of us opens it, they'll realise something's wrong. If the one in the car escapes and contacts their office, it will give them time to shut the operation down before we can stop them. But I know just the person who fits the elderly person bill."

"Who?" asked Scrump, "Sir Duncan?"

"No." Mac smiled at the thought of his boss playing the role he had in mind. "I think my father fits the bill perfectly."

"Good call," said Smithy. Although Mac's father was an officer, Smithy regarded him differently to the other senior ranking officers he'd met. Mac's father was always willing to stand and chat to all ranks and to buy them a round of drinks. It made him one of the lads in Smithy's eyes.

"Are you sure Mac?" Scrump asked.

"Yes, I'm sure. I'd put money on it that he'll jump at the chance, although he won't like being called old and vulnerable." He smiled to himself when he thought of what his father's reaction would be. "But he won't be meeting them on his own, we'll be there with him when they call so he won't be in any danger."

Scrump still looked dubious. "Okay if you're sure, that's if he agrees to do it."

Mac smiled. "Oh, he'll agree. In fact, I expect we'll have a job from stopping him trying to take the whole operation over."

They knew from their army days that any successful operation relied on meticulous planning, so they spent the next hour fine tuning their plan, looking for weaknesses or alternatives. Once Mac decided it was as robust as possible, he thought it time Sir Duncan knew what they intended. He picked up the phone and dialled Emma's extension. "Hi Emma, it's Mac. Could you ask Sir Duncan if he can spare us a couple of minutes? We want to run a couple of things by him."

Five minutes later Sir Duncan entered the boardroom and took a seat at the far end of the table from Mac. "Sir Duncan," Mac began, "before I outline our plans, I'd like Jock to go over what he's researched on these types of scams. Jock if you'd go through your presentation again please, it won't do the rest of us any harm to hear it one more time."

Jock stood by the flip chart and went through his presentation again. When he'd finished, he asked Sir Duncan if he had any questions.

Sir Duncan sat thinking for a moment. "Just one. I know it's irrelevant to what we're trying to do but does anyone know where is this money eventually ending up? I've been to presentations about scams before, but I never realised the amount of money being stolen. The amounts you've talked about are huge, so either someone is getting extremely rich or the money is funding something that's incredibly expensive."

"We don't know for sure where the money is going," Jock answered. "In some cases, once the person at the top of the scam has made enough, they'll pull out, usually to start up another criminal money making-activity. The long-term scammers are usually part of a bigger organisation. They need the vast amounts of money involved to fund terrorist activities across the world and fund armies fighting coalition forces in places like Afghanistan. We all know from experience that war is an expensive business, they would need every penny of what they make from scams such as the one your son was a victim of to buy arms and equipment."

"Thank you," Sir Duncan said. "I have no more questions."

Mac stood and walked to the flip chart. "We have two plans to put to you. The first would recover Sam's money and put a stop to this scam. The second would recover Sam's money and possibly make you some money and cover the expenses you'll be incurring in trying to get his money back."

"Let me stop you there, Mac," Sir Duncan interrupted. "I want us to take as much money from these people as we can, but I don't intend to make any money out of this for myself, that would make me no better than the people committing these crimes. I saw what effect it had on Sam and I'm sure it affects other people far worse than it did him, particularly the elderly and vulnerable. I will not make money out of other people's misery. I think as a minimum we should aim to recover the money Sam lost and make sure these people are stopped from scamming anyone else. If we recover more than Sam lost I'll decide what we do with it once we know how much we're talking about. What you do with these people if you catch them is up to you, as long as they're stopped from stealing anyone else's money in the future."

"Understood," Mac said. "Both plans are essentially the same. First, we place what these people will believe is an old and vulnerable person in a remote house and get them to call the number Sam has given us."

"But won't they know they haven't called that number?" Sir Duncan interrupted.

"No, that's the beauty of it. They use an automated call system phoning random numbers to cast their net as wide as possible. They don't know who they've called. They're relying on people to call back after getting a fright from the automated call."

"Sorry Mac, carry on," Sir Duncan said.

"So," Mac continued, "the supposed old person calls the scammers, we have the advantage because we know what they will say. I suspect they have a script and they probably go through the same dialogue as they did with Sam. When they ask this old person how much they have in their bank account we give them a figure they can't resist. Our old person will tell the scammers he's infirm, can't drive and doesn't bank online. When it comes to getting the money, the old person will suggest he could transfer it to them if he could get to his local branch. With the amount on offer, we hope the scammers will think it worthwhile sending someone to take the old person to the bank. We'll be waiting for them when they arrive. We persuade them to tell us where their office is, then pay them a visit and, with a little luck, recover as much money as we can."

Sir Duncan took a moment to take in the details of Mac's plan. "Sounds simple, but I'm sure it won't be as easy as that. How will you persuade them to give you their address?"

"We have our ways," Mac said. "Skills learned in the regiment. Probably best you don't know."

"Yes, probably best. Sorry I asked." Used to having all the information on any new venture he was running in his business Sir Duncan couldn't break the habit of wanting to know all the facts, even if this was somewhat different to his usual business ventures.

"You need to be aware that there are any number of things that could go wrong," Mac said. "The scammers may not take the bait; they may be at the other end of the country and not willing to make the journey. If we do manage to find them, they could have more security than we can cope with. They may be armed, we won't be, and as Jock explained they may have a panic button connected to the computer transferring funds. If the button's pressed there'll be no way for us to recover any money. The computer will automatically shut down alerting the people at the other end that there's a problem. The money held at that end of the operation will be transferred meaning we can't get to it. If that happens all we can do is put a stop to their scam.

"The biggest risk to recovering big amounts of money is that the person here doesn't have access to the account the money is being transferred to overseas, or the login details have been changed since they last worked at the office abroad. I think we'll be okay with the login change; these people don't believe anyone would do the same to them. We really are relying on speed and surprise to stop the people at this end alerting the people receiving the transfers. And finally, they could be operating from somewhere abroad where we can never find them, but Jock is fairly confident they're somewhere here in the UK.

"You do know you're risking a lot of your own money by doing this Sir Duncan?" Mac said. "You may not get it back if they realise there's something wrong".

Sir Duncan nodded. "Yes, I realise that, but if they are operating from this country your plan looks like our only option, and I'm prepared to take the risk. Even if we don't recover any money, I will consider it a success if you can get to these people and stop them scamming anyone else. Any money we take from them will be a bonus."

Sir Duncan looked around the table. "Which of you will be posing as the old person?" he asked.

"None of us," Mac replied.

"Who do you have in mind for this old person?" Sir Duncan asked. "Not me I hope, I said I wasn't going to take an active role in this."

"No Sir, not you, my father." Mac smiled at the look of horror on Sir Duncan's face when he thought he was being put forward to play the role of the old infirm victim.

"Are you sure, Mac?" Sir Duncan asked slightly surprised and relieved. "We don't want to put him in any kind of danger. You'll be giving them your father's address if you want them to come to his house. They could pay him a visit after this is all over. I hate to think what they might do to him."

"Don't worry sir, we'll all be there when they pay him a

visit. They probably wouldn't send more than two people on a call like this. I think we can take care of him. And once we've finished, I don't think they'll be in a position to pay anyone a visit. Besides, if I know my father, I think he'll enjoy it."

"Well, if you're sure. Just remember if there's the slightest chance that any of you, including your father, are in any kind of danger or likely to get hurt I want this stopped immediately. As for what you do with these people if you do catch them, you're right, probably best I don't know."

"Yes Sir, probably best," Mac replied even though he hadn't thought about what they would do with the scammers should they catch them. That was a decision totally dependent on the success of the first part of the plan and one he would put off until the time arose.

There was a knock at the door and Emma entered. "Three vans have been left in the car park for a Mr. Smith, I assume that's one of you gentlemen." She walked to the boardroom table and placed three sets of keys in front of Mac.

"Thanks, Emma." Mac picked up the keys and put them in his pocket.

Sir Duncan rose from his seat and stood next to his secretary. "I'll let you gentlemen get on with your planning, just keep me updated, and remember, no heroics. I don't want any of you hurt doing this." He left the boardroom with Emma, closely followed by Mac. He didn't want the others listening to his conversation with his father, he'd make the call from the privacy of his own office.

Mac's father, Andrew MacDonald, had also served in the army but not in special forces, and after a lifetime of service had reached the rank of major before retiring. After his wife died five years earlier he moved to a remote cottage in North

Wales where he passed his time walking, playing the occasional game of golf, trying to keep the rabbits out of his vegetable patch and telling tall tales in the village pub a few miles away. He was in no way old or infirm, in fact, he was just the opposite.

Mac dialled his father's number. After four rings his call was answered, "Hello," Andrew said.

"Hi Dad, it's Alistair. How are you?"

"Alistair, it's good to hear from you. I'm good thanks, what about yourself?"

"I'm fine thanks. How's the golf?"

"I don't get out as much as I'd like to, and the weather's been a bit iffy lately. I'm not really sure where the time goes, you know how it is."

"Yes," Mac said. Not being a golfer himself he never saw the attraction, a good walk spoiled as the saying went. "Dad, I have something to ask you and time is pressing so I'll get straight to the point. Some of the lads from the regiment have got back together on an operation to catch some scammers. My boss's son was scammed out of just short of four thousand pounds two days ago and he's asked me to try to get it back. We're setting up a sting to try to trap some of them and part of the plan means we need someone to pose as an old infirm person to lure them to a remote location. I wondered if you'd be willing to help us?"

"As the old person?" Andrew asked, his voice giving away the fact that he was obviously indignant at the thought of anyone thinking of him as old and infirm.

"Yes, Dad."

"Bloody cheek, I could still take on a man half my age. You know I walk the hills around here, and I walk the couple of miles to and from the pub and shops in the village? I'm as fit as a fiddle."

"Yes, I know Dad, but this would be playing a role to catch these crooks. I can't guarantee it won't get a bit hairy, or that they'll take the bait, but I think with the amount of money we'll be offering they will. So, we need someone to play this part. We'll be there to make sure no harm comes to you."

"Sounds like it could be fun," his father said with a hint of mischief in his voice, relishing the thought of spending a little time with his son and some of his colleagues. It would be just like his days in the army. "I can take care of myself you know, as well as the walking I do try to keep fit. When would this be taking place?"

"Well, as I said, time is of the essence so we would come up to your cottage tomorrow if that's okay? We'll brief you, set up, then try to contact them. If you're willing to help we would be with you around nine tomorrow morning. We need to get this done as soon as possible otherwise these people may disappear and we'll have no chance of catching them."

"Of course I'll help," his father said. "I'm supposed to be playing golf tomorrow, but I can cancel that. Maybe I'll pretend that I'm too old and infirm to walk around a golf course," he joked. "It's a long time since I've been on an op. If your lads are anything like mine used to be, they'll want plenty of tea while they wait around so I'd better go into the village and buy some more milk."

On the other end of the line, Mac shook his head. His father really should have been in the catering corps he thought. "Ok Dad but not a word to anyone. No popping into the pub for a swift half and a quick natter either. We don't want word getting out of what we're doing. If we manage to catch these people and recover the money what we've got planned isn't strictly legal and we could be in all sorts of trouble, so we need to keep it strictly between us."

"Yes, don't worry son. Mum's the word, loose lips and all that."

"Good, I'll see you tomorrow around nine."

"Yes, see you then son, bye." Right, Andrew thought as he put the phone down, milk. I'd better get to the village shop before it closes, and I expect Alistair's lads will want food too, an army marches on its stomach. He realised he should have asked how many of his son's old team would be coming. He put on his shoes, jacket and cap, put a carrier bag in his pocket and stepped out of the cottage closing the door behind him. He pointed his keys towards the car but stopped himself before pressing the key fob to unlock it. No, he thought to himself, it's a nice day I'll walk, got to keep fit. Old and infirm indeed!

Mac returned to the boardroom to inform the others that his father had agreed to help. "There are a few more things we're going to need," he said. "Scrump, you're our camo expert, we need camouflage, five sleeping bags and binoculars. You're a local Smithy, do you know anywhere nearby we can get them?"

"Yes guv, there's a camping shop about twenty minutes away, and a camera shop next door. They should have everything we need. It won't be what we were used to in the regiment, but it will be good enough for what we need."

"Probably better than we were used to," Jock grumbled in the background.

"Okay enough. You know the area Smithy, go with Scrump and show him where these shops are, you can help carry everything back here." Mac handed Smithy the envelope containing the money Sir Duncan had given him. "And don't forget...."

"I know, I know. Don't forget the receipts." Smithy walked towards the door. Scrump stood and followed him out.

"And no stopping at the pub on the way," Mac called out as Scrump closed the boardroom door.

While Smithy and Scrump were on their shopping trip the others went through Sam's account of the scam again. Mac decided that, like the scammers, his father should follow a script. They thought they already knew what the scammers would say, what they needed were the correct answers to entice them to the cottage, and Mac knew his father, left to his own devices the whole plan could blow up in their faces. After an hour they were happy with the script they'd put together, one his father would follow and one they hoped would bring the scammers to them.

An hour later Smithy and Scrump returned with the equipment Mac thought they would need. The team went through the plan one last time trying to find anywhere, apart from the scammers not taking the bait, it may fail. After an hour of trying to find holes in their plan, Mac decided it was time to head back to the hotel. "Okay lads, it's at least a five-hour drive tomorrow so we need an early start. I'll let Sir Duncan know we're leaving and let the security team know what time we'll be here to collect the vans." He picked up his laptop and the envelope containing what was left of Sir Duncan's money and headed for the door. The rest of the team tidied the boardroom, a habit from their time in the regiment, they didn't want to leave any evidence of the plan they hoped to put into action the following day.

~

AT FOUR THE next morning Mac and his team woke a startled security guard dozing in the car park gatehouse. They threw their gear in the back of the vans and set off on the long journey to North Wales, only too aware that it could be a wasted journey, and possibly a very expensive one for Sir Duncan.

16

Five and a half hours after leaving the underground car park in London Mac's team finally arrived at their destination. "This really is the middle of nowhere" Smithy said as they pulled onto the drive just after nine-thirty. "I can't understand why anyone would want to live out here, there isn't even a pub close by. What do people do for entertainment in a place like this?"

Alerted of their imminent arrival by the sound of the vans coming down the quiet country lane, Mac's father stood at the door waiting to greet them.

Mac's team climbed out of their vehicles and stood on the driveway stretching their aching limbs. He looked around the men he'd served with on tours in trouble spots all over the world. They had all kept themselves in shape since leaving the army but there was no defeating Father Time. He worried that they may be taking on more than they could handle if the scammers had a security team younger and fitter than themselves, especially if they were outnumbered and came up against anyone who was armed. But they'd set their plan in motion and were enjoying being back together and working as a team again. He'd need to be careful and keep their enthusiasm in check, he didn't want any repeat of the disaster they'd experienced on his last day with them in Afghanistan.

After greeting his visitors with a handshake and a hug for his son, Andrew asked if anyone would like tea or coffee before unloading the vans. "The kettle's on," he said, "I expect you lads could do with a brew after such a long journey?"

"Dad, let us get sorted first then we'll have a cuppa while we go through the plan with you. First, we need to store the vans somewhere out of sight, they'll stick out like a sore thumb to anyone coming down the lane if we leave them here. Is there anywhere close by where we can hide them?"

"Yes, there's a derelict farm about a quarter of a mile down the lane with a barn big enough to put them in. It's the perfect place to hide them and they'll be safe there," his father pointed towards the end of the lane.

"Are you sure they won't be discovered? What about someone coming from the other direction?"

"It's a dead end," his father said. "The council closed the road last year to stop the boy racers using it as a cut through. That farm is the end of the road, anyone going there needs to pass here first. You'll know if someone's approaching if you post a lookout. But don't worry, no one comes this way, I can't remember the last time anyone went down there."

"Perfect, and you need to put your car in the garage too, you're not supposed to be driving remember."

"Okay, I'll get the keys," his father said heading for the door.

They unloaded the bags containing Mac's laptop, the equipment they would need if they took hostages and the holdalls with the few personal belongings they'd brought for an overnight stay. "Smithy, Taff, Scrump, take the vans to the end of the road and put them in the barn out of sight, please. Make sure they're secure and can't be seen from the road." They wearily climbed back into the vans and made their way slowly down the lane to find the hiding place.

Mac and Jock entered the cottage loaded down with the laptop and bags. When they entered the kitchen, Jock saw a shotgun leaning against the table. He smiled and nodded towards the gun. "That could come in handy Mac."

Mac picked the gun up and check the safety was on. "Dad, you know this should be locked up."

"Don't worry son, it's not loaded. That's just an old thing I use for shooting the bloody rabbits. I like to keep it close by so I can get out there quickly if I see the little buggers in my veg patch. They're out of control around here you know. They'll eat everything I've got growing in the garden if I don't keep their numbers down. I got a couple this morning but there are plenty more out there to take their place. I'll lock it up with my good gun after I've made the tea."

"How many guns do you have sir?" Jock asked, addressing Mac's father as though they were both still in the army. He found it a hard habit to break.

"Just the two," Andrew replied. "That old thing and a Purdy that's locked in the gun cabinet. I used the Purdy when I went pheasant shooting before I moved here. I don't get to use it much now, but I keep it for sentimental reasons. My wife bought it as a present for my 60th birthday."

"Mac, I know what you said back at the office about us using weapons, but we really don't know what we might be up against. The guns will at least give us the look of an armed gang that means business if nothing else. That's if your Dad doesn't mind us using them?" Jock said.

"Not at all, be my guest. I'll go and get the other one." Andrew picked up the keys for his gun cabinet, "I won't be a minute."

"We weren't supposed to be armed," Mac said when his father had left the kitchen, "but I suppose we could use them as a deterrent." After weighing up the risks Mac thought they should use every advantage available to them. "We'll take the guns, but they'll be unloaded. We don't want any accidents, and if we did have to use them things will have spiralled too far out of control and it would be time to pull the plug. You know what Sir Duncan said, he doesn't want any of us getting hurt doing this." After what had happened the last time they'd all worked together Sir Duncan wasn't the only one who didn't want any of Mac's team hurt.

A couple of minutes later Andrew returned with the gun and a box of shells. He handed the Purdy to Jock who looked it over with the eye of someone who appreciated the quality of workmanship that had gone into the shotgun. "Nice gun," he said, "more than enough to persuade someone to give us the info we're going to need."

Mac picked up the box of shells. "Dad, put these back in the gun safe please, we'll be using your guns, but they'll be unloaded."

Mac looked at Jock who was still admiring his father's best gun. "You know we won't be using these for real, they'll be for appearance's sake only," he reminded him.

"Aye, I know, but they're nice to have all the same," Jock said feeling the weight of the gun in his hands and admiring the intricate patterns on the stock.

Once the rest of the team returned after hiding the vans

everyone gathered in the kitchen, all but Jock sat at the table, he stood leaning against the kitchen units watching the others. "Right Dad," Mac began, "you know the basics of our plan, but we need to go through it in detail until you have it word perfect." Mac handed his father the typed script they'd prepared in the boardroom before they'd left. "This is what we want you to say, word for word, no ad-libbing. Have a read through it then we'll go through it together."

After making everyone tea Andrew sat at the kitchen table, picked up the script and started to read. "The name's left blank," he said after reading the first line.

"That's right," Mac said, "we want you to choose a name for yourself, one you will easily remember. We don't want you to use your own. These people operate to a set formula, firstly they try to scare their intended victim, then offer a way out, but all the time they have someone on the phone they try to keep them confused with a feeling that the situation is out of their control, the only way out being to transfer money to them. If the conversation starts to get heated, you need to have a name you'll remember. If he calls you Mr. Jones and you don't respond he may get suspicious and end the call. We have the advantage of knowing who we're talking to and what they're likely to say, that way their scare tactics won't work."

"A name is easy", Andrew said. "I always admired Robert Scott when I was a young boy."

"Who the hell is Robert Scott?" Smithy asked.

Andrew shook his head. "Don't they teach you youngsters anything at school? Robert Falcon Scott. He was a captain in the Royal Navy, awarded the grade of Commander of the Royal Victorian Order. He's been a hero of mine since I was a young boy. You may know him better as Scott of the Antarctic, young man," he said looking at Smithy. "He died along with all his men in a terrible storm in 1912 just after losing the race to be the first man to the South Pole to a Norwegian named Roald Amundsen. Terrible waste of such a great man and a tragic loss of his brave team."

"If he's someone famous won't they be suspicious?" Smithy asked.

"I suspect the people we'll be dealing with will have as much idea who Robert Scott was as you did, young man," Andrew said.

"Okay Dad," Mac said, interrupting his father before he could launch further into Scott's life story. "Back to the job in hand, please. The key points are; One;" Mac started counting off the points on his fingers, "you have just over fifty-thousand pounds in your bank account. That should be enough to tempt them. Two; you don't have a laptop or internet access for online banking. Three; you are old and infirm, and you don't drive," Mac smiled as he counted this last point off, the one his father had been indignant about the previous day. "There is no bus service here and the taxi drivers won't come out this far into the country, so you need help getting to the bank. Four; your local branch is only fifteen minutes away. Five; and this is the most important point, you are willing to go to the bank to make the transfer if they are willing to come here and take you to your local branch."

For the next two hours, Mac sat at the kitchen table with his father repeatedly going over the script. Despite Andrew having ideas of his own he wanted to include Mac eventually persuaded him to stick to the script and rehearsed with him until he was word perfect. The rest of the team kept out of sight, not wanting to distract Mac and his father or draw attention should any of the locals ramble down the lane and see them, despite Andrew's assurances that no one ever walked past his house.

"At last," Mac said putting the script on the table, "I think we're ready. The time's getting on, so I think we go for it tomorrow morning around nine-thirty. Wherever they're based it's bound to be a long journey, so we need to give them plenty of time to get here. Dad, I'll put the gear in the cellar, you show the lads where they'll be sleeping tonight then we can get some food on the go."

Later that evening after finishing their meal, Mac's team sat around the kitchen table while his father loaded the dishwasher. When he'd finished, he disappeared for a moment then reappeared carrying a bottle of whiskey and six glasses.

"I don't think that's a good idea Dad," Mac said. "We need clear heads in the morning. Maybe we can come back and celebrate when this is all over, if there's anything to celebrate, but until then we don't touch a drop." Jock looked disappointed, it was a bottle of excellent malt and he fancied a wee dram.

"Ok son, you're in charge, I just thought one drink would be a nice way to finish the evening," Andrew put the whiskey and glasses on the side.

"Put the whiskey back in the cabinet please Dad, out of sight. If you leave it there it may be too much of a temptation." Mac knew Jock liked a wee dram and one drink would lead to another, sometimes he didn't know when to stop. They needed to be sharp when the scammers arrived the next day. If the scammers arrived.

"As you say, Son." Andrew picked up the whiskey and glasses and left the kitchen to return them to his drink's cabinet.

As evening turned to night, they sat around the kitchen

table reminiscing about old times and old colleagues. Inevitably the subject came back to their time served in Afghanistan and the friends and colleagues they'd lost. After his revelation in the pub two days before, Mac was only too aware that Scrump had suffered more than the others adjusting to life as a civilian and repeatedly tried changing the subject to happier times, but eventually gave up. Maybe Scrump needed to talk about what he'd been through with people who'd been there with him, those who'd shared the same experiences. The feeling of helplessness while you watched a friend slowly bleed to death or carry one away on a stretcher screaming after an IED had inflicted terrible injuries. Mac hadn't suffered the same way Scrump had but he would never forget what he'd seen, especially on that last fateful day of his tour in Afghanistan when Gav was injured, and the innocent boy killed. He thought that maybe subconsciously he'd agreed to take this job because if the scam was funding terrorism he saw it as some way to pay the terrorists back for the pain and suffering they'd caused, not only for those who'd lost their lives or been injured in the conflict, but for those like Scrump who were still reliving the nightmare of what they'd seen and were still suffering.

"We don't know where this money is going but if it's going to terrorists and we can stop it getting to them it may just save a life or two," Scrump said. "I wouldn't wish what we went through out there on anyone. I'm doing this for my mates who were injured or those that didn't come home at all. It's not revenge," he said, "it's just some kind of way to lend a helping hand to the lads still out there fighting these bastards. We know better than anyone they need all the help they can get."

Mac smiled, he realised he'd been wrong to try to steer

the conversation away from what they'd experienced in Afghanistan. It was part of Scrump's therapy to talk about his experience and feelings both while there and now he was home. Perhaps this would help his ongoing recovery, it would probably help all of them, even if they didn't like to admit it.

"Wherever the money's going you can be sure it's doing no one any good other than the people at the top of this scam," Mac said, "and causing a lot of pain and suffering to the innocent people who are losing their money."

Andrew sat listening to Mac's team talking of old times, he thought a glass of whiskey really would have been a perfect end to the evening.

～

THAT EVENING IN KARACHI, Omar's phone rang. He didn't recognise the number and wondered who could be calling at this time. "Hello," he said warily.

"Omar," the voice at the other end of the phone said.

The old man. Omar wondered why he would be calling at such a late hour. He was immediately concerned. He couldn't think of any trouble at the office, or could it be trouble with Hadia? "Hello," he said again.

"Omar, I am sending you a replacement for one of your team first thing in the morning."

"Why, has there been a problem?" Omar asked.

"No everything's fine. We're setting up a new operation in America and we're sending your man to be the person responsible for transferring money back here. You know we like to use people who've worked for us here in Karachi in such an important and trusted position. The young man we're sending you as a replacement has been injured in the war just like you. Make sure you look after him."

Whenever the old man spoke to him Omar felt there was always a hint of menace. Didn't he trust him? After all the time he'd worked for the organisation there had never been reason to doubt his work or his trust and yet Omar always felt the old man was waiting for one slip and he would pounce. He would look after this new recruit and prove to the old man he could be trusted and that his loyalty shouldn't be doubted. He couldn't put himself, his brother and his family in any kind of danger. He knew the dire consequences that would follow if the old man was crossed.

"I will look after him," Omar said.

"Good, see that you do."

"What about the woman we sent to the UK?" Omar asked. "We sent her as an emergency replacement. When can she come home?"

Your niece, the old man thought to himself, you wouldn't be asking that question if the woman wasn't related to you. "She's only been there for six months. We need people we can trust transferring our money. With our expansion in America we don't have any suitable replacements at the moment, and she's done a good job for us over there, we have more money coming from the UK than ever before. We can talk about it some other time."

The phone went dead. Another piece in the jigsaw, the old man thought. After the last conference where he'd informed another of the groups financing the war about how much was being stolen from them, he had taken over their operation. The man he was sending from Omar's team was an important part of his retirement plan, and one of a number of staff he'd sent to replace the existing staff. His cut of the money generated was modest when he'd first taken over, he'd slowly increased it and now his retirement fund was growing nicely. It would soon be time to disappear and enjoy the fruits of his labour before those at the top of these organisations realised exactly how much money he was stealing from them.

OMAR STARED AT HIS PHONE. He knew Hadia was desperate to come home. What would he tell her when she called him next?

17

That same evening, Haida transferred the last of the day's takings to the bank account in Karachi and shut down her computer. Hassan logged the last name and amount on his laptop and totalled the amount scammed that day. Two hundred and fifteen thousand pounds, not the most they'd taken in one day but almost. Her uncle and his bosses back home would be pleased, she thought.

Hadia had been in the UK for six months and desperately wanted to return home. She hated living in the UK. She hated the people; she hated the food and she hated the weather. It always seemed to be cold and wet, even in summer. When it was hot the people complained, when it was cold, they complained. Whatever the weather it was never right, too hot, too cold, too wet, too windy, the wrong kind of snow. They were obsessed with the weather. She also hated how the West was insidiously infecting the culture of her homeland.

Because of the nature of their operation they were always

on the move. If they believed there was a chance the authorities would discover what they were doing they would change location, even if they'd been there for only a few days. She was tired of moving every few months, sometimes they stayed in at a location even less, and she hated living with the stupid men in the team. She wanted to see her mother and father, her friends and her uncle.

Before she left Pakistan Omar had told her to pack for a couple of weeks, she was to be a temporary replacement and he would do everything he could to bring her home as soon as possible, but despite talking to him regularly he hadn't mentioned any plans to bring her home. Maybe as she'd turned the situation around and the UK operation was now transferring more money than it ever had she was a victim of her own success and they would leave her in the UK until her visa expired. Even then, she thought they would have some way of getting around visa restrictions to extend her time in the country she hated.

Hadia faced constant hostility from the other members of the team when she first arrived. They resented working with a woman, especially one who thought she was responsible for the most important part of the operation, and as the only member of the team who'd worked in Karachi, believed she was therefore more senior. They seemed to have the same attitude as the company she had worked for back home, women were inferior, suited only to housework or jobs men felt were beneath them. But her strong will meant she would not bow to these men's outdated attitudes. She stood her ground and gradually gained their grudging respect. Everyone except for one of the guards. No matter how hard she tried all she felt from Nasir was a constant menacing hostility and a sense that he was constantly keeping watch over her, waiting for her to make one mistake before he could pounce.

Despite their reluctance, and in Nasir's case open hostility, she introduced a scheme where two scams could be carried out at the same time. When Amir and Imran told their victim they were being put on hold while they talked to the legal team and prosecutors, they would transfer to another victim who was on hold and had been told the same story. For the first few days of trying concurrent scams, Amir and Imran became confused switching between calls, the victims became suspicious and, realising it was a scam, many had hung up. Income fell and Hadia worried the Karachi office would suspect there was a problem, possibly that she was stealing their money. Nasir pointed out that he'd told her the idea was stupid and bound to fail and that they should revert to the old system that was proven to work. She called her uncle to tell him of the new process she'd put into place and to let him know that despite the teething difficulties they were experiencing she was confident, given a little time, that it would generate even more cash. Omar told her to continue the process for another week, after that if income hadn't returned to at least its former level she was to revert to the old system of one scam at a time. He suggested she could try training Imran and Amir after work, but she doubted they would be willing to give up their time.

To overcome Imran and Amir's confusion, Hadia gave them both a script and tick list for each of their victims. She told them to write the person's name at the top of each list and follow the new script she'd printed for them. After five days, income returned to the level prior to the new process, and gradually increased, eventually going up by twenty percent.

After shutting the computers down, they gathered their belongings and set off for the rented house they were currently living in. She knew the others would expect her to cook when they arrived at their temporary home, just as they did almost every day after work. In their eyes cooking was women's work, but she'd had a long day and was tired, she couldn't be bothered to cook for everyone again. Why should she work all day then be expected to cook when she got home while the others relaxed watching television or playing games on their phones? She wondered what they'd done about eating before she'd arrived.

She closed the front door and told them of her decision. "I'm not cooking tonight, so unless one of you is willing to do woman's work it's a takeaway again." She walked into the kitchen, picked up the numerous takeaway menus they'd accumulated and asked if anyone had any preference.

Nasir glared at her. "All you've done is sit in front of a computer all day. How can you be too tired to cook?"

"And all you've done is sit around and stare at your phone all day," Hadia replied, "why don't you cook?" As soon as she'd spoken, Hadia knew she'd overstepped the mark. Nasir's open hostility towards her was bad enough already, she suspected her outburst would further antagonise him. Once again, she couldn't hold back her headstrong nature.

Nasir glared at her menacingly, aware that everyone was staring at him after Hadia's humiliating comments.

Hadia stood frozen to the spot, horrified at what she'd said, convinced if the others weren't there Nasir would be tempted to take some kind of retaliation against her. Hassan took the menus from Hadia and passed them to the others. "Takeaway it is then," he said, trying to defuse the situation.

After deliberating over the menus for half an hour they

finally decided what each of them wanted. "I'll go," said Tariq.

"But there's no need, we could have it delivered." She hoped the other hadn't picked up the note of desperation she recognised in her own voice. She had a strange premonition of what was to come. The last thing she wanted was to be left alone in the house with Nasir.

"I said I'll go," Tariq said glaring at her. "If you can't be bothered to cook don't interfere when we make plans to pick the food up."

"I'll come," Amir said.

"I'll come too," Hadia said in a desperate attempt to ensure she wouldn't be left alone with Nasir.

"No, you won't. As you've decided you won't be cooking for us you can stay here and clean up the breakfast things and lay the table ready for when we return. Now, anyone else want to come?" Tariq asked.

Leaning against the kitchen units Nasir remained silent, his arms folded across his chest, a smug look on his face.

Both Imran and Hassan said they would join Tariq and Amir to collect the food. Tariq picked up the menus marked with their orders and headed for the door followed by the others.

Hadia's worst fears had been realised. She was to be left alone with a man who hated her, a man who held all women in contempt, and one who had a violent streak in him. She now regretted her refusal to cook. Unwittingly she had orchestrated a situation where she would be left alone with Nasir. It was almost as if he'd planned the whole thing and she'd fallen into his trap.

Despite the takeaway only being a short distance from the house, Hadia knew it would not be a quick trip to collect the food, then home. They would be gone for at least an hour. She knew where they were going. Their first stop would be the late-night betting shop and then on to the pub before collecting the food and returning home. Even though alcohol was forbidden by their religion they took every chance they could to go to the pub, often stopping on the way home from work while she walked home to cook the evening meal. They'd been infected by western culture just as was happening back home in Pakistan.

The door slammed as the others left the house. Hadia was left standing in the kitchen with Nasir, the one person in the team she hated and feared the most. He stood in the doorway blocking any attempt she might make to escape to her room. She hoped that if she kept herself busy clearing the breakfast things as Tariq had said, cleaning around the kitchen and preparing for the meal, Nasir may get bored and leave her alone. If she got the chance, she would lock herself in her room until the others returned.

As she turned to get plates and cutlery, Nasir grabbed her and spun her around. "Let go of me," she said, "you're hurting me." Nasir pulled her closer, but despite his superior strength Hadia managed to push herself away then slapped him across the face. She stood staring at Nasir, stunned, frozen in horror at what she'd done. For a woman to strike a man in her culture was unforgivable, whatever the provocation.

Equally stunned for a moment, Nasir stood motionless. Slowly the full realisation of what had just happened dawned on him. Being spoken to in front of the others as he had been earlier was bad enough, but the humiliation of being hit by a woman was something he wouldn't tolerate. "How dare you," he growled. Before she could move away Nasir took one step toward Hadia and hit her across the face. She stumbled, her head spinning from the blow, she grabbed the table to steady herself. Nasir took another step forward and hit her again, a blow much harder than the first. Hadia's legs buckled beneath her and she fell to the floor. She could feel blood running down her face from a cut above her eye as she tried to regain her composure. Terrified of what Nasir might have in store for her next she sat in silence, staring at the kitchen floor, trying to appear submissive and full of remorse. Although the others had only just gone, she prayed they would return soon before he could do any worse.

As Hadia sat still cowering on the kitchen floor Nasir stood over her. "Don't ever touch me again," he said. "If you do, I will kill you. And don't breathe a word of this to the others or it will be much worse for you next time. It's about time someone put you in your place. You should be at home, married to someone your parents have approved of with children running around your feet. I'll be watching every move you make. One slip and I'll report back to Karachi that you're not to be trusted and you should be removed. Then who knows what your fate will be."

Sitting on the kitchen floor with blood running down her face, Hadia thought maybe that would be for the best. It would get her away from these men and the country she hated, back to her family and friends, back to her homeland she so longed to return to. Using the table for support, she slowly pulled herself to her feet. Keeping her eyes fixed on the kitchen floor she staggered towards the door, never once looking at the man who'd attacked her. As she tried to leave Nasir stepped into the doorway blocking her escape.

"Remember what I said, not a word to the others. If I find out you've spoken to any of them about this, I will make things much worse for you." He stepped aside letting Hadia pass. She walked unsteadily from the kitchen, grabbed the bannister for support then slowly made her way up the stairs to her room.

An hour later she heard the others return with the meal. After a few minutes, she could hear excited raised voices and laughter. They must have had a few drinks at the pub and done well at the betting shop, she thought. Not for the first time in the country she hated, she cried herself to sleep.

The next morning Hadia was first to the kitchen for breakfast. Dirty cutlery, plates and takeaway cartons from the previous evening's meal littered the worktops and table. No doubt they expected her to clear up after them, after all, it was women's work. But she wouldn't do it. These men she was forced to live with had embraced the parts of western culture that suited them, now they could embrace the West's attitude towards women and clear up after themselves. The events of the previous evening had finally pushed her over the edge. She didn't care anymore, she would no longer be their cook, cleaner and servant, whatever the consequences and whatever abuse she would face from Nasir. She would call her uncle and tell him exactly what abuse she was being subjected to and the type of people the organisation they were working for employed. She just hoped he had enough influence to have Nasir removed, or better still, and what she longed for the most, to have herself removed and returned home.

When Hadia first sat at the breakfast table the next morning she wondered if she should arrange her hijab to cover as much of the cut and bruising inflicted by Nasir as she could. Or she could make up a story to explain her injuries. But why should she? The others all knew what a thug he was. Even if she couldn't tell them she wanted them to be aware of what he'd done while they were at the betting shop and pub.

She stood and walked to one of the kitchen drawers. Looking over her shoulder to make sure none of the others had entered the kitchen without her realising, she quickly opened the drawer and removed a long-bladed knife. She wrapped it in a tea towel then quickly returned to her seat. She slipped the knife into her bag then put it under the table. Nasir's animosity towards her had now escalated into physical violence. She partly blamed herself, she knew she shouldn't have talked to him the way she had in front of the others and she should never have hit him, but if Nasir attacked her again she would now have something to defend herself with.

Amir was first to the kitchen for breakfast. He stopped in the doorway and stared at Hadia. She returned his stare, holding his gaze for longer than she normally would. Even if she wouldn't dare explain to him how her injuries had been inflicted, she was determined that everyone should know what Nasir had done to her while they were out enjoying themselves. She hoped they would feel ashamed that they had allowed the situation to deteriorate to a point where this could happen. Maybe they would summon up the courage to confront Nasir and make sure it didn't happen again, but she doubted it.

"How...," Amir started to ask.

"Please, don't ask," Hadia interrupted. "I'm sure you can guess how I got this," she pointed to her bruised and cut face. "I've been told I can't talk about it, but while you were all out last night collecting our meal I was left alone here with Nasir. I can say no more."

Amir thought he had a good idea of what had

happened. He felt guilty but would do nothing. He knew how much Nasir hated Hadia, and how violent he could be, especially towards women. Except for Tariq they were all afraid of him and wouldn't raise a finger to stop his violence. The rest of the team agreed that Hadia didn't help herself by assuming an aloof nature and air of superiority. Nasir just needed to make sure he didn't go too far. There would be awkward questions from Karachi if Hadia's injuries were bad enough to stop her from doing her job. Nothing would be allowed to interfere with the flow of money.

Hadia knew she would get the same reaction from the others when they saw her injuries. She wondered what story Nasir had told them during their evening meal to explain why she wouldn't be eating with them. It was obviously a good one from the amount of laughter she'd heard coming from the kitchen. She decided she would sit facing the door, each of the team would have no choice but to see the injuries Nasir had inflicted. Over the next fifteen minutes the others arrived for breakfast, each of them stared at Hadia but said nothing before sitting at the table to eat. All except Nasir, who was last to join them.

"Feeling better this morning?" he asked as he sat at the table. "You may want to put some ice on your eye, it would reduce the swelling."

Hadia stared at him, a fierce hatred in her eyes. "Thank you for your concern but no, I'm not feeling better," she said sarcastically. "I'm going to get my things and walk to work. I need some fresh air, I can't stand the smell in here, maybe it's from the takeaway cartons you've left all over the kitchen, or maybe not." She picked up her bag from under the table and headed towards the kitchen door. She would be forced to take matters into her own hands if her uncle didn't get her out of here soon, before she was badly injured, or worse.

"The kitchen needs tidying before you go to work," Nasir called after her, his voice full of contempt.

Hadia stopped in the kitchen doorway, slowly she turned and glared at Nasir with what she hoped was as much contempt as he was showing towards her. "It's your mess, you clean it up." She wondered if she'd gone too far this time speaking to Nasir like that again in front of the others, but she knew he wouldn't do anything while they were present. After speaking to him as she had she would need to avoid being alone with him over the next few days. The situation was getting out of control, what had just happened at the breakfast table galvanised her resolve, she would call Omar that evening and tell him what was going on. She prayed he could help. It was clear the other men here were afraid of Nasir or shared his animosity towards her and would do nothing to stop him if he turned violent against her again. She could feel their eyes boring into her back as she turned to leave.

Hadia arrived at the industrial unit they were using as an office before the others. Five minutes later the others arrived, three in the black BMW that was Tariq's pride and joy and two in Imran's battered old Ford. The journey from the house was no more than a mile but they insisted on driving. They had become lazy, another western trait they'd picked up, she thought. They would start to get fat if they carried on eating takeaway meals and not exercising. But why should she care? After all, none of them were concerned for her welfare or prepared to stand up for her.

Tariq unlocked the door and they entered the unit to prepare for the day's work ahead. Hassan turned on the background office noise, Amir turned on the machine making the random automated calls, Imran placed the scripts and tick lists Hadia had devised on his and Amir's desks, Hadia turned on her computer to await the first money coming into the account. They were ready for their day's work, ready to scam money from the unsuspecting public.

While the other members of the team prepared for the day ahead Tariq and Nasir, the *security guards*, walked over to the kitchen to make themselves a coffee. Their job was mainly standing around all day watching the others work or staring at their mobile phone screens, or in Nasir's case keeping a close eye on Hadia for the old man.

Hadia watched them making coffee, they never offered to make drinks for the other members of the team. A smile crossed her face, a rare occurrence since she'd returned to the UK. They can do women's work when it suited them, she thought.

After thirty minutes the first money arrived in the account, two thousand four hundred and twenty pounds. Hadia transferred it to the holding account in Karachi. Amir and Imran were now in full flow, the scripts and tick lists Hadia had devised were paying dividends. It was going to be another profitable day for them, but a miserable one for the people at the other end of the phone lines.

18

At nine-thirty just over sixty miles away in a cottage hidden in the Welsh hills, Andrew Macdonald picked up his landline telephone and dialled the number written on the script in front of him. Mac sat at the table next to his father to make sure he didn't deviate from the dialogue they'd agreed on.

"Remember Dad, no ad-libbing, stick to the script."

"Yes, I know." He waited while his call was connected. "Hello, my name is Robert Scott, someone from your office called me regarding some outstanding legal action against me."

Imran made a note of the name and the callers number displayed on his phone at the top of the tick list, Mr. Robert Scott. "Thank you for returning our call Mr. Scott. Can you confirm your postcode and date of birth please?"

Andrew read out the postcode and date of birth written on the paper in front of him, even though he knew it by heart. After all, he thought, it was his own postcode and date of birth, the only information he was about to give that was actually true.

Imran noted the date and postcode then looked up the address on his computer. "That's Dolwen Road, Dolwen, North Wales. Can you confirm the house number please?"

There was no house number, Andrew gave him the cottage's name.

Imran wrote down the name.

"Mr. Scott my name is Ken Martin, I'm part of an investigation by the National Crime Agency into suspected money laundering. My officer number is 36369," Imran read from his script. "We've called you today in connection with case number DC7010. A car hired in Manchester under your name and using your postcode has been found by police inside of which was found a large amount of money and drugs. There were also weapons and blood found in the car. Have you ever hired a car in Manchester, Mr. Scott?"

So far almost the same as the conversation written on the script in front of him, Andrew thought. "No, I'm not allowed to drive anymore," he said. "I had to give my license up a couple of years ago. I'm a bit unsteady on the legs you know, and my eyesight isn't what it used to be. Are you sure you have the right person? I think this may be a case of someone else using my name to hire a car."

It was the usual reaction to the automated call Imran heard on most calls, as always, he ignored whatever the person at the other end of the line said and continued with the script in front of him. "The case against you involves drug trafficking and money laundering. These are very serious allegations sir. Do you have a bank account, Mr. Scott?"

"Yes, but as I said this must be a case of someone using my identity to hire this car."

"So, do you deny these charges, sir?"

"Yes, I certainly do. I've never hired a car in Manchester," Andrew answered.

"In that case, I'll pass you over to the senior officer investigating this case. Please hold the line while I transfer you."

One minute later, Amir put another victim he was trying to scam on hold. He looked at the name of his next potential victim on Imran's notes, took a drink of water and picked up Andrew's call. "Hello, my name is James Douglas, officer number KRM469238. I should make you aware that this call is being recorded and that we are on a three-way call with the legal team and prosecutors dealing with this case. Do you understand sir?"

"Yes," Andrew replied.

"I believe my colleague has explained the charges against you, is that correct sir?"

"Yes but.."

Amir interrupted, "I understand that you have a bank account sir, do you have any other investments?"

"Yes, a couple of ISA's and a few shares."

"How much is in your current account Mr. Scott?"

Although he could only hear his father's side of the conversation, Mac knew from following the script that they'd arrived at the point of offering the scammers the bait. Sitting beside his father, he hoped whoever was on the other end of the line was somewhere in the UK and the amount his father was about to tell him was in his bank account would be enough to lure them to the cottage.

"Just over fifty thousand pounds," Andrew said.

The amount took Amir by surprise. "That's a lot of money to keep in a current account sir, if you don't mind me saying so," he said going off-script.

"There's no point putting it in any of the other accounts the banks have now, none of them pay any interest. I might as well keep it under the mattress," Andrew replied.

Mac looked on as his father worked his way through the script, still hoping the balance was enough to tempt them. He was confident it would be. So far his father had managed to stick to the script, provided the scammers took the bait everything was going to plan.

Going back to his script, Amir continued. "Sir as this case involves money laundering, we need to freeze your bank account for up to ninety days while the investigation takes place. We want to prevent whoever is committing these crimes access to bank accounts, to stop them moving drug money in and out of the country, possibly using your account, and from taking your hard-earned money."

"Look as I said to the other officer, I'm sure this is a case of someone using my name and postcode to hire this car in Manchester. After all, I've told you I'm not allowed to drive now."

"Sir, this is a very serious matter. We need to convince the prosecutor and legal team listening to our conversation that you are not the person committing these crimes. At present, you are liable for prosecution for very serious crimes and could face jail time if found guilty. If you choose not to cooperate you will be arrested and will need to seek legal representation to defend yourself which could cost up to thirty thousand pounds. Can you really afford that Mr. Scott? If you help us catch the criminals committing these crimes it will cost nothing but a little of your time. I'm sure you'd agree that it would be worth it. You do understand the seriousness of these charges don't you sir?" Amir asked.

"Yes but..."

"Sir," Amir interrupted again, "let me put you on hold while I speak to the prosecutors. Please do not hang up, if you do, we'll assume you are using the time to move money and cover your tracks. We'll assume it to be an admission of guilt." Amir pressed the hold button on the phone before Mr. Scott could interrupt again and ticked the next section on the list in front of him. It was at this point the seriousness of the charges really hit home, he thought, confusion and panic would be setting in. To get out of this situation most people would agree to almost anything, especially an old and frail one like he imagined this man to be.

On the other end of the line, far from old and frail and certainly not in a state of panic or confusion, Andrew was enjoying playing his role. He could see how, when confronted with these circumstances, someone who didn't realise they were being scammed could panic and agree to transfer money to these people to avoid prosecution in the belief they were helping the police, especially an older person.

After a couple of minutes, Amir came back on the phone. "Sir, the prosecutor and legal team have agreed they do not believe that it's you who's committed these crimes, but we need your cooperation to help us catch the criminals who have, and to clear your name. Are you willing to help us Sir?"

"Yes, of course."

"Good, then this is how we need to proceed. Your bank account will be frozen preventing both yourself and anyone else from accessing the account. Before we freeze your account, we need you to transfer the balance to a government treasury escrow account which will keep your money safe while the investigation proceeds. Do you know what an escrow account is sir?"

"No," Andrew replied.

"Sir, do you have internet access?" Amir asked. "I can direct you to a government website that explains what an escrow account is and how it works."

"No, I'm afraid I don't have internet access. We have terrible reception around here in the Welsh hills, virtually no internet or mobile phone signal, but my local branch in the village is only fifteen minutes away. I could transfer the money from the branch if I can get there."

Sitting by his father following the script Mac, knew after being tempted by the balance in the bank account this was the next big hurdle, getting the scammers to come to them.

Amir was starting to get confused and a little frustrated, this wasn't how calls usually went. Ignoring what Mr. Scott had said he continued to read from his script regardless, even if it seemed to make no sense. "Then I will briefly explain what an escrow account is," he said, although he didn't fully understand how they worked himself and this would be an unscripted explanation. Not that he was too worried, he didn't think this old man would understand anyway. "An escrow account is an account held by a third party on your behalf," he began, "in this case HM Treasury. If you agree we will send two officers to your house tomorrow with various documents for you to sign, they will give you a cashier's cheque so that you have funds to live on while the investigation continues. Once the investigation is concluded your account will be unfrozen and the difference between what you transfer, and the cashier's cheque will be returned to your account. Can you get to your branch and make the transfer today Mr. Scott?"

"Oh no, I won't be able to get to the bank on my own. As I told you I'm a little unsteady on my legs. I can't drive and there are no busses around here anymore, and the taxi drivers won't come this far out into the country for such a short journey."

"Do you have any family or friends, or maybe a neighbour, who could take you to the bank Mr. Scott?" Amir asked.

"I'm afraid not. My son's in the army and he's posted abroad, and my house is very remote so there's no one close by to ask for a ride to the bank."

"Please hold the line sir while I talk to the legal team. Remember, please don't hang up Mr. Scott." They didn't usually do home visits but depending on how far away this man's house was it would be worth the journey for fifty thousand pounds. Amir opened his laptop and logged in to an online route planner. He typed in the office address as the start location, looked at his notes and entered Mr. Scott's address as the destination. Just over sixty miles, but the journey would take an hour and a half on the country roads. But for fifty thousand pounds he thought a three hour round trip would be worth it. As Mr. Scott had said the location looked remote. Away from prying eyes, it was an ideal location for what he had planned, and an old person would be no threat to anyone in his team. Amir reconnected the call.

"Mr. Scott, I've talked to the legal team and we're prepared to send officers to you now. They should be with you in about an hour and a half. They'll have documents for you to sign and the cashier's cheque. They'll take you to the bank and will give you the details of the account we need you to transfer the money to when you get there. Is that clear Mr. Scott?" Amir asked. "Can I just confirm your address again please?"

"Yes, thank you it's all clear. My address is Dolwen Road, Dolwen, North Wales. You can't miss me, it's a dead-end road.

I'm the last cottage before you get to a derelict farm at the end of the road. I'll keep an eye out for your officers."

"Thank you for helping us with our investigation, Mr. Scott. Our officers will be with you as soon as they can, probably in about an hour and a half traffic permitting, two hours at the most. Goodbye."

"Goodbye." Andrew put the phone down and looked at his son.

"Well done Dad, let's just hope they can find us. How long before they arrive?"

"He said it would take them between an hour and a half to two hours before they get here."

"Thanks Dad, I'll let the others know." Mac left his father sitting at the table to gather the rest of the team together. Moments later they were all sat at the kitchen table. "Okay, they've taken the bait, they'll be here in about an hour and a half, which gives us more than enough time to set up a welcoming committee. Scrump, grab the camo gear and bins then set up somewhere along the road leading to the house. I want a couple of minutes warning before they arrive. Take your mobile with you and let me know when you're in position. Text Scam to me as soon as you see them."

"How will I know it's them?"

"Have you seen any other cars pass while we've been here?" Mac asked.

"Good point." He stood up and made his way to the cellar to collect the camouflage and binoculars.

"Dad, do you have any power tools?" Mac asked.

"Doing some DIY, guv?" Smithy asked.

"Let's just call it the power of persuasion," Mac said, he looked back to his father. "Dad?"

"Yes, I've got a drill and sander in the shed."

"Smithy, can you get them both and put them in the cellar please. And put some of the cable ties down there with them. There's a table in the cellar but we need chairs as well, four should be enough until we know how many of them we're dealing with. I'll get those," Mac said.

"You're not going to use the drill and sander on them are you guv?" Smithy looked horrified.

"Of course not, just a little phycological warfare. Once we've got everything ready in the cellar, we'll go through the plan one more time," Mac said.

Ten minutes later, sat around the kitchen table, they went through each of their roles again. Although this part of the operation should be straightforward, they all knew meticulous planning was the best way to avoid any unforeseen problems. Once they'd been through the plan, they settled down in the kitchen to wait for their visitors, all except Scrump who was walking down Dolwen Road looking for the best spot to hide in the hedgerow.

19

A mir put the phone down and looked at the clock on the wall. Provided there were no traffic hold-ups there should be more than enough time to get to Wales before the banks closed. He needed to organise what looked like a lucrative trip before he could get back to the phones. "Tariq, I have a job for you," he called across the unit gesturing for him to come to his desk.

Tariq looked up from his phone screen, annoyed the game he was playing had been interrupted. Reluctantly he hauled himself from his chair and slowly made his way to Amir's desk. While he walked the short distance to his desk Amir gestured for Hassan to join them. Once they were both standing next to him Amir explained what he wanted. "I need you to go Wales and take an old man to the bank. He's going to transfer fifty thousand pounds to us. He's got no internet access so he can't do it from home, and he's got no one to who can take him. I need you to pose as police officers and take him to his local branch. He's expecting two officers with paperwork to sign so you need to be wearing suits and carrying ID." He wrote down the address and postcode then handed it to Tariq. "Here, you'll be calling on a Mr. Scott. Go back to the house and change then get on the road as soon as you can. Mr. Scott said phone reception's terrible where he lives so there's probably no mobile signal but try to keep me informed if you can."

Tariq and Hassan left the unit and returned to the house to change into suits they hardly ever wore. The takeaway meals they'd been eating over the last few months were taking their toll and the suits were feeling a little tight. They picked up their fake police ID badges, a briefcase for the illusion of a cashier's cheque and paperwork, then set off for Wales in Tariq's BMW.

For the first twenty minutes of the journey, they hardly spoke. They had nothing in common, Tariq was the muscle, and no one was quite sure what Hassan was still doing as part of the operation. He'd been an emergency replacement for the last fool who thought he could steal from his bosses, who Tariq knew were ruthless when it came to the protection of their money. That man had disappeared overnight. Tariq had seen what they did to people who tried to steal from them, it was something he wouldn't wish on his worst enemy. Hassan was supposed to be a temporary replacement until someone was sent from Pakistan to take the role, but when Haida arrived Hassan remained with the team. His job now was one he'd created for himself, entering the names and addresses of all the people they took money from, along with the amount, onto his laptop. It was a job Hadia's predecessor had performed alongside the money transfers, and as far as Tariq was concerned, one she should be doing now. Like Nasir, Tariq thought all she did all day was stare at her computer screen and transfer money to the bank in Karachi as soon as it landed, he could see nothing complicated in that. He knew that before coming to the UK she'd worked in the Karachi office receiving the transfers, now she was at the other end of the operation sending money to whoever had taken her place. The Karachi role was a trusted position, whoever had that role saw just how much was received from accounts across the world, it was why Hadia believed herself to be more senior than the other members of the team.

Although he disliked Hadia's aloof nature and superior attitude, Tariq thought Nasir's treatment of her had gone too far. Anyone sent from the Karachi office had experience at the heart of the operation and usually knew someone in a more senior role in the organisation. Nasir could be in serious trouble if it was discovered he was mistreating her as badly as was evident from the injuries inflicted while they were collecting the takeaway the previous night. And, as a consequence, they could all be in trouble for not stepping in to stop the violence. Although the hierarchy in Karachi were of the old school and saw women as inferior, if anything interfered with their money-making operation there would be serious repercussions. After the previous night's incident he decided it was time to speak to Nasir. He would have a quiet word with him when they returned from this trip, the others didn't need to know. Nasir was a bully and Tariq was convinced that the violence would stop if he was confronted. His one concern was that if Nasir thought Hadia had approached him for protection it would make things worse for her. He would need to make it clear to Nasir that he was confronting him over the violence for the protection of all of them, not Hadia alone. They would all be in serious trouble if she couldn't do her job as a consequence of Nasir's actions.

"I could do without this," Hassan said suddenly breaking

the silence. "But then it is fifty thousand pounds. That's a lot of money in anyone's book."

"True," Tariq nodded.

"Have you ever wondered what you would do with fifty thousand?"

"Hasn't everyone?"

"What would you do with it?" Hassan asked.

"I don't know," Tariq thought for a moment. "Maybe buy another car and go on a nice holiday. What would you do?"

Hassan sat in silence for a moment staring straight ahead at the road, suddenly unsure whether he should divulge his secret to Tariq. "I'd clear my gambling debts," he finally muttered.

"What?" stunned by such a confession, Tariq took his eyes off the road and stared at Hassan for a moment, not sure he'd heard correctly. "Are you joking?"

"No, I'm not joking. I wish I was." Hassan continued to stare at the road ahead, ashamed to be admitting he had a gambling problem. "You know I like the betting shops? Well it's much worse than just liking them, I'm afraid I'm addicted. I've racked up huge debts online as well as in the shops. Now the people I owe money to want it back and I don't know where to turn. I need to get my hands on some cash, and as soon as possible."

Tariq had an uneasy feeling he knew what Hassan was about to suggest, he kept his eyes on the road, hoping he was wrong.

They drove in silence for a few minutes before Hassan finally said what was on his mind. "Look, I was thinking, Amir doesn't know exactly how much this old man we're paying a visit to has in his account. The man himself didn't know exactly, he said *about* fifty thousand pounds. What if we got him to withdraw ten thousand in cash then transfer the balance left in his account? We could take the cash and split it equally. It will only clear a little of my debt, but it will keep the people I owe money to off my back for a while. I know it's asking a lot and I don't want to get you in any trouble, but please Tariq, this is my only chance to buy a little time."

The silence in the car was almost overwhelming. Tariq's original suspicion had been confirmed. From his constant trips to betting shops, he knew Hassan had a gambling problem but hadn't realised it was so bad. He wondered if Hassan had thought of the consequences if their bosses found out what he planned. After the incident with his predecessor, Hassan knew what their bosses would do to them if they found anyone stealing their money. Knowing this, he thought Hassan's situation must be desperate to suggest such a plan. He mulled it over for a few seconds. But how would they find out? If they both kept quiet how would anyone ever find out? They could tell Amir the old man was a bit senile and didn't know how much he had in his account. It could work, but could he trust Hassan to keep his mouth shut? The danger was that he'd go back to his gambling and would end up back in the same position, or worse, and Tariq's part in his plan may come out. If Hassan was addicted as he said he was, Tariq could see no way that he wouldn't return to his gambling. Five thousand pounds, was it really worth the risk?

"Tariq, please," Hassan pleaded, breaking the awkward silence. "I don't know how I'm going to get the money they want if I don't take this chance. This will only pay off a small part of my debt, but it will buy me a little time while I try to figure out how to get the rest."

"Hassan, please be quiet for a minute. I need to think

about this." They rode in silence for another five minutes. In his mind, what Tariq thought he could do with five thousand pounds shut out the consequences of their paymasters discovering what they were thinking of doing. The temptation was too great. And besides, what was ten thousand pounds to an organisation that generated millions?

"Okay," he finally said, "I'll tell you the only way I'll agree to this. We do as you say, we take the old man to the bank and he withdraws ten thousand pounds in cash which we split equally. We tell Amir that there was only forty thousand in the bank and the old man transferred it all, it's still a lot of money so he should be happy. We stop at two different banks on the way back to the office and pay the money into our own accounts, that way we won't have a lot of cash on us when we return. When we get back to the office, you tell Amir you've heard from your family that your father is unwell and that you need to return home immediately. It's up to you whether you pay the people you owe money to before you leave, I don't care, so long as you keep your mouth shut about what we're doing. I'll take you to the airport to make sure you get on the plane back to Pakistan. You return home and never come back to this country. If I hear you've told anyone I will find you and kill you, unless our bosses find you first, then you know it will be much worse for you."

"Thank you," Hassan said, relieved Tariq had agreed to his plan. They travelled the rest of the journey in silence, Hassan with a growing sense of relief, Tariq wondering if he'd done the right thing and whether he should change his mind and call the whole thing off, but at the same time wondering what he could spend his half of the money on.

The longer they travelled in silence the more Hassan liked Tariq's plan. If he told Amir his father was sick and he needed to return home immediately he could disappear with the five thousand pounds. He had no intention of paying his gambling debt. But he wouldn't disappear to Pakistan, he would go to America. Hassan wouldn't know which plane he was boarding once he'd gone through passport control, even if he went with him to the departure lounge. Yes, he thought, this was going to be a worthwhile trip for everyone. Why shouldn't he take a little extra money from the business? He worked hard and was sure the people further up the organisation took money for themselves, why shouldn't the people at the bottom get their share? Thanks to Tariq and the old man they were about to visit, his troubles would soon be over. He would disappear to America, start a new life away from his gambling debts and away from the clutches of the organisation he was now working for.

20

S crump walked along the lane looking for the best
position to hide from their visitors. As he walked, he
gathered some grass, moss, hay and small branches
which he stuck through the camouflage netting he was carrying. After spending fifteen minutes looking for the best spot
in which to hide, he settled into a ditch behind the hedgerow
in Dolwen Road. Once in his hiding spot, he poured water
from the bottle he'd brought with him over a handful of mud
then smeared it over his face. He pulled the netting over his
head, covering his body from head to toe. He knew his
camouflage wasn't to the exacting standard required if
inspected by his old regimental sergeant major but from the
road he was invisible, especially as their visitors weren't
expecting the welcoming committee that awaited them. He'd
done this hundreds of times while in the regiment, sometimes for days crouched in the cold and wet. At least he knew
on this occasion it was only for an hour or two, and it was
warm and dry, not the sleet, driving rain and biting cold he'd
experienced the last time he did this in Wales on a training

exercise in the Brecon Beacons. He checked his phone; the battery was fully charged and the signal strength good. He sent a text to let Mac know he was in position, turned the ringtone off in case of any unexpected calls, then settled down to wait.

Just over an hour and a half later, the sound of an engine broke the silence of the Welsh hills. Scrump picked up the binoculars and focused on the end of the road. A black BMW was coming toward him, almost at walking speed. The two men in the front seats both stared fixedly ahead, searching for Andrew's cottage. Scrump let the car crawl towards him a little further before picking up his phone and texting "Scam" to Mac's number.

A black BMW with tinted rear windows, a spoiler and custom wheels, not the type of police car I would recognise, Scrump thought, even for undercover police officers. He remained motionless as the car crept past him on its way toward the cottage, invisible to the men inside who were completely unaware of what fate held in store for them.

In the cottage, the rest of the team were waiting in the kitchen when the phone on the table vibrated. Mac looked at the one-word message then put the phone in his pocket. "They're here," he said. "Jock, in the cloakroom by the front door. Taff, outside the back door. Smithy, in the cellar. Dad, are you ready?"

"Yes, and looking forward to a bit of action." Andrew picked up an old walking stick he'd found in his cellar. Try to look old and frail, he reminded himself.

"Good, you all know the plan. Time to teach these people a lesson." Mac's team moved silently to their assigned positions to wait for their visitors.

· · ·

TARIQ PULLED up outside the farmhouse. This really is the middle of nowhere, he thought. If this old man couldn't drive and there were no busses why was he living in such a remote spot? Still, it was a welcome escape from another day cooped up in the unit they were currently using as an office and, with a bit of luck, he would be five thousand pounds better off when they returned. He just needed to make sure Hassan kept his part of the bargain and left for Pakistan as soon as they got back. He picked up his phone from the centre console and got out of the car. Strange he thought, the old man had told Amir there was no signal in these hills, but the phone's display said the signal strength was good. Perhaps the old man was with another network or had an old phone. He sent a text to Amir to let him know they'd arrived.

IN THE OFFICE, Amir heard the tone from his mobile phone to alert him a message had arrived. He told their latest potential victim that he was putting them on hold while he talked to the legal team then picked up his phone to read the message. It was from Tariq. They had arrived at Mr. Scott's house. Strange, he thought, the old man had told him there was no mobile signal where he lived. Maybe he was on a different network, or more likely was too old to work out how to use a mobile phone properly. He put his phone back on the desk and re-connected his call without giving it another thought.

HASSAN GOT out of the car and stretched his aching limbs. He put his jacket on and pulled the fake ID from his pocket, picked up the briefcase and walked to the cottage door with Tariq following. Before they could knock the door opened and an old man appeared. Not as frail as Tariq had imagined he would be, or as old.

"Mister Scott?" Hassan asked.

"Yes," Andrew answered, "you must be the police, I've been waiting for you. Sorry for being such a nuisance. Thank you for coming, I hope you had a good journey?"

"Yes, thank you. We are officer's Khan and Ali from the National Crime Agency," they both held up their fake Warrant cards. Neither had any idea what names or whose pictures were on the cards, but it didn't matter, the old man didn't look closely at them. No one ever did.

"Please come in while I put my shoes on and get my hat and coat," Andrew said. "Or would you like a cup of tea before we go, you've had a long journey."

"No thanks, we need to get to the bank before it closes and we need you to sign some documents." Hassan held up the briefcase, "but we can do that after we've been to the bank."

Andrew turned and walked towards the kitchen, hoping he was giving them no option but to follow him. Try to look frail, he reminded himself once more as he walked along his hallway leaning on the walking stick. Tariq and Hassan looked at each other. Hassan shrugged his shoulders and walked through the door. Left standing on the driveway, Tariq looked around, nothing but rolling hills and sheep. He took the car keys from his pocket, pointed them at the BMW and locked the doors. The last thing they needed was his car being stolen leaving them stranded in this remote location. He stepped into the cottage, closed the front door and followed Hassan and the old man along the hallway towards the kitchen.

Jock heard their visitors pass. He silently stepped out of the cloakroom and stood in front of the door Tariq had closed seconds ago. He hadn't held a gun since leaving the regiment, but Andrew's Purdy shotgun felt comfortable in his hands, a deterrent to anyone unaware that it wasn't loaded. He stood in the hallway blocking any escape route from the front of the house.

Tariq and Hassan entered the kitchen to see a man standing behind the door aiming a shotgun at them. "Welcome gentlemen, we've been expecting you." Tariq glanced over his shoulder to see Jock blocking the front door they'd just come through. He too had a shotgun aimed at them. "Please take a seat," Mac said.

"What's going on Mr. Scott? We are police officers." Hassan stared in horror at the man pointing a shotgun at him. "You are making a terrible mistake here, one that could get you into serious trouble."

"You will regret this," Tariq said, "you don't know who you're dealing with or the consequences of what you're doing."

"Don't waste your breath," Mac pointed his gun at Tariq immediately identifying him as the biggest threat. "We know exactly who you are and what you do. Now put the briefcase, your mobile phones, and car keys on the table."

Tariq would have liked to take these men on, but with shotguns aimed at them from both front and rear, he had no alternative. Staring defiantly at Mac, he reluctantly placed his mobile phone and car keys on the table next to Hassan's.

"But we are police officers," Hassan said trying to prolong the façade.

"Really?" Mac said. "Jock, search them for any weapons and more phones, and take their police ID cards, which no doubt are fakes."

Jock handed the shotgun to Andrew then searched them both. Neither had any weapons on them, he threw the fake IDs onto the table beside the phones, keys and briefcase. Mac picked them up and studied the pictures and information on each warrant card. "What name is on your card?" he asked, staring at Hassan.

Hassan closed his eyes, desperately trying to visualise the warrant card in his head. Although he'd never studied the ID maybe the name would come to him. But it was no use, after a few seconds shook his head. "I don't know."

"Good," said Mac. "Now that we've established you are not police officers we have a few questions for you. We know who you are and what you've been doing, so please don't prolong this by lying to us. If you do, or you try to withhold the information we want, you will experience pain like you've never known before."

As Tariq and Hassan stood in front of Mac, Taff came through the back door, followed by Scrump, carrying the camouflage and binoculars, mud still smeared over his face, straw and twigs sticking out of his hair.

Smithy heard voices from the kitchen, a sign it was safe to leave the cellar and join the others. He arrived in the kitchen doorway and stood behind Jock.

Mac handed his father's shotgun to Taff. "Jock, Taff, take these two to the cellar. Strip them to their shorts and tie them to the chairs please."

None of the team needed telling what was expected of them. They'd been over the plan numerous times and knew where they had to be and when they had to be there. Smithy left the kitchen and stood at the end of the hallway blocking any escape attempt. Taff led the way out of the kitchen to the top of the cellar stairs. He opened the door and looked at Hassan. "Down you go," he said. Slowly Hassan descended into the gloom followed by Taff, the shotgun pointed at his hostage's back all the way to the bottom.

After a shout to confirm they'd both reached the cellar Jock repeated the exercise with Tariq. Once their hostages had stripped to their underwear they were ordered to sit while Taff secured their arms and legs to the chairs with the cable ties.

"Are we going to let them sweat for a while guv?" Smithy asked after returning to the kitchen.

"I'd like to Smithy, but we don't have time," Mac said. "If they're gone too long the rest of their team will get suspicious and wonder where they are. We don't want them closing their operation down and scarpering before we get a chance to catch them and recover some money. But we do have a little time before we need to get on the road, time they would have spent taking my dad to the bank. We told them there was no mobile reception around here so hopefully they won't be suspicious back in the office if they haven't heard from our guests in the cellar, but the sooner we get what we need from them the better, then we can be on our way."

Mac picked up the briefcase, gave it a shake then returned it to the kitchen table, he popped the catches open and emptied the contents. "Just as I thought, nothing but pieces of blank paper."

Mac headed for the cellar, leaving Scrump washing the dirt from his face while his father made the team yet another cup of tea. Descending the steep cellar stairs, he could see Hassan and Tariq secured to chairs at either end of the table, both staring at the drill and sander Jock had placed on the table in front of them. Hassan looked terrified, as if he was about to burst into tears. Jock stood by the stairs, Taff to one side, both holding the shotguns.

"Well gentlemen," Mac began, "we can do this the easy way, or we can do this the hard way. The choice is yours. Whichever way you chose we *will* get what we need from you. It just depends on how much pain you are willing to endure," he paused before slowly picking up the drill, "or not."

Despite the chill of the cellar, beads of sweat were beginning to appear on Hassan's forehead. "What do you want to know?" he asked, almost whispering. "I'll tell you everything, just please don't hurt me."

"Don't tell them anything, Hassan," Tariq tried to make eye contact with his colleague, but Hassan kept his focus fixed on the drill Mac was holding. "Nothing they can do could be worse than what the people from Karachi will do to us if they discover we gave them any information."

"I think the time for worrying about what the people in Karachi will do to you has passed, don't you?" Mac said. "As I said, we can make it easy for you if you tell us what we want. If not, you're going to be in unimaginable agony, but eventually you will give us the information, so why not save yourself from all the pain and tell us now without us having to use this?" He slowly placed the drill back on the table.

"I'll tell you whatever you want to know," Hassan blurted, "just please don't hurt me." From the other end of the table, Tariq glared at him.

"Jock," Mac nodded towards Tariq, "take him back upstairs and tie him up somewhere while I have a chat with this one." By separating the hostages, Mac hoped any influence Tariq may have over Hassan was removed. He needed information and he needed it as fast as possible. "Taff, can you ask my Dad for a pen and some paper. I think we may be getting all the information we need."

Jock cut the cable ties securing Tariq to the chair. He stood and glared at Jock, rubbing his wrists where the cable ties had cut into his flesh even after such a short time. Jock returned his glare with a smile. "Don't even think about it, laddie. Now move," he waved the shotgun towards the stairs.

Taff climbed the cellar steps first. When he reached the top, he turned and pointed the shotgun down towards the cellar as Tariq appeared at the bottom of the steps. Tariq looked up at Taff pointing the gun at him. With men pointing shotguns at him from both front and rear, he knew there was nothing he could do to stop Hassan from giving these men what they wanted. His shoulders sagged, all defiance draining away from him. Wearily he trudged slowly up the stairs, followed a few steps behind by Jock pointing a shotgun at his back. Together they led Tariq into the dining room, secured him to one of the chairs and closed the curtains.

After collecting a pen and paper Taff returned to the cellar where Mac and Hassan waited in silence, another tactic learned in the regiment. With the drill and sander still sitting on the table in front of him to focus his mind and without conversation Hassan had time to think about the consequences of not giving these men the information they asked for.

"You probably realise we know all about your scam operation so please don't insult our intelligence by spinning us some yarn," Mac said. Taff waited at the cellar table, pen in hand ready to take down the information Hassan was about to give them on the notebook in front of him. "We want to know the address from where you're transferring the money, how many of you are there, what security you have, is anyone in your team armed, is there an alarm or panic button, the number of entry points, and how much you take each day. First, the address."

Hassan paused. "Before I answer your questions you do understand that the people I work for will kill me if they can find me. I will give you all the information you want if you get me a visa and a ticket to America, they will never find me there. I want to disappear and start a new life," and be free of my gambling debts, he thought.

Although Hassan was in no position to bargain, Mac thought they would get the information they needed quicker if they went along with the sham of offering him a deal. "Okay," he said. "We can sort that out once we've recovered our money. Now, the address where you are operating the scam from?"

Hassan told him the address. Taff noted it down.

"Got that Taff?" Mac asked. Taff nodded. "Postcode?" Easier to program the satnav, he thought.

"I don't know the postcode. We're never in one place long enough for it to matter, or for us to remember."

"Okay, how many people are operating at that address?"

"Six. Tariq, who you have upstairs, and Nasir are the security guards, Amir and Imran work the phones, Hadia transfers the money to Karachi, and me."

"And what do you do?"

"I keep a list on my laptop of the names and addresses of the people we take money from, plus the amount."

"Why do you need to keep the details of the people you've scammed?"

"We don't need to, it's just a type of insurance. After what happened to the last person doing Hadia's job we have proof of the amounts we've taken if there are any questions. My list should match what Hadia transfers each day."

"What happened to the person before Hadia?"

"He was stealing money, transferring some to his own account. He disappeared one day. We never saw him again. I think Tariq and Nasir know what happened to him, but they've never told the rest of us. But from the rumours I've heard whatever happened to him, it would have been terrible."

"You haven't got much of a role, just listing the people you've scammed," Mac said, "hardly a full-time job."

"I used to transfer the money until Hadia was sent by the people running the operation back home."

"And where's home?" Mac asked.

"Karachi in Pakistan."

"Is anyone in the group armed?"

"Not that I know of. If anyone has a weapon it would be Nasir, he may have a knife, but I don't think anyone has a gun."

Now the crucial question, Mac thought. "And is there an alarm or panic button to cut the computer off?"

"Yes, there's a panic button in the desk drawer next to the computer Hadia sits at. She's supposed to press the button if we ever have an emergency. It closes her computer down and alerts the office in Pakistan of a problem. There are no other alarms."

"Entry to the office and any other exit points?"

"There's a keypad on the main door and a fire escape at the back."

"What's the code for the keypad?"

Hassan told him the six-digit code.

"Did you get that Taff?" Mac asked. Taff nodded and read it back.

"And how much do you take each day?"

"Usually around one hundred thousand pounds but on a really good day we can take twice that amount."

Sitting at the opposite end of the table from Hassan, Taff shook his head, still unable to comprehend the amounts of money such scams could generate and the total disregard for the people they were stealing from. He briefly thought of his grandmother.

"So, you transfer the money to a bank in Karachi which is then transferred to another bank. Do you know where that bank is?" Mac asked.

"No, not even Hadia knows, and before she was sent here it was her job to transfer the money from the account in Karachi. The top people in this organisation keep that a closely guarded secret."

Mac made a mental note, the person transferring the money to Pakistan was a woman who'd worked at the other end of the operation. Her former role was receiving money transferred from around the world before transferring it on to another secret account. It was information he knew would be crucial to the amount of money they may be able to recover. "Do you know what the money is used for?"

"No, not for sure, but Hadia told me that most of it goes towards the fight in Afghanistan. Her boss in the Karachi office was wounded there and was recruited by an old man who said he could continue the fight by helping to raise money for the fighters still trying to rid the country of foreign invaders."

Mac still had friends stationed in Afghanistan. He was pleased to know they would be cutting off some of the money going to arm those fighting against them if they could put a stop to this scam.

"Do you know how many other teams like yours are operating here in the UK and around the world?" Mac asked.

"I think we're the only team operating here in the UK, but from what Hadia said the organisation has teams working all over the world."

From Hassan's answer and Jock's presentation, Mac knew the amounts of money they were talking about were probably huge.

"I want you to draw the layout of the office showing where everyone sits, where the doors are situated and I want you to include measurements, as accurate as you can be." Mac stepped forward and cut the ties securing Hassan's hands to the chair.

Taff tore a sheet of paper from the notebook and handed it to Hassan along with the pen. Hassan drew the plan with names on each desk showing where each of them sat. Although they were hardly ever sat there, he drew Tariq and Nasir's chairs either side of the main door, his own and Hadia's desks with their backs to the entrance, and Imran and Amir at desks opposite, facing them and the unit's door. When he'd finished, he handed the floorplan to Mac. As soon as he looked at the plan Mac thought whoever was responsible for security had done a poor job. It was a very small space and if the measurements were correct, Hadia's desk was only a few paces inside the door and she faced away from the entrance. With the element of surprise and speed, they may be able to get to her desk before she could reach the panic button in her drawer. If they burst through the door with enough speed the guard sat on his chair would be rendered useless, by the time he was out of his seat they would already be at Hadia's desk, hopefully in time to stop her pressing the panic button.

"Is there anything else I need to know?" Mac asked. "Is there a daily call to Karachi to confirm the total amount sent? Or any kind of communication that lets them know everything is okay which if they don't get will alert them to trouble?"

"No, Hadia occasionally calls the head man in the Karachi office but it's not a daily call. I think she just likes to keep in touch with the people she used to work with."

"One last thing," Mac said, "does the person who makes the transfers to Karachi speak English?"

"Yes, she speaks good English, we all do. She studied English at home and did her degree here in the UK." Hassan was now in full flow, happy to give whatever information was requested in the belief that he would receive the precious ticket and visa to America and escape whatever vengeance would come from Karachi.

"Okay," Mac said, "I think we have enough for now, but if I think of anything later, I'll ask. Is there anything else you think I should know?"

"No, I don't think so. I've given you all the information you've asked for, now what about our deal?" Hassan looked at Mac hopefully.

"Let us get our job done first, then we can sort out your travel arrangements. Taff untie his legs, get him dressed and bring him up to wait with the other one, and bring the other one's clothes please," Mac nodded towards Tariq's clothes heaped in the corner. He turned and climbed the steep cellar stairs and returned to the kitchen where the rest of the team were drinking tea with his father.

"Scrump, Smithy, could you go with my Dad and bring

the vans back, please. Put the gear in them and get ready to leave. I think we've got all the info we need. We'll draw up a plan while you're gone and go over it with you when you get back. Dad, do you mind if we take your drill and the shotguns? We may need them when we get to the other end. I promise to bring them back as soon as this is over."

"But I thought I'd be coming with you," Mac's father looked disappointed.

"No Dad, you've done a great job but your part in this is over. Thanks for your help but it's down to us now. The drill and guns, can we take them?" Mac asked again.

"Of course, you can take them but don't leave it too long before you bring my guns back or I'll be overrun by the bloody rabbits and won't have a veg patch left."

"Thanks, I'll bring them back as soon as this is over, and perhaps I could stay for a while if that's okay." Mac picked up the car keys, Hassan and Tariq's mobile phones and joined Jock in the dining room.

"Jock, the others have gone to collect the vans. When they get back, untie him and get him dressed," Mac pointed at Tariq. "Then tie him up again and cover his mouth with tape."

He held the phones out in front of Hassan, "which one is yours?" he asked.

"That one," Hassan pointed to the phone in Mac's left hand. He handed Hassan his phone and put the other and the car keys in his pocket.

"Unlock the phone and open the contact you'd send a text to at your office then give it back to me so I can send a text." Hassan unlocked the phone, found Amir's number then handed it back to Mac. "Tell me how you would let the office know that you were delayed at the cottage but are on your way to the bank so it won't sound suspicious, and that his phone has run out of charge," Mac nodded towards Tariq. He typed what Hassan said word for word then pressed send. Seconds later Amir's reply appeared on the screen. "Make sure you get to the bank before it closes. Remember don't go into the bank with the old man and stay away from the entrance. We don't want anyone getting suspicious." Mac smiled and put the phone in his pocket.

"What's the code to unlock your phone?" Mac asked.

"1-2-3-4-5-6," Hassan replied.

Easy to remember, Mac thought. "Not the most secure code is it?" He hoped the office in Karachi was equally as lax with their security.

"Jock, tie him up too," Mac pointed at Hassan. "We're ready to move as soon as the vans are back."

"But what about our deal?" Hassan asked. "I've given you everything you asked for, you said you would get me a visa and a ticket if I helped."

"We haven't finished yet. We may need more information from you later. This is just for appearance's sake; we can sort your ticket out once we have what we want." Mac wanted to string Hassan along and keep him on side in case they needed anything more from him. "You wouldn't want the others to know you sold them out until you're on your way to America, would you?" Mac nodded to Jock who spun Hassan around, quickly securing his ankles and wrists with cable ties and tape over his mouth.

After the vans returned from their hiding place at the abandoned farm they gathered in the kitchen. Until now, the details of their plan had only gone as far as capturing someone involved in the scam and extracting information from them. With the layout of the office and knowledge of the person transferring the money, Mac now had a better picture of what they were up against. He wanted to go over the plan he'd quickly drawn up in his head to see if the others had any better ideas.

"Okay," he said, "we all know the basics of the plan but now we have the layout of the office they're operating from," he laid the office plan Hassan had drawn on the table to give the rest of the team a feel for the office and approximate distances involved. "The key is going to be speed. We need to get from the door to this desk before the woman responsible for transferring the money has a chance to press the panic button," he pointed to the drawing of the desk with Hadia's name written on it. "If she gets there before we do, all we can do is put a stop to their scam, it will be all over as far as recovering any money is concerned."

"We've got the keypad number for the door. We'll have the element of surprise if they think it's their colleagues returning. Providing these measurements are accurate I can't see why we can't get to her before she has a chance to press the button," Smithy said, "it's only a couple of paces in, no trouble."

Mac wasn't so sure. If they were suspicious after not hearing from Hassan and Tariq for such a long time, and the lack of a transfer to their account from a Mr. Scott, the scammers may be alert and waiting for trouble. He thought he would try to allay any fears by sending a text while they were on their way to the office.

They returned to the dining room, put bags over the heads of both Tariq and Hassan, pulled the drawer string tight then carried each of them out of the cottage and put them in the back of separate vans. They loaded their gear into the back of the unoccupied van, all except Mac's laptop which would travel with him on one of the passenger seats. Once everything was loaded, they stood on Andrew's driveway ready to go.

Mac walked over to his father. "Dad, thanks for all your help, we couldn't have done this without you." He opened his arms wide pulling his father to him to give him a hug.

"I'm sure you could have done it without my help, but thanks for including me. It's been fun to be part of a team again and it's brought back some fond memories." After holding his son close for a moment, Andrew held him away at arm's length. "And don't forget my shotguns, or those bloody rabbits will take over and eat all of my veg patch."

Mac smiled and gave his father one last hug then broke away ready for business again. "Jock, you and me in this one," he said pointing to the van with their gear in. "Taff, Scrump, take a van each. Smithy you take the BMW. And keep together. If anyone needs to stop, flash your lights, otherwise we'll stop at the service station we talked about just before we get to the unit. See you when we get there." They each climbed into their vehicles, started the engines and slowly pulled away from the cottage.

Andrew stood on his drive watching the three vans and black BMW slowly disappear down the lane. He turned and walked back towards his garden. Well, that's my excitement for the week done, he thought, I'd better put some netting up, it's the best I can do for now, otherwise there'll be no veg left once those bloody rabbits get in.

21

For the next hour, Amir repeatedly glanced at the clock on the wall. He was beginning to worry that something had gone wrong. He'd received texts from both Tariq and Hassan, despite Mr. Scott telling him there was poor reception where he lived, but there had been no update from either of them for nearly two hours. He was sure there was somewhere they could get a signal and let him know what was going on? In his last text, Hassan had said Tariq's phone was nearly out of charge. Perhaps both phones had run out of charge? His mind was racing, going over a multitude of reasons why they hadn't been able to contact him.

To add to his worry there had been no transfer of fifty thousand pounds into the account from a Mr. Scott. Surely nothing could have gone wrong, they were only visiting a frail old man. He'd stressed to them not to accompany him into the bank, and reminded them before they left and again when Hassan had sent his text message, stay in the car and wait for him, don't raise the suspicions of bank staff or anyone outside the bank, they may start asking awkward questions. Transferring such a large amount alone would be enough to alert bank staff, they would ask Mr. Scott who he was making the transfer to and the reason why. If he had two Asian men standing in the bank waiting for him the cashier may refuse to make the transfer.

As the worries raced around his head, his mobile phone vibrated on the desk. He unlocked it and read the message. "Old man too ill to take to bank. Lost mobile signal in hills. Tariq's phone out of charge. My phone also nearly out of charge. On our way back." Strange, he thought, it didn't sound like Hassan and his last message said they were already on their way to the bank. Perhaps Mr. Scott had been taken ill on the journey and they'd had to return to his house before the transfer could be made. When he finished his current call he would try contacting Hassan to find out what had happened and where they were. As he put his mobile back on the desk Imran passed him another call. He checked his tick list to remind himself where he was with his latest victim, then reconnected the call.

"Hello, my name is James Douglas, officer number KRM469238," he began, "I should make you aware that this call is being recorded and that we are on a three-way call with the legal team and prosecutors dealing with this case. Do you understand Mr. Heath?" Amir read from his script but was finding it hard to concentrate on his latest victim with concerns about Hassan and Tariq constantly nagging at the back of his mind.

THE THREE VANS and BMW pulled into the motorway service station four miles away from where Amir was continuing his call. Mac jumped out and told the others to fill the vans, but not the BMW, then pull over to the Costa at the other end of the car park and get coffee, some sandwiches, crisps, water and a few other snacks to keep them going overnight.

After he'd paid for the fuel for all three vans, Mac joined the others standing in the quietest corner of the car park they could find. "Okay let's go over it one more time." Worried they hadn't had enough time with the layout of the office to memorise the plan in detail, he laid Hassan's drawing of the office on the bonnet of the BMW. It would be their last opportunity to go through the plan before arriving at the scammers' office. Mac thought they were as prepared as they could be given the amount of time available to them, but he was still worried. Recovering Sam's money depended on getting to the desk before the panic button could be pressed. They needed to get in fast and cover what appeared on Hassan's drawing to be three or four paces to Hadia's desk before she could put her hand in the drawer and press the button. The element of surprise was the first key to the operation's success, after that, they were relying on luck and complacency on the part of the scammers. Even if they couldn't recover Sam's money at least they could stop them from causing more grief to an unsuspecting public.

"When we get there, try to park the vans close to the office so our entry is hidden as much as possible. We don't want anyone seeing a group of men entering the building, especially as some of us will be carrying shotguns. Smithy, you stay outside and keep an eye on the vans. If anyone comes snooping while we're in there make an excuse and get rid of them. If they won't leave come and get Jock, he's enough to scare anyone off. We'll move the two in the vans into the unit with the others as soon as it gets dark."

"What if she gets to the button before we can stop her?" Scrump asked.

Finally, one of the team had voiced the fear all of them had in the back of their minds. It was something that had been going around Mac's head during the journey from his father's cottage and was a distinct possibility, but one they could only hope their planning and the element of surprise would prevent.

"I think we all know the answer to that. Sam's money will be gone, and we'll have no prospect of recovering any money. But as Sir Duncan said, this is as much about stopping them scamming anyone else in the future as it is about recovering any money. With a bit of luck, it won't come to that." In Mac's opinion not recovering Sam's money would mean they had failed. He pointed to the desk on the plan with Hadia's name written on it. "She has her back to the door and we'll be at the desk before she can react. Who knows, we may be lucky, she may not even be sitting at her desk when we go in, she could be in the toilet or making a drink. Now, is everyone sure they know what they're doing?" They all nodded. "Okay let's go." They climbed back into their vehicles and set off for the scammers.

Mac could see the unit they wanted in the corner at the far end of the car park as they pulled into the industrial estate. No prying eyes would be able to see them enter the unit if they parked the vans as discussed. The vehicles pulled up in front of the door and Mac's team got out, hidden from view behind the vans, Scrump and Taff concealing the shotguns as best they could. Mac pulled a piece of paper from his pocket and entered the six-digit number into the entry keypad. As he released the last keypad button, Taff pulled the door wide open and Jock burst through the doorway closely followed by Mac, Scrump and Taff.

It was late in the day and sat on a chair next to the entrance Nasir was playing yet another game on his mobile phone. He was bored, tired, stiff from sitting in a chair all day and paying no attention as the door to the unit burst open. For a moment he was startled and hesitated before standing to see who was making such a dramatic entrance. Before he could confront the intruders, Jock hit him in the stomach with a punch powerful enough to lift him off his feet and force the air from his lungs. As he doubled over, Jock brought his knee up to meet Nasir's face, a loud crack reverberated around the unit before he slumped to the ground, his face covered in blood, his nose obviously broken and from the strange way his face was contorted probably his jaw as well.

With Tariq secured in the van outside, Nasir was the scammers only remaining security guard, unconscious on the unit floor in an ever-increasing pool of blood streaming from his shattered nose there was now no one able to protect the scammers from the intruders.

Amir and Imran looked past Hadia to the commotion at the unit's entrance. Left speechless by sight confronting them, they both stopped talking to the people they were trying to scam and watched in horror at what was happening over Hadia's shoulder.

Concentrating on her computer screen as she transferred the money taken from their latest victim, Hadia was totally unaware of the drama unfolding behind her. She looked up and saw Amir and Imran were no longer talking on the phones but staring at something happening behind her. She swivelled her chair around to see what they were staring at and couldn't believe the sight that greeted her. Nasir slumped on the floor, blood pouring from his nose, a huge man standing over him and three men coming towards her fast, two of them carrying shotguns.

"Hadia," Amir shouted.

Suddenly remembering what she was supposed to do in an emergency, she quickly swivelled her chair and started to open the desk drawer.

Mac strode towards Hadia, the distance between the door and her desk was further than it looked on the drawing, he thought. As Hadia put her hand into the drawer Mac jumped, leg outstretched, and slammed the drawer shut with his foot, the full weight of his body behind the lunge, trapping Hadia's hand with a sickening crunch. Hadia screamed in agony. She could feel her finger resting on the button she needed to press but the shattered bones in her hand wouldn't allow her to move her finger enough to generate the pressure needed to depress it.

Standing on one leg, with his foot still firmly pressed hard against the drawer to keep it closed on Hadia's hand, Mac steadied himself on the desk and without easing the pressure on the drawer pulled her hand free. She screamed again and held her hand against her trying to support the broken bones, tears streaming down her face. Mac grabbed her chair and pulled her away from the computer, and more importantly the panic button. Through her sobs, she screamed something at him in a language he didn't understand. From memory he'd heard something vaguely familiar while serving in Afghanistan, something which he guessed was not complimentary.

While Mac moved Hadia away from her desk, Taff and Scrump quickly covered the ground to Amir and Imran's chairs, pulling them away from their desks. Taff motioned towards the wall at the back of the unit with his shotgun. "Get up and stand over there."

"Scrump, search the others for phones and weapons. Put whatever you find on the desk, then get the gear from the vans. When you've done that, bag and tag this lot, all except this one," Mac said, holding on to the back of Hadia's chair. "We are going to have a little chat. Don't tape his mouth," Mac pointed to the figure of Nasir slumped beside the door. "Looking at the state of his nose he won't be able to breathe if we put tape on him." Jock stood guard behind Scrump, his shotgun pointed at their hostages as his colleague completed his search.

"Taff, see if there's any way you can disable the panic button without alerting the people at the other end of the line. If not when Scrump's finished, see if you can seal the drawer closed. We don't want anyone playing the hero and making a desperate lunge for the button. When you've done that, have a look around to see if you can find anything that might be useful. And see if you can turn the automated call system off and shut that bloody office noise off."

Mac breathed a sigh of relief. It had been a close-run thing, he thought to himself. A split second later and the button would have been pressed and the money gone. Now they could put the rest of their plan into action, a plan he hoped would recover not only what Sam had lost but what many others had too.

Scrump returned from the vans and fastened cable ties

around Amir, Imran and Nasir's wrists and ankles, tape over Amir and Imran's mouths, then slipped the hessian bags over each of their heads. After securing the hostages, he opened Hadia's desk drawer and looked at the panic button. There were so many wires coming from the box the button sat on he decided it wasn't worth the risk of setting it off. Admitting defeat, he sealed the drawer with some of the tape. With Taff's help, he put the phones on the floor then turned Imran's desk on its side. Together they manhandled it in front of Hadia's desk, shutting off access to the panic button.

Once everything was secure, Scrump placed Mac's holdall under the desk next to where Hadia sat watching them work, just as their plan said he should.

After walking around the small office, Taff returned to the desk where Mac was standing, his hand still on the headrest of Hadia's chair. "I found this, sarge," he held out a laptop. "It must be the one with the names, addresses and amounts they've taken from everyone they've scammed." He pointed under Hadia's desk. "It looks like her handbag is under there."

"Thanks, leave the laptop on the desk with her computer." The laptop Hassan had told him about, Mac thought. Somewhere on there, along with countless others, Sam's name would appear, the reason why they were now standing in this industrial unit. "I'll have a look in her bag once I've finished talking to her."

Mac wheeled one of the chairs over and sat in front of Hadia. "It's no use," she said, a smug look on her face despite the intense pain in her hand, "you're too late. There's no money in our account and the balance of the main account in Pakistan is transferred at six o'clock."

Mac looked at his watch, it was just after five o'clock.

"Six o'clock in Pakistan, they are four hours ahead of us. It's nine o'clock in Pakistan, you're too late, there's no money in the account," Hadia said again, a note of defiance in her voice.

"How do you know there's no money in the account in Pakistan?" Mac asked.

"Because it was my job to make the transfer when I worked there." Hadia stopped herself as she realised what she'd said. Her headstrong nature had caught her out once more. She clutched her broken hand to her chest and started to cry again.

Mac smiled. "Then I don't think we are too late," he said. "In fact, I think we're too early. If you're transferring money after they make the daily transfer at six there will still be money in the account, but not as much as there will be tomorrow afternoon. I think we can wait."

Mac stood up, Hadia now seemingly inconsolable slumped in the seat next to him. "Taff, put her with the others please, bag and tag her too." Taff took Hadia by the elbow and led her to where the others were seated on the floor and told her to sit.

"Please, be careful with my hand," she said still sobbing. Taff looked over to Mac.

Mac nodded. "Okay, cuff her hands in front of her, not behind her back like the others." He couldn't decide whether Hadia's tears were because of the from her shattered hand or because she'd revealed the fact that she'd once worked at the main office in Karachi. Now all they could hope for was that the login details in Karachi hadn't changed since she'd left.

Mac took Hadia's bag from under the desk and emptied the contents next to the mobile phones, keys and wallets Scrump had taken from the others. He took her phone and keys and put them with the others. He was surprised to see two passports and a tea towel among the contents. He picked up the towel and carefully unwrapped it. Inside was a long-bladed kitchen knife. He looked over to where Taff was securing her. Why would she be carrying a weapon when they had security at the door? If he remembered, he would ask her about it later. And why did she have two passports? Was Hadia her real name and which, if either, showed her true identity? He returned the contents to the bag and put it back under the desk.

In the back of Taff's mind was the thought that these may be the people who'd scammed his grandmother, and were, in his eyes, ultimately responsible for her death. If that was the case, he would like to inflict as much pain on them as possible, but he had no way of knowing unless her name appeared on the laptop now sitting on the desk next to Mac. Tempting as it was to scroll through the names on the computer, he didn't want to sink to their level and did as Mac said. He finished with the cable ties and tape then slipped the hessian bag over Hadia's head, pulling the draw sting just a little tighter than was necessary.

"Mac, shall we get the others in? Just in case. We don't want anyone snooping around the vans. I know we're secluded here in the corner of the car park but if those two in the vans start kicking the sides and making a noise it might bring some unwelcome attention."

"Yes, good idea. Get Smithy to reverse the vans up to the entrance, once the doors are opened it should screen us from any prying eyes and it will help when we leave." While Taff was outside with Smithy, Mac took the clock from the wall and wound the hands forward four hours. It now displayed the time in Karachi.

Fifteen minutes later the hostages were sat together at the back of the unit, Hadia cradling her broken hand and still crying, Nasir still slumped on the floor unconscious, the others anonymous under the bags over their heads. Hooded, bound and gagged, they made a pathetic spectacle.

After securing the hostages, Mac and his team settled down for what promised to be a long night. He now realised they were unprepared for an overnight stay as far as food was concerned, all they had was what they'd bought at the service station on the way and he knew it wouldn't be enough to keep them going for the next day and possibly longer. He decided they should send someone out to get some hot food. "Smithy, Scrump, take one of the vans and find a takeaway. Anything will do, pizza, fish and chips, kebab, and some drinks, whatever you can find close by." He gave them what was left of Sir Duncan's cash and told them to be careful.

Two hours later when they'd finished eating, Mac decided it was time to prepare for the following day. They moved the phones from Amir's desk onto the floor and Hadia's computer onto the free desk along with the laptop containing the details of their victims. Mac walked over to the hooded figure of Hassan and pulled him to his feet, removed the bag from his head, cut the ties around his ankles then led him to the small kitchen area, the furthest point from the other hostages. Mac leaned Hassan against a cupboard and pulled the tape from his mouth. "We need to talk," he said.

Once recovered from the pain of the tape being torn from his face Hassan looked hopefully at Mac. "What about our deal?" he said expectantly.

"Don't worry, I haven't forgotten but we've got a whole days' work ahead of us before we can think about that. I have a few more questions for you first," Mac pulled some paper and a pen from his pocket. "What's the Wi-fi code here?"

Hassan gave the code confident that he would be separated from the other hostages and would soon be on his way to America where he would be out of reach to anyone sent from Karachi to investigate. Mac wrote down the code as Hassan told him.

"What time do you usually start in the morning?"

"We usually start work at nine o'clock."

"How long before you make the first transfer to the bank in Karachi?"

"It usually takes between half an hour and an hour before the first money comes into our account," Hassan said, "we transfer it as soon as it arrives to stop anyone trying to recover it."

"And how much do you usually take from each victim?"

"As much as they have in their bank account. Sometimes it's only hundreds, sometimes thousands. It's not worth the time if the balance is really small so we disconnect the call and move on to the next person."

"Do the people in Karachi know any details about the people you take money from?" Mac asked.

"No, they don't care. They don't ask questions so long as the money is being transferred to the account in Karachi."

"How long has the woman been working here?" Mac was trying to appear as friendly as possible, the information he needed now would determine how much, if anything, they could recover.

"Hadia?" Hassan said, "she's been here just over six months."

"Has she talked about her role in Karachi?

"A little. She doesn't say much, I don't think she likes any of us really, especially Nasir. He treats her really badly. It was him that inflicted those cuts and bruises on her face."

"Tell me all you know about her, especially anything you know about what she did in the Karachi office."

Hassan thought for a moment. "I'm not sure how she was recruited. It's unusual for a woman to be working in this organisation, she's the only one I know of. When she worked in the main office in Karachi she monitored the cash coming in from all over the world and transferred the balance to another secret account at the end of each day."

"Does she have access to the account she was sending money to from the one in Karachi?"

"No, I think it's only the people at the top of the organisation who have access to that account."

Mac wrote down everything Hassan told him. "So, she had the login details for the account in Karachi?"

"Oh yes," Hassan answered, "she couldn't do her job without it. She was trusted by whoever was running the Karachi office, and the people above him."

"Does she still have the login details?"

"I don't know. Provided they haven't changed them then I suppose she does, if she can remember them after six months. We haven't changed our logins for the two years I've been working here so I don't suppose they've been changed in Karachi."

"Do you know the login details for the account in Karachi?" Mac asked. He knew it was a longshot but worth a try.

"No, I've never worked there. I was only filling in here until a replacement was sent. I used to work the phones until I was moved to transferring the money."

Mac now knew Hadia had the login and password for the

main account in Karachi, she was the only one of the scammers who could do what they had planned.

"The laptop," Mac pointed to the computer on the desk, "is that the one with the details of everyone you've scammed?"

Hassan nodded. "Yes, that's my laptop. I log names and addresses of all the people we take money from, along with the amounts we've taken."

"Is there a login password?" Mac asked.

Mac wrote the password down and read it back to Hassan to check he'd written it correctly.

"One last thing, do you have any idea why she has a knife in her bag?"

"No," Hassan looked surprised. "I didn't know she had a knife."

"And two passports?"

Hassan shook his head, "no."

"Okay, that's all for now. If I think of anything else, I'll come and get you."

Satisfied he'd delivered his side of their agreement Hassan expected his captors to honour theirs. "Now please, our deal. If the people back home find out we've been caught, and they lose money they will find us and kill us all. I'm the one who's given you the information and will be made an example of. I can't tell you the horrors that await me if I'm caught. Please, I must get to America," he pleaded.

"We still have a lot to do and you're going to be needed tomorrow. Just be patient." Mac put another strip of tape over Hassan's mouth before he could complain any further then led him back to the other hostages. He pushed him to the floor, tied his ankles and slipped the bag back over his head.

"Okay lads," Mac said, "grab a sleeping bag and get some

sleep, it's the big day tomorrow. I'll watch over this lot with Jock for a couple of hours, then Smithy and Taff can take a turn. Taff, wake me when your shift is over, I can get a few bits ready for the morning with Scrump." They each picked up a sleeping bag and made their way to the opposite side of the unit away from the hostages. It's going to be a long night, Mac thought. He knew he wouldn't be getting any sleep.

22

As the hostages woke the next morning, Mac and his team were ready to put what he hoped would be the final part of their plan into action. Scrump stood in the small kitchen area making tea and coffee for the team while Jock sat on Nasir's chair watching over the hostages. After pulling the bag from Hadia's head, Taff removed the tape from her mouth and ties from her ankles and wrists. Grabbing her uninjured hand, he pulled her to her feet, put his hand on her shoulder and led her to the computer where Mac was waiting.

"What do you want?" she asked as she took a seat.

"I want you to log in to the bank in Karachi," Mac answered.

"I don't know the login." Hadia hoped Mac had forgotten what she'd told him during her outburst the previous day.

"We know you worked in the main office in Karachi, Hassan told us. And you told me yourself yesterday. He also told us you had the login details for the bank there, the bank you transfer money to each day from here."

After admitting she'd been responsible for transfers from the bank in Karachi, Mac knew Hadia had the login details for the bank before she'd been sent to the UK, but that was six months ago. Was he correct in his assumption that the scammers' security was so lax that they hadn't been changed since she'd left?

Hadia looked over to the hooded figure of Hassan then returned her gaze to Mac, hatred in her eyes. "I won't do it," she said. After breaking down following the previous day's admission that she'd worked in the Karachi office her defiant nature had returned.

"You will do it, or the pain in your hand will be nothing compared to what we will do to you." Mac took the holdall from under the desk and made a show of slowly unzipping it. He took the drill from the bag and placed it in front of Hadia. She sat for a moment staring, the fear of what awaited her if she didn't cooperate evident by the look of terror on her face. "We know you used the login when you worked in Karachi. If you refuse or try to fool us by entering the wrong details you will be in a world of pain. You really don't want that, do you Hadia?" Mac said calmly. He knew the calmer he appeared the more terrorising it was for his prospective victim.

"No," she said barely above a whisper. "But what about ..."

"You don't have to worry about anything else Hadia, just do as I ask. I really don't want to hurt you anymore, but I will if you don't do what I ask. Now, are you going to do what I tell you?"

"Yes," she said meekly, again barely above a whisper. Tears were beginning to stream down her face, already streaked with black eye makeup from her tears the day before.

Mac thought Hadia's body appeared to be shrinking in on

itself. The fight seemed to have drained from her just as it had the day before. He picked up the drill and put it back in the holdall under the desk. It had served its purpose, hopefully for the last time before being returned to his father.

Slowly Hadia turned her chair, opened the internet browser and clicked on the icon for the bank in Karachi. This is the make or break moment, Mac thought as she began typing the login details. If the password details had changed the money they'd stolen from Sam and everything Sir Duncan had paid out so far was lost.

Hadia tapped one handed at the keyboard, her injured hand cradled in her lap. "I'm in," she said shakily.

Mac felt a sense of relief wash over him. The screen in front of Hadia displayed the account details and balance, a healthy amount for such an early hour in the morning but he knew it would be considerably bigger later in the day when they intended to make their final move.

"Thank you," Mac said, "not so difficult after all was it? Now log out of the bank, please."

Hadia looked at Mac in confusion. "But I thought..." she began.

"I know what you thought, but you were wrong. That comes later this afternoon. Just log out please."

Hadia did as instructed then turned to face Mac.

"Tell me, are you proud of what you do?" he asked.

"Yes, I am proud, why shouldn't I be? I'm helping the brave men in Afghanistan trying to rid my country of men like you, men who have no right to be in our country. We want our country back to rule as we see fit, not how the West wants it to be ruled," Hadia's passion for her cause surprised Mac. Suddenly the fight in her had returned, she sat up in her chair and appeared to grow in stature.

"And that's worth the misery you cause to the people you steal money from and all of the killing and maiming the war inflicts?" Mac asked.

"Unfortunately, as in any war, there will be casualties." She looked at him with piercing eyes. "Casualties on both sides."

Mac had seen the same look before in the eyes of fanatics willing to die for their cause. Provided they took some of their enemies with them they were willing to sacrifice an innocent child so long as a foreign soldier died along with him. "Have you ever watched one of your friends bleeding to death after being shot, or a child standing so near to a bomb that when it explodes there's nothing left of him for his parents to bury?" Once again, the image of the little boy standing in front of Gav reaching out for the chocolate bar being offered before being blown to pieces came to mind as clear as if it were yesterday. It was a vision that would stay with him for the rest of his life. "If you had, you wouldn't be here funding these people who bring misery not only to the troops out there fighting against them but also to your own people."

"Do you think my people don't suffer?" Hadia replied. "We bleed just as your soldiers do when we are shot. We die when your planes drop bombs on us. Is taking prisoners and transporting them thousands of miles away from their homes and family to torture them for information any better than what our soldiers are doing? We don't want to fight, we want to live in peace and rule our own country as we see fit, but you give us no option. We are trying to fund a holy war to rid our home of invading armies. I see that as a noble cause."

Mac could feel the anger in him rising, something he hadn't felt about his service in Afghanistan for some time. Maybe it was Scrump's revelation in the pub about the effect the war had had on him and his family that made him feel so animated. "And what about all of the foreign fighters coming to help your countrymen? They're not in Afghanistan to free their homeland. They travel to there because they want to kill Western soldiers or to train to take the war to the West. They are nothing but terrorists. And have you thought about what life would be like for you if the West leaves? There'll be no walking around wearing your hijab, a Taliban government will pass laws to make you wear a full burka, and you'll have to be accompanied by a male member of your family each time you leave the house. Do you want to live in a country where there is no education for girls and barbaric laws involving stoning to death and amputation?"

There was a moment of hesitation before Hadia replied. "I don't believe you," she replied with the first sign of doubt in the voice, "but whatever laws we pass will be our own, not ones the West has imposed on us."

He was about to continue the argument when Taff appeared behind Hadia. "Put her back with the others please Taff," Mac said trying to keep his anger in check, "then bring Hassan over please."

During the night, Mac had toyed with the idea of changing their plan. Should they take whatever money was in the account in Karachi at the first opportunity or stick with the original plan and take the bigger balance at the end of the day? He knew by delaying the transfer more people around the world would be scammed out of their money, but making the transfer at the end of the day would mean there was more money in the account. He thought the bigger the amount they could take the more of an impact it would have on the people running the scam in Karachi. Hadia's latest outburst made him more determined than ever to cause as much pain to the people running the scam as possible. They would stick with the original plan.

As Hadia rose from her chair, Mac remembered the knife. "One minute, why do you have a kitchen knife in your handbag?" he asked.

"So I can defend myself the next time the thug who did this to my face tries to attack me," she pointed to her bruised and cut eye while looking over to where Nasir lay slumped on the floor.

"And two passports?"

"I was given a false one before I came here. They said it was to protect the people I work for from being traced by the authorities."

"Which of them is the real one?" Mac asked.

For a moment Hadia hesitated, but what was the point of lying? These men had taken them hostage and were planning on recovering money from the scam, they were obviously not part of British law enforcement. She pointed to her own passport. "That one," she said.

Mac put both passports in his pocket. If the police had them maybe they could go further up the organisation and possibly arrest the people running the scam.

Taff led Hadia back to the other hostages, cuffed her wrists and ankles and sat her with the others. He pulled the bag from Hassan's head and helped him to his feet, after removing the tape and ties securing his hands and feet, he led him to the desk where Mac sat waiting.

"Yesterday you told me you used to transfer the money to Karachi before Hadia was sent to replace you," Mac said.

Hassan sat in the chair opposite Mac rubbing his sore wrists while trying to work out what these people wanted from him. He would do whatever they asked, so long as there was a ticket to America at the end. "Yes, but it was only temporary until they sent Hadia to replace me."

"You'll be doing that job today."

Hassan looks puzzled. "Will Imran and Amir be working the phones?"

"No, all you have to do is transfer the money just as you used to before Hadia arrived. Did you use the same login as her?"

"Yes, there's only one login for the bank here."

"Good, do you need anything else to do the job?"

Hassan was still confused. "But where will the money be coming be from?"

"You don't need to worry about that, just transfer it as it arrives in the account the same way you used to." Mac was trying to put on a friendly face, he needed Hassan's cooperation for a little while longer. "Now do you need anything else to do that?" he repeated.

"No, I don't think so. A coffee and some water would be good though, and I haven't eaten anything since breakfast yesterday."

Mac looked over to where Scrump was standing outside the kitchen area. "Another coffee please Scrump, water and something to eat if there's anything left." He turned back to Hassan, "I'll be watching you, Hassan. Remember our deal, don't try anything that might jeopardize it. If you want a ticket to America, you'll do everything I say."

"Don't worry, I'll do whatever you want, I really need that ticket."

At nine-thirty Mac logged into one of Sir Duncan's offshore bank accounts and transferred two thousand four hundred and sixty-five pounds to the account in the name of William Ried's, the account Sam had given them. Once he'd confirmed the transfer he logged out of the bank and wheeled his chair the short distance to where Hassan sat waiting at his computer for money to arrive. Together they waited for almost fifteen minutes, staring at the screen before the transfer appeared. "Okay," Mac said, "transfer the money to the bank in Karachi." Hassan looked at Mac in confusion. "Transfer the money please, Hassan," Mac repeated. He watched closely as Hassan did as he'd been instructed.

Hassan was still confused, what were these people doing? Why were they giving the scammers their money? But he did what Mac asked and transferred the money, he didn't want to do anything that would risk his deal with these men. The thought of disappearing to America debt-free was now the only thing on his mind. If he did what they asked he would leave for America to begin a new life before anyone from Karachi could arrive to investigate what had happened in the UK. He promised himself that once he arrived in America he would never gamble again. He would find a job and live quietly somewhere he could never be found.

Over the next two hours, Mac transferred money in varying amounts from Sir Duncan's account to the scammers. There were no huge amounts, he didn't want Sir Duncan to lose too much if he'd overlooked something and the plan went wrong. After making each transfer he wheeled his chair over to Hassan's desk to watch him make the onward transfers to the bank in Karachi. So far everything was going to plan.

As Mac wheeled his chair back to the laptop to make another transfer, one of the phones on the floor began ringing. Everybody in the unit stopped what they were doing and stared as it continued to ring. Mac knelt on the floor and picked up the receiver. "Hello," he said.

"Oh, hello," the voice on the other end of the line said.

"My name is Eleanor Barnes. I've had a message asking me to call this number because there are some outstanding legal proceedings against my name. I've been away on holiday and I've only just picked the message up. I'm sure there must be some mistake, I've never been in trouble with the police before."

Mac thought the lady at the other end of the line sounded a little shaken by being caught up in what she believed to be a police investigation. "Don't worry madam, our investigations have now been concluded," he said, trying to reassure her. "I'm sorry but it was a case of mistaken identity and you should never have been contacted. We're currently in the process of wrapping this operation up, it should be closed down later today. Thank you for calling, have a nice day."

"Oh, thank goodness for that. I can't tell you how worried I've been, it's kept me awake all night. Thank you, goodbye." The line went dead.

Still kneeling on the floor, Mac replaced the receiver and smiled to himself. A lucky escape for one lady, he thought. She would probably be poorer by whatever was in her bank account if she'd called a day earlier. He crawled under the desk and disconnected the phones Imran and Amir had been using to scam their victims. He returned to his seat ready to make another transfer.

At the arranged time of one o'clock, Taff walked over to Mac's desk and stood behind Hassan. Mac looked up at him and nodded.

"Time for you to go, mate." Taff spun Hassan's chair around and pulled him to his feet. Holding him by the shoulder, he marched him back to where the other hostages were seated, securing him again. He pulled the bag from Haida's head.

"Looks nasty," Taff said as he cut the ties binding her wrists. Hadia screamed in pain. Her broken hand was now twice its normal size and already a deep shade of blue and purple. The ties had cut into her swollen flesh, worsening her injury

Hadia looked up from her hand and spat at Taff. The spittle missed her intended target, landing on his shoulder. "You will all die for this," she screamed, "you don't know who you are dealing with."

"Do that again and I'll give you a black eye to go with the other one," Taff growled. Knowing Mac would be watching, he had to keep his fiery temper in check. Hadia screamed in pain as he grabbed hold of her broken hand and pulled her to her feet, then led her to where Mac sat at the desk waiting. She stood in front of him sobbing, clutching her broken hand to her chest knowing she had no choice but to do as these men said.

"Sit down," Mac gestured to the seat Hassan had just vacated. "And no more histrionics. Remember what I told you earlier, you know the consequences of not cooperating and the terrible pain you'll suffer if you don't do as we ask."

While Taff was returning Hassan to the other hostages, Mac had moved the holdall containing the drill from under the desk. It would serve as a reminder of what would await her should she decide not to cooperate. If she chose not to do as he asked there was nothing Mac could do, he had no intention of using the drill on Hadia, but all the time she believed he would it was the only weapon he had to persuade her.

Mac was becoming concerned about Hadia's state of mind, each time he spoke to her she was becoming increasingly volatile and he thought she may be losing her grip on reality. He'd seen the fierce passion she had for the fight she thought was just when he'd spoken to her earlier, but her mood swings were becoming more pronounced. Her outburst toward Taff convinced Mac that he needed her to perform the last task he would ask of her with as much patience as he could muster.

Hadia sat at the desk, the computer in front of her still logged into the bank. "What do want?" she asked, still bristling with defiance. It was a question she already knew the answer to but one she hoped she could avoid.

"I think you know what I want," Mac said. "I want you to do your old job when you were back in Pakistan, but with a slight twist."

The consequences of what these men were asking her to do had been going through her mind ever since Mac had asked her to log into the bank in Karachi. If she did as they asked Hadia knew she would be putting the rest of her family in terrible danger, and she wondered what these men had in mind for them once they had what they wanted. She looked at Mac with an icy glare. "You want me to transfer the money from Karachi to your bank account. Never. I won't do it."

"You will do it." Mac looked towards the holdall containing the drill, "Remember what I showed you earlier, you don't want me to use it on you do you?"

Hadia glanced at the holdall. "No, but..."

"No buts Hadia, unless you want to feel excruciating pain. Do you really want that? And you know eventually you will do what we want. We have plenty of time. If you're awkward and we have to persuade you to do what I tell you we can do this all over again tomorrow, and the next day, and the next until finally, you do what we want. If you don't do as I say you'll be putting yourself through indescribable agony. Please save yourself the pain and suffering and just do what I tell you, then it will all be over."

The sight of the holdall and the memory of the drill sitting on the desk was still fresh in her mind. After a moments silence, Hadia's shoulders slumped, her body sagged as she admitted defeat. "Okay," she whispered, "I'll do it."

"Good. Now go to your computer and be ready. And remember, I'm watching every move you make." Mac looked at his watch. One forty-five. He looked to the clock on the wall. Five forty-five in Karachi. Time to make the transfer. "Now log in to the Karachi bank account please."

Hadia typed the login details once again. "I'm in," she said meekly.

"Good, now transfer the balance to this account." Mac placed a piece of paper with the details of one of Sir Duncan's offshore accounts in front of her. "And remember I'm watching every move you make so don't try anything. If we don't get this done today, we'll do it all again tomorrow." Mac knew they only had today and possibly the following day to complete this part of the plan. They hadn't come prepared for a long stay and they couldn't keep the hostages indefinitely. Everything he'd transferred from Sir Duncan's account so far would be lost if they didn't get the money today, and to avoid suspicion he would need to continue transferring money throughout the rest of the day and again the following day. If the office in Karachi saw there was nothing coming from the UK, they would know something was wrong.

Watched closely by Mac, Hadia typed the details of Sir Duncan's offshore account where the money was to be transferred to, followed by the total held in the Karachi bank. She checked she'd entered everything correctly and pressed enter.

The balance in US dollars was huge. Mac had a rough idea how much it was in sterling, certainly many times more than the amount he'd transferred from Sir Duncan's account during the day and much more than he ever dreamed they could recover.

Hadia stared at the screen showing the amount to be transferred. She moved the cursor slowly across the screen to the *confirm transfer* box, closed her eyes and pressed the button on the mouse. She slumped in her chair. "It's done," she said, almost in a whisper.

Hadia began to sob again. She knew what she'd just done would put the lives of her family back home in terrible danger. Her father had been proved right, she should never have taken this job, his warnings were now coming true. She prayed that somehow her uncle could get word to her parents to flee the city before the old man and his bodyguards could pay them a visit.

Once again Taff appeared behind Hadia and placed his hand on her shoulder. "Time to go back to your friends."

Hadia looked pleadingly at Mac, tears coursing down her face. "Please can I take something for the pain in my hand? There are some painkillers in my bag."

Mac took the bag from under the table and passed it to Hadia along with a bottle of water.

"Thank you," she said, her voice almost inaudible. When Hadia opened her bag the first thing she saw was the tea towel. For a moment she wondered if she could unwrap the knife before the man sitting next to her noticed. She glanced at Mac hoping he wasn't watching.

Mac smiled. "I wouldn't if I were you. There are five of us, two with shotguns. Do you really think you can unwrap the knife, attack me and escape without one of us stopping you?

Just take the painkillers out of the bag then put it back under the desk."

After taking the painkillers, Hadia slowly rose from her chair and walked wearily across the office to where the others sat hooded and bound. She sat next to Hassan while Taff bound her hands and feet again then finally slipped the bag back over her head. As Taff turned to re-join the rest of the team Hadia slumped forward sobbing again.

While Taff was securing Hadia, Mac wheeled his chair back to the desk where his laptop waited. For twenty minutes he stared at the screen while nothing happened. Just as he started to doubt the transfer had gone through the account balance changed. He stared at the screen in disbelief. "I don't believe it," he said.

Taff walked over and looked at the screen displaying the new account balance. "Bloody hell," he said. "We really are in the wrong game."

Smithy joined the two of them, looking over Mac's shoulder at the laptop screen. "Jesus," he said, "how much?" He walked away whistling a tune Mac recognised as *We're in the money.*"

"Well sarge, how much?" Jock called over from his seat by the door.

Mac stared at the screen still unable to believe they had successfully transferred the amount he was looking at on his laptop. "We've just transferred almost ten million pounds into Sir Duncan's account," he said after roughly converting the US dollars to sterling.

Scrump pumped his fist. "I think Sir Duncan will be pleased we've managed to get a little more than his son's money back."

"I think that is a bit of an understatement," Jock said.

"Now I don't feel so bad about being paid so much for one week's work."

There was an air of elation in the unit. They had achieved much more than they'd set out to, but Mac was aware they still had work to do and a difficult decision ahead of them. "Okay lads back to work please, this isn't over yet." Somehow, he had to try to bring his team down from their high and back to the task in hand.

Mac took an envelope from his pocket and navigated to the money transfer page on his laptop. He transferred the balance they'd just received from the bank in Karachi plus what was left of the initial half a million pounds Sir Duncan had opened the account with to the second offshore account. As far as the money was concerned it was job done, Mac thought. If the scammers in Karachi tried to recover the money there would be nothing in the account that their money had been sent to. He smiled at the thought of the scammers being scammed. He didn't think the individuals involved would suffer financially but he hoped they would feel as bad as the people around the world they'd been stealing from. From what the hostages had told him, the people at the top of this scam were ruthless and may take retribution against those working for them. Too bad, Mac thought, live by the sword die by the sword. They may get mad, but now they couldn't get even.

23

In Karachi, Omar was also staring at a computer screen, his emotions a complete contrast to those Mac and his team were feeling back in the UK. How could this happen? Who outside his own office could access the account and make such a transfer? And where had the money been transferred to? The office was in total silence, everyone in a state of shock. What would he tell the old man? *Should* he tell the old man or just leave before he discovered what had happened? He had no doubt any retribution would be swift, far-reaching and horrific in nature. Once they found who was responsible heads would roll, probably literally.

As the questions ran through his head a nagging doubt crept in and one name came to the fore: Hadia.

Hadia had access to all the login details and passwords at both ends of the operation. As far as he knew, apart from himself and the old man, she was the only person with access to both. The young man sent to America also had the login and passwords, but he hadn't started work there yet, he was probably still on a plane somewhere over the Atlantic Ocean.

Why hadn't they changed the passwords? Any security-conscious business asked its employees to change passwords regularly and to never share login details. They had become complacent, never believing that someone could do the same to them as they had been doing to thousands of others around the world all this time.

Should he contact the bank and try to recover the money? If he did, what would he say? How could he explain the amounts of money coming into the account each day from all around the world? Omar knew from his time working at the bank that such huge transfers would look strange. The bank would suspect the money was from some kind of illegal activity, probably money laundering, and would refuse to attempt any recovery.

He felt sick. What had Hadia done? If the old man suspected this was her doing, he would assume Omar was also part of any plan to steal money along with the woman he'd recruited. But did the old man know Hadia was his niece? There was no way he could know. Omar hadn't told him when he'd put her name forward for the job.

He knew Hadia didn't want to be sent to the UK to work but he was certain she wouldn't do something like this out of spite. But who else could it be? Why had she betrayed him after everything he'd done for her? Didn't she realise she wasn't only putting a death warrant on her own head but also on his and the rest of her family?

His thoughts turned to his brother, the one person who'd warned him not to take this job and had pleaded with him not to involve Hadia. He must call Salman and tell him to leave the city immediately. Leave the city and get as far away to the most remote part of the country he could. Even there he may not be safe. The old man's tentacles reached across the country far and wide. God help all of us if they find us, Omar thought. He could feel his heart pounding in his chest. He was starting to panic. The air conditioning in the office was on the maximum setting but beads of sweat were forming on his forehead and he could feel sweat slowly trickling down his back.

Omar looked up from the screen he'd been staring at for the last five minutes, the account balance remained unchanged, zero. Everyone in the office stood motionless, staring at him. "You must all leave, now," he said. He had no doubt everyone was thinking the same as him and wanted to get away before the old man arrived with his henchmen. Although none of them was to blame, retribution would be swift and ruthless if the old man chose to include all of them in his wrath. "I'll let the old man know what's happened. Go home and take whatever measures you must to keep yourselves and your families safe. It's nearly six o'clock now, I'll delay my phone call to the old man for as long as I can, it will give you a little time to return home and do whatever you think is best. Use what little time you have wisely my friends. Goodbye and good luck."

The others needed no further invitation. They left the computers on and everything where it was, gathered their personal belongings and scurried out of the door. Rats fleeing the sinking ship, Omar thought. He only wished he was going with them.

Omar dialled his brother's number. He cut in before his brother could say a word. "Salman, I have terrible news. Someone has stolen our money. You need to get out of the city as quickly as you can."

"But what does this have to do with us?"

"Salman, please don't ask questions, there isn't time. I'm

doing this to try to protect you. You need to leave the city as soon as you can. Please go now. Go now and disappear, you can't let them find you."

For a moment there was silence on the line. "Omar, what have you done?"

"I've done nothing, but there may be some kind of misunderstanding."

"What kind of misunderstanding?" Salman asked.

"Hadia...," Omar began.

His brother shouted down the phone before he could say another word, "I told you, Omar. I told you I didn't want Hadia to take this job. I told you to keep those men away from my family. What have you done?"

Omar could hear the emotion in his brother's voice, he sounded almost on the verge of tears. Salman could do nothing to help his daughter, she was thousands of miles away and he knew what terrible fate awaited all of them if they were caught by the old man.

"And what about Hadia? How are you going to protect her?"

"I'm sorry, but there's nothing I can do to protect Hadia now. If she's done what I think she has there's nothing I or anyone else can do. I just hope she has a plan to escape somewhere before the old man can find her. I'm sorry, Salman," Omar was almost whispering now, suddenly realising how he'd entwined his whole family in this disaster and the terrible consequences that awaited all of them if they were caught.

Omar tried to remain calm, trying to keep the panic from his voice hoping it would have the same effect on his brother. "Salman, listen to me. I don't know for sure exactly what's happened, but you need to leave your house and get out of the city as soon as you can. Disappear into the countryside. Go somewhere no one knows you, where no one can find you."

"But this has nothing to do with us," Salman began, contradicting everything he'd said when Omar had recruited his daughter.

"There isn't time to argue," Omar interrupted. "If you don't go now, they'll kill you, they'll kill all of us. Please Salman, go." There was silence on the line for a moment. "Goodbye, brother." Omar disconnected the call before his brother could say any more.

Omar sat at his desk, almost in a trance. He couldn't believe his life was unravelling before him. He'd returned from Afghanistan a broken man without the family he loved but had rebuilt his life. He realised now that rebuilding was always the old man's plan. He would always be indebted to him and would never be allowed to sever the ties the old man had on him. Despite his brother's pleadings, he'd been foolish enough to involve Hadia. Now she was in the same position, work for the old man until you died, or when the old man decides you should die. Omar knew he had to delay making the call to the old man for as long as possible. He hoped it would give his brother time to escape, and possibly for Hadia to escape somewhere in the UK if she hadn't already.

Omar's phone rang startling him. He glanced at the clock on the wall, almost seven in the evening, he looked back at the number displayed on his phone. The old man. An hour had passed since the money had been stolen from their account, he must surely know by now no transfer had been made from Karachi. His phone continued to ring. Should he take the call? The old man would assume he was guilty and was already on the run if he didn't answer. He felt had no choice but to accept the call.

"Hello," he said, trying to keep the growing sense of panic he was feeling from his voice.

"Omar, you didn't call me at the usual time. I understand we have a problem." It was a statement, not a question.

"Yes," Omar saw no point in lying, the old man probably knew everything already.

"How did this happen, and why didn't you call me as soon as it happened?"

"I don't know how this could happen. Someone must have hacked into the account. I've been phoning the bank trying to get the money back," he lied, a last-ditch attempt to buy some time for his brother and to divert the old man's attention away from who Omar feared the real culprit to be.

"I don't think we'll get our money back Omar. We both know how the banking system works, it's been too long now. I think we both know who transferred the money." There was a short pause. "Don't we Omar? It was your niece Omar, wasn't it? It was your niece Hadia."

"But..."

"No Omar, you know it was her, don't you? Hadia, your niece. A member of your family. The woman you conveniently forgot to tell me was your niece when you recruited her." The old man sounded calm, but his voice conveyed real menace. Suddenly his mood changed, and he started shouting down the phone. "We are fighting a holy war to rid our country of the West and you and your family have betrayed us. You've stolen our money."

Omar knew whatever he said the old man wouldn't listen, he'd already made up his mind about who was guilty and nothing Omar could say would change it, even if he was wrong about Hadia. He wondered again why he hadn't left as soon as this had happened. "I had nothing to do with this," he said in a last desperate attempt to save himself. "There must be a reason why Hadia would have done this. She must have been forced to transfer the money." He stopped himself from saying more. He'd admitted that he also believed Hadia had transferred the money. There must be someone else involved, he thought, someone who had forced her to transfer the money. She would never do such a thing on her own. She was proud of her Afghan heritage and believed in the war being fought in her homeland. He felt terrible that by naming her he'd betrayed Hadia just as she'd betrayed him and the rest of her family.

Suddenly Omar thought he should follow the advice he'd given his brother and escape. Get away quickly before the old man could catch him and exact a terrible revenge. Before the old man could say any more, Omar ended the call, picked up his jacket, put his mobile phone and its charger in his pocket and headed for the door. As he neared the exit he changed his mind. He would leave by the fire escape and slip away through the alleyways at the back of the unit. With luck, no one would expect him to leave by the back door. He hoped anyone waiting would be at the main front entrance. He stepped into the alleyway at the back of the unit and closed the door as quietly as he could.

At the front of the unit, the old man's bodyguards entered the keypad code and stepped into a deserted office. The computers were still on, coffee cups were on the desks, music was playing on the radio, but the office was empty. They made a routine check, but it was obvious everyone had fled in a hurry. One of the bodyguards called the old man with the news.

"I don't want excuses," the old man yelled down the phone, "I don't care what it takes just find him and bring him to me. I will make an example of this thief." The old man's rage knew no bounds, he ended the call and threw his phone across the room, smashing it against the wall.

The two bodyguards looked at each other. They'd never heard the old man in such a rage. They knew their task was simple, bring Omar to him so that he could be made an example of, and possibly recover the stolen money. But where to start looking among the city's fifteen million inhabitants, and what would the consequences be if they failed?

DARKNESS WAS BEGINNING to envelop the city as two figures disappeared into the gathering gloom. Salman and his wife reached the corner at the end of their road, the few belongings they'd managed to quickly gather in a rucksack over Salman's shoulder. He stopped and looked back to his house as two men climbed the steps and knocked on the door. While the two men waited for their knock to be answered, Salman and his wife disappeared into the labyrinth of alleyways.

24

Mac looked at his team. The elation of recovering the money was wearing off, they looked tired. The long early morning drive from London to his father's cottage followed by another long drive to the scammer's location and broken sleep while guarding their hostages had taken its toll. In their younger days while in the regiment, they would think nothing of a sleepless night or two, they had trained and been conditioned for it, but those days were long gone. Adrenaline would carry them only so far. As fit as they were, age and fatigue were taking their toll and they needed rest. "Okay lads, we leave as soon as it gets dark. Pack everything except the laptops and their mobile phones into the vans then tidy this place up. We don't want to leave any trace we were ever here. Once you've done that, I want all of you to get some rest. I'll call Sir Duncan and let him know we've got his son's money back."

"And then some," Smithy said.

Mac picked up his phone and dialled Sir Duncan's

number. After three rings his boss answered. "Mac, how is everything going?" he asked.

"We've put a stop to the scam and we've got the money. It was transferred to the second offshore account about half an hour ago."

For a moment there was silence. Despite his complete faith in Mac and his team, Sir Duncan couldn't quite believe they'd pulled it off. Finally, he spoke. "Well done Mac. To be perfectly honest I never really believed we could do this. Is everybody Okay?"

Despite Sir Duncan's doubts about their chances of recovering any money, Mac thought it was a nice touch that his boss asked about his team before asking how much was now deposited in one of his offshore accounts. "Yes, thanks Sir, everybody's fine. We're just tidying up now, as soon as it's dark we'll be on our way."

"How much did you manage to recover?" Sir Duncan finally asked.

Mac told him the total they'd transferred. The amount that was still staring at him from the laptop screen, an amount he still couldn't believe himself, even though he'd been looking at it repeatedly for nearly thirty minutes.

Despite being accustomed to the huge amounts of money transferred in the business world, Sir Duncan was astounded by the amount of money they were talking about. For once, he was at a loss for words. "Well, to say that was a worthwhile exercise is a massive understatement. Even if we were successful I didn't for one moment think we would recover anywhere near that amount. When Jock gave us his presentation, the numbers involved were so huge it was hard to comprehend. Even now it doesn't seem possible the amount of money we're talking about can be real. I still find it hard to believe that these people really are stealing billions of pounds a year from innocent victims. I'm glad we've stopped at least one of the groups responsible for this". There was a pause while Sir Duncan gathered his thoughts. "I assume you have the people who've been committing this crime. What do you intend to do with them?"

"Yes, we do have them, but I'm not sure what we're going to do with them yet. As we said in the boardroom, it's probably best you don't know once we do decide."

"Yes, sorry Mac I forgot, probably best. So long as they can't set up somewhere else and start all over again as we agreed. I'll see you and your team in a couple of days. And thanks again. Call me as soon as you've dealt with the scammers and we can arrange a final meeting, then I can pay you and your team and thank them personally for a job well done."

"Okay Sir, we'll see you in a couple of days." Mac disconnected the call.

He reflected on what Sir Duncan had said, "*as soon as you've dealt with the scammers.*" It was a problem he'd been thinking about since the money had landed in Sir Duncan's account. What to do with the hooded figures sitting across the unit from him? Detached from the emotion of what his team had been through over the last two days and what they needed to do to ensure they all stayed out of the spotlight, Mac thought Sir Duncan was looking at the problem through rose-tinted glasses. Despite being a hard-nosed businessman, he would never have encountered a problem such as the one now facing Mac and his team. In Mac's mind, the reality was far grimmer than anything Sir Duncan could imagine.

Mac sat down and thought of the consequences of what needed to be done to ensure their own safety. He knew Sir

Duncan would realise the enormous implications of any decision they made about the hostages. If his part in what they'd done came out it may ruin his business. It had been at the back of his mind ever since they'd entered the unit the scammers were using as an office. He'd been putting off that decision, but the time was rapidly approaching when he would have to decide. They'd agreed with Sir Duncan that whatever their fate, the hostages should not be in a position to start scamming people again. But how could he ensure that if they were set free? He put it to the back of his mind once again. They had other matters to attend to first. He knew he was putting the decision off, but he would try to decide their fate on the journey home.

Once everything in the office was back as it was when they'd arrived, Mac and his team settled down to wait for the cover of darkness. After an hour waiting to make a move, the silence in the unit was broken by the ringing and vibrating of one of the hostages' phones. It was an incoming call that wouldn't be answered. Mac wondered which of their hostages the phone belonged to. He walked to the desk and picked it up while the phone continued to ring. It was the phone he'd tipped onto the desk from Hadia's handbag. The ringing stopped. As Mac placed the phone back on the desk there was a chime to alert the phone's owner the caller had left a message.

Intrigued by what the message could be, Mac walked over to the hostages and removed the bag from Hadia's head. "You had a phone call, someone's left you a message. I want to know if it's from the office in Karachi." He cut the ties around Hadia's ankles pulled her upright by her uninjured hand and led her back to the desk, handing the phone to her.

"Play the message on speakerphone." With her hands still

bound by the cable ties, Hadia slowly unlocked her phone, dialled the number to listen to her messages and turned the speakerphone on.

"Hadia, it's your Uncle Omar. I don't know what's happened there, but we've received no transfers from your account in the UK for the last two hours. I'm guessing something has happened and someone has forced you to transfer the money from our account here. I'm sure you realise the terrible consequences this will have on all of us. I've called your father and told him what's happened and urged him to disappear before the old man's henchmen call on him and your mother. Please call me if you can and let me know what's happened and that you are safe. If I can, I'll let your parents know you're okay."

The message ended but Mac was none the wiser. Whoever had called left the message in Urdu, a language he didn't speak. He looked at Hadia. "Well, who was it and what did they want?"

Hadia saw no point in keeping the information from her captors, the damage was already done. As she was telling Mac who'd called and what was said, her phone chimed again, alerting her of another incoming message. Hadia looked at Mac for permission to look at the text. He nodded and she opened the message.

"Hadia," the text began, "what I feared all that time ago before you took the job has come true. Omar called to tell us what's happened and told us to flee the city. We are on a train and plan to cross the border into India. We hope to disappear somewhere in the south of the country. Once we are settled, we'll send you a text to let you know where we are. If you get a chance please call me, we just want to know you are safe and unharmed. Despite what's happened we want you to know we love you and hope to see you as soon as we can."

As Hadia read her father's message, she could feel tears welling up in her eyes and eventually flow down her makeup streaked face. Mac was unsure about asking who the message was from as she was obviously upset, but Hadia volunteered the information without being asked. "My father," she said. "He and my mother are fleeing the city. Do you realise you've signed the death warrant not only for the people involved in your theft of our money but all of their family members as well?"

"Your money!" Mac was still astonished that the scammers considered the money their own and had a callous disregard for those they'd stolen it from. "How can you call it your money when you've stolen it from innocent victims?" Hadia seemed to believe that Mac and his team were the thieves and she and the rest of the scammers the victims. "Might I remind you how you got the money that we transferred," he said. "I think you'll find that the money was not yours and the initial theft was by you and the organisation you were working for. If you choose to steal and are caught you must face the consequences. I'm sorry that your family, and probably many other innocent people, may suffer because of this, but you should have thought of the danger you'd be putting them in when you took this job. Maybe you should take a minute and think of the suffering you've inflicted on the innocent people you and your organisation have stolen money from. It's as you said about the war in Afghanistan, unfortunately there will be casualties. As the old saying goes, live by the sword, die by the sword."

Mac took the phone from Hadia and placed it back on the desk with the others. He led her back to where the other hostages sat and replaced the bag over her head and cable ties around her ankles.

Sitting in darkness Hadia recalled her father's protests when Omar had first offered her the job. Tears streamed down her face as she went over what he'd said in his text, "*we want you to know we love you and hope to see you as soon as we can.*" Why hadn't she listened to him when he'd told her not to take the job? What was going to happen to her now? Would she ever see her parents again? She sobbed uncontrollably as the enormity of what had happened, and the desperate situation she was now in, hit her.

Three hours later, satisfied it was dark enough and unlikely there would be anyone else around, Mac decided it was time to leave. "Smithy, take a look outside, make sure the coast is clear. While you're out there wipe the BMW down inside and out, we won't be taking it with us. Jock, Taff and Scrump, once Smithy gives you the all-clear load this lot into the vans and make sure you put those two in vans on their own," he nodded toward Hadia and Hassan, "the rest can travel together. Smithy, once you're done outside help me wipe everything down in here, we can't afford to leave a trace we were ever here." They put on the nitrile gloves and set about their tasks.

Late that night, three vans left the car park of the industrial estate. As they turned onto the main road a Mac looked in the mirror. A fox made its way past the lone vehicle remaining in the car park. A black BMW, unlocked with keys in the ignition. After the journey to and from Wales, it had only a few miles of fuel left in the tank, but Mac was confident it wouldn't be there in the morning.

25

Mac drove alone, Hassan's laptop along with his own next to him on the passenger seat. He wanted some time to himself to think about what to do with their hostages. He went through the options he thought that were open to them as he drove down the seemingly endless motorway.

Their easiest option would be to hand them over to the police, but if they did their part in recovering the money would come out, and despite the fact they wouldn't be gaining financially they may face prosecution. They had taken the scammers money, money that belonged to the people named on the laptop next to him and the thousands of other anonymous victims from around the world. If the authorities got their hands on the money it would probably be swallowed up by lawyers across the world and the bureaucratic machine. If the people who'd been scammed discovered the UK government had their money it would probably lead to endless court cases costing the taxpayer millions of pounds, benefitting nobody but the lawyers. Was it theft to steal from a thief? One thing he was certain of was the taking of hostages wasn't legal. If links to Sir Duncan were made public the press would have a field day. In his opinion, handing them over to the authorities was not an option.

They could try to put them on a plane to Pakistan, but he doubted they would go willingly, and whatever fate Mac decided on would be infinitely better than what he imagined would await them back in Pakistan. If everything he'd heard about this type of set-up was correct, what they would endure if caught was too horrible to contemplate, and despite having no sympathy for them it was something he didn't want on his conscience. And besides, he suspected some of them were UK citizens, they couldn't just buy a ticket and put them on a plane. Sir Duncan could charter a private flight, but again it left them too exposed if the police and media discovered what had happened and who was involved. And what was to stop them from returning and starting the scam again? Especially if they were given no option by the people in Pakistan running this scam.

They could release the hostages in some remote spot, possibly abroad, but he suspected they would restart their operation and start scamming innocent people out of their hard-earned money within days of being released. And again, would their paymasters in Pakistan track them down and wreak terrible retribution for losing the money?

Releasing the hostages could also put his father in terrible danger. The scammers knew his address, they could return to take their own revenge.

If both they and the money disappeared, maybe the people running the scam would suspect a conspiracy which could cause infighting and recriminations back in Pakistan and Afghanistan. The people who ran these types of operations weren't known for getting along with each other. Mac had seen it first-hand during his time serving in Afghanistan. Outside of the capital the country wasn't run by the government but by various militias and factions. Once they fell out, they would spend days fighting and killing each other, giving the troops a well-earned break and reducing the numbers fighting against the army, although there always seemed to be an endless stream of willing replacements to take up the fight. All the people at the top of operations such as this were skimming money off the top from their scams, lining their own pockets while sending their men out to fight poorly equipped and hungry. They would suspect each other of taking the money.

Maybe they'd made a mistake by not wearing masks, but he'd dismissed that idea when they'd first come up with their plan. Hassan and Tariq needed to believe they were dealing with a frail old man when they'd arrived at his father's house. A hooded man or someone wearing a mask opening the door would have alerted them and they could have escaped. Even if the hostages didn't know the identity of their captors, Mac and his team still had the problem of dealing with them.

The more Mac thought about the problem, the more he thought there was only one thing they could do with the hostages to ensure their part didn't come out, but it wasn't a decision he wanted to make on his own. He would ask the others once they reached his house. He was senior in rank when they were in the regiment, but this was different. Because of his position with Sir Duncan's company and his rank while they were in the army he'd taken the lead throughout this operation, but they were all in this together, they all deserved a say in the fate of their hostages. Not that his team would thank him for putting such a difficult decision on them, even if ultimately the final decision would rest on his shoulders.

After driving through the night, they pulled onto the driveway of Mac's old farmhouse in the remote rolling countryside. He smiled for the first time since leaving the industrial unit. Just like my father, he thought, living alone in a remote house in the countryside. There must be something in the genes. And the bloody rabbits ate his vegetables too!

Standing on the driveway, the team stretched their tired limbs. It had been another long journey, and hopefully their last. Mac threw a set of keys to Jock. "Put them in the barn please, Jock. Make them as comfortable as possible while we decide what we're going to do with them." Jock opened the back of the first van and pulled Hassan out.

Hassan looked at Mac imploringly.

Mac shook his head. "After the misery you and your friends have inflicted on the citizens here in the UK I don't think the American's would want someone like you living there, do you? Nobody wants a thief living amongst them." He turned towards his house. "Besides, you don't have the money for a ticket now."

Once the hostages were secured in the barn and the doors padlocked, Mac and his team sat around the kitchen table, steaming cups of coffee in front of them. It had been a long night, everyone ached from the long drives they'd had over the last couple of days. They'd all come down after the adrenaline rush of storming the unit and the high of recovering the money. They were all bone-tired, drained and in need of rest. The coffee was the only thing keeping some of the team going. Mac worried that the last part of the operation he had in mind would be a step too far, both physically and emotionally, but he could see no other option. With the huge burden of responsibility weighing on his shoulders, he needed to discuss his decision with the others, even if only to confirm the conclusion he'd come to was their only option.

"I'm sorry to bring this up," he said, "but we have a difficult decision to make. What do we do with our guests in the barn? As we've been through this together, I think each of us should have a say about their fate. I don't want to make this decision on my own, it's one that could potentially have repercussions for all of us, but I will if you don't want to be party to the decision. Since we recovered the money, none of us has said a word about their what we do with them, but ever since we sat in Sir Duncan's boardroom and formulated this plan I think all of us knew that if we were successful it would come down to this. If we do the wrong thing there could be some serious repercussions for all of us, including Sir Duncan and my father, so we all need to agree on what we're going to do with them."

They discussed each of the options Mac had thought of on the long drive home plus a few the others came up with, but they kept coming back to the same conclusion. After an hour, they reluctantly made their decision, one Mac thought that was really their only option, the same conclusion he'd come to on the long drive home from his father's.

"So, are we all sure about this? I know it's a decision none of us wants to make and one that will stay with us for as long as we live, so we need to be one hundred percent sure about it." Mac looked at each of them, "Scrump?"

Scrump looked down at the table, seemingly unable or unwilling to look the others in the eye. "I think it's a decision none of us has taken lightly but unfortunately I can't see any other way without it coming back to bite us."

"Smithy?" Mac asked.

"Yes guv, afraid so."

"Taff?"

"Agreed."

"Jock?"

"Aye. I think we've got to consider the misery these people have inflicted on countless others in the past, and where the money's going. I know it's the people in charge of this lot that really deserve what we've decided on, but we can only deal with what we've got. We'll be stopping them from setting up again and causing misery to innocent people just as they did to Taff's Nan, which is what Sir Duncan asked us to do."

It was rare for Jock to voice such an emotional opinion. Because of this, his words seemed to carry extra weight.

The decision was unanimous. The hostage's fate was sealed. The mood in the room was sombre. No one spoke for a couple of minutes as each of them contemplated the difficult decision they'd come to and the implications it may have for each of them. Mac stood up, trying to lift the mood. "Taff and I will go and make sure our guests are secure and as comfortable as possible while you finish your coffee, then I suggest you get some rest. Unfortunately, we've got another late night ahead of us."

Despite believing it was their only option, Mac was still uneasy with the decision they'd reached and worried the conclusion he'd come to on the drive from his father's was one he'd wrongly put into the rest of the team's heads. Maybe they would have thought of an alternative if he hadn't put his own conclusion into their minds. "Are you comfortable with the decision we've just made?" he asked as they walked towards the barn.

"No-one would be comfortable making a decision like this, Mac, but there's no other way unless we want our part in this to come out, or this lot going back to scamming innocent people. Like Jock said, I just think of my poor old nan. Before she was scammed, she was full of life, as bright as a button. As soon as it happened, she went downhill fast. She died six months after they stole her money. My family hold the people who scammed her responsible for her death, but we'll never have the satisfaction of seeing them prosecuted for what they did to her. If it was this lot that scammed her, I think they deserve everything they get. You know what they say Mac, live by the sword, die by the sword."

Mac smiled, the same sentiment he'd voiced to Hadia earlier, or as Sir Duncan would say, *don't get mad, get even.* He knew that even if these weren't the same people who'd scammed his grandmother, Taff felt he was in some way getting even.

Mac took the key from his pocket and unlocked the padlock. The screech of rusty hinges shattered the silence as he pulled the huge barn doors open. When they stepped into the gloomy interior, they could just make out the shape of one of the hostages sitting on top of another. Taff ran over and dragged the hooded hostage to his feet and away from the prone figure on the floor. He pulled off the hood and tore the tape from the hostage's mouth.

Tariq glared back at him. "This dog got what he deserved," he turned his head and spat on the hooded body lying on the floor next to him. "If you hadn't interrupted, the woman was next."

Taff slapped him across his face. "Don't you think you've caused enough misery already you bastard?"

Tariq braced himself for further blows, but none came. Slowly he turned and fixed Taff with an intense stare. "I will show you what misery I can cause when my hands are free. I will break every bone in your body, then you will know what real pain is."

Taff took a step backwards then kicked Tariq between the legs as hard as he could. "How's that for real pain you murdering bastard? Take it from me, your hands will never be free again." His fiery temper was taking over, he took another step backwards, about to launch himself at Tariq.

"Taff, pull yourself together man," Mac shouted. "Just secure him and the rest of them while I check on this one."

Mac knelt next to the lifeless body, gently pulling the bag from the figures head. While it had disguised the identity of the person lying next to him, he knew who it would be. Hassan, his lifeless eyes stared past Mac up to the barn roof. He wasn't breathing, his face a strange ashen colour, his lips a pale blue. His eyes conveyed the terror he must have felt while Tariq had suffocated him, the tape they'd put over his mouth aiding his murderer. It was obvious any attempt to revive him would be useless.

Taff dragged the squirming figure of Tariq across the floor to the far side of the barn then returned to where Mac was kneeling next to the prone figure. "Aren't you going to try to bring him round, Mac?"

Mac shook his head. "There's no point, and anyway I think we're too late. If we did manage to bring him back, he's been out of it for too long. Starved of oxygen I think he'd be brain damaged." Mac continued to stare at Hassan's lifeless body. "I thought with their hands and legs cuffed they wouldn't be able to move around the barn and they'd all be safe, but obviously I was wrong. Can you go back to the cottage and get some rope and a knife please. We need to secure this lot spread around the barn far enough apart so they can't do each other any more harm during the rest of their stay. We don't want any more trouble. I'll take care of this one while you get the rope."

He picked up Hassan's lifeless body and carried it to a quiet corner of the barn. Despite his loathing of what these people did he would afford the man a little dignity for the short time before they set off on their final journey later that night.

While Mac was distracted, Amir worked furiously rubbing the cable tie around his wrists against a rusty nail embedded in one of the barn's old beams. With his hands behind his back, he had to do everything by touch. He'd slipped a few times, cutting his hands and wrists, the tie now slippery with blood, but he didn't care, this could be his only chance of escape. Suddenly the tie broke. He pulled the bag from his head and looked around for something to break the cable around his ankles. A few feet away he could see an old pitchfork leaning against the wall. He rolled through the hay as quietly as he could and grabbed it. Forcing one of the prongs into the join of the cable tie, he pushed as hard as he could. His bloody hands made gripping the handle difficult, but eventually the cable snapped.

Mac laid Hassan's body down and turned to see a figure coming towards him holding a pitchfork. As he got closer the figure pointed it at him.

"Out of my way," he said, jabbing the pitchfork at Mac.

Mac remained silent, staring at the man in front of him quickly assessing his options. In the gloom, it was difficult to see which of their hostages was confronting him, but from his build, he knew it had to be either Amir or Imran.

"I said out of my way," the figure repeated, jabbing the pitchfork towards Mac again.

"I don't think so," Mac replied.

The figure lunged out of the gloom aiming the pitchfork at Mac's stomach. He parried the thrust deflecting it downwards. Suddenly he felt an excruciating pain. One of the prongs had sunk deep into his thigh muscle. He screamed in agony.

TAFF WAS RETURNING to the barn with Jock when they heard Mac's scream. He dropped the rope he was carrying and they both ran toward the barn. As they arrived at the door, a figure emerged. The figure stopped in front of them, his hands covered in blood, his eyes huge like a rabbit caught in the headlights. Jock stepped forward, grabbed his hair and smashed his forehead against the barn door, immediately knocking him unconscious.

They left the figure in the doorway and rushed into the barn where Mac was sitting on the floor, the pitchfork still stuck in his leg. "I'm okay," he said when they reached him.

"It doesn't look that way to me, Mac," Jock said.

Taff ripped open the leg of Mac's trousers and inspected the wound. "Looks nasty, but I think it's only a flesh wound. You need to get to the hospital and have this looked at by a professional."

"I can't do that Taff, not until we've dealt with this lot. There's a first aid kit in my bathroom if you could get it please."

"We can't do it here, there's not enough light. I'll get the others then we can get you back to the house."

Accompanied by the rest of the team, Taff returned with the first aid kit a few minutes later, stepping over the still unconscious figure of Amir in the doorway.

While Smithy shone a torch on Mac's leg Taff carefully

inspected the wound. "You know we shouldn't remove this, if it's gone through an artery you could bleed to death."

"Just do it please, Taff. You can't carry me back to the house with this thing still stuck in my leg." Mac said through gritted teeth.

As gently as he could Taff removed the pitchfork from Mac's leg and pressed a gauze pad on the wound. There was very little blood, a good sign. With Smithy's help, they took Mac back to the kitchen to clean and dress his wound.

After replacing the cable ties and hood on Amir, the rest of the team set about securing the other hostages to the sides of the barn, making sure they were well away from each other and there was nothing sharp nearby they could use on the cable ties.

Mac sat in the kitchen, his leg elevated and an icepack on the wound. He thought it ironic that he didn't want their hostages to come to any harm during the rest of their stay in his barn considering the decision his team had agreed on and what fate had in store for them later that night. After taking some pain killers, and putting on a new pair of trousers, Mac gingerly made his way back to the barn.

Scrump was busy in the hayloft getting the equipment they would need later that night. He lowered it to Taff and Jock who loaded it into one of the vans. With everything ready and their prisoners secured, Mac locked the barn doors ready to return to his kitchen.

"Mac, I know we've secured them, but after what's happened do you think it would be a good idea if one of us stayed in there to keep an eye on them?" Jock asked. "I'm happy to sit with them until we leave."

Mac nodded. "I suppose it won't do any harm. I'll bring you a cuppa in about an hour." He handed Jock the key and made his way with the others back to the farmhouse to wait for nightfall.

Jock pulled the barn doors open and sat on the first bale of hay he could find. He could hear Hadia quietly crying somewhere in the gloom. None of the others made a sound. It was going to be a long wait for darkness.

After returning from the barn, the remaining members of the team sat around the kitchen table, each with a hot cup of tea. Hassan's laptop sat in the middle of the table along with the hostage's mobile phones, keys, the knife and Hadia's two passports. Taff nodded towards the laptop. "Can I take a look on the computer, Mac?" he asked. "Just so I know."

"We've made our decision, Taff. Whether your grandmother's name is on there or not makes no difference now." Mac was reluctant to let his friend search for his grandmother's name. He wondered how Taff would react knowing his fiery temper.

"I know. But put yourself in my shoes. I want to look just so that I know. If it was them it makes me feel a little better about the decision we made earlier."

"Okay. I can't see that it will do any harm, but if you find your grandmother's name on there I don't want them mistreated for the rest of the time they're with us, or to affect the way you conduct yourself later. Is that clear?" Mac picked up the laptop and handed it to Taff. "You know the password?"

"Yes. Thanks Mac." Taff took the computer and sat at the far end of the table, away from the others. He opened the only file and looked at the first line of data. A date, a name, the first line of an address, a postcode and an amount of money. People such as his grandmother reduced to a line on a spreadsheet, the only reason for each entry being how much had been stolen from them. After what Mac had said, he tried to control the anger he felt. Despite the slight chill in the air, Taff could feel sweat breaking out on his forehead.

Now he had the information in front of him, he wasn't sure he wanted to know. But eventually, his curiosity proved too much. He moved the cursor and clicked on the find icon, typed his grandmother's surname, then pressed the *find next* option. The cursor jumped down the page to the name he was searching for but wasn't sure he wanted to find, along with the address and amount of money stolen from her. He stared at the line, remembering the sudden decline in the woman he'd looked up to and loved. A tear slowly trickled down Taff's face as he continued to stare at the screen, remembering the good times he'd spent with his grand-mother and how the scam had ultimately taken her life. How many more innocent victims had suffered the same fate as his grandmother, he wondered.

Taff wiped away the tear, closed the file and turned the laptop off. In his mind, the decision concerning their hostage's fate was now fully justified. Nobody said a word. The team watched Taff hand the laptop back to Mac. "I just need a little time alone, sarge, if that's okay? I'll be outside for a couple of minutes."

Mac nodded. "Take as long as you need."

JUST AFTER MIDNIGHT, torches in hand, Mac and his team returned to the barn. Once again, the door hinges screeched in the still night air, waking the hostages inside. After cutting the cable ties around their ankles, they led the hooded figures to the vans. Nobody said a word. The mood among the team had remained sombre since deciding the hostage's fate. After Mac had informed his team of Hassan's death, their resolve had strengthened. They were not only dealing with thieves and fanatics, but now with at least one murderer, and in Nasir a man who had no qualms about beating women. Hadia's crying was the only sound breaking the silence as they led their hostages to the vans, no one knew whether from the pain in her broken hand or the worry of the uncertain fate that lay ahead of her.

Mac's heart was heavy, and he was sure the others were feeling the same way, but they had made their decision. However difficult, what they were about to do was the only way they could see to end this without the chance of it coming back to haunt them and to be sure these people wouldn't start up their scam again somewhere else. They were professionals, they had faced unpleasant tasks and been in life and death situations before, but never one like this. They would complete this job in the same professional manner as they had others during their military service, but each of them knew what they were about to do would remain with them for the rest of their lives.

A full moon glistened off the frosty road as three vans pulled out of Mac's driveway to begin the short journey to the coast. Not conditions ideal for what they were about to do, Mac thought. He would like cloud cover and total darkness to shroud this final act, but they had no choice. They couldn't wait for perfect weather conditions.

In the van behind Mac, Smithy tried to inject a little of his East End humour into proceedings. "You know if we get stopped by the law it will look like we're people trafficking."

Scrump took his eyes off the road for a moment, looked over at Smithy and shook his head. "I don't think this is a time for humour Smithy. None of us are happy about what we're about to do, so please don't try to lighten the mood, it just doesn't seem right."

"Sorry."

The rest of the journey was made in silence.

The three vans turned into the car park at their remote destination. Mac was relieved to see no other vehicles and a chilly mist beginning to roll in off the sea. It was the cover he was hoping for while they completed this last task, one he still had misgivings about.

Aware of Scrump's ongoing therapy, Mac decided he wouldn't include him in what he hoped would be the conclusion of the operation. Despite Scrump agreeing to the hostage's fate, he didn't want to risk setting him back on his fragile road to recovery. He had no doubt what they were about to do would have a profound effect on each of the team who would be present, the gravity of which they all understood and wouldn't be able to forget, but if Scrump was vulnerable he couldn't risk undermining the progress he'd made so far. If he remained on the beach and didn't witness the conclusion of the operation it may not lessen the burden of guilt he was sure they would all feel, but at least he wouldn't be there to see the final act itself.

Mac took Scrump to one side while the rest of the team unloaded the equipment. "Scrump, I want you to be our eyes and ears here while we're out there finishing this. We don't need any early morning fishermen or dog walkers poking their noses in and we need someone here to guide us back to shore when we're done. I want you to stay with the vans. When I text you, flash the lights to give us an idea of where we need to land."

"Thanks, Mac." Scrump smiled. He was fully aware of what Mac was doing.

Mac's team went about their work in silence, preparing to launch the two inflatables into the gathering misty gloom, the only sound was the lighthouse foghorn in the distance and the crunch of shingle underfoot. The hostages remained in the back of the vans, but despite the hessian bags over their heads they seemed to sense the mood of Mac's team and were becoming agitated. Mac knew they needed to get them into the boats and off the beach as quickly as possible before they became difficult to handle.

After twenty minutes of running up and down the beach, they were ready. The two inflatables moved gently back and forth where the waves were gently breaking on the shore, ready to make one final journey. His team put on their life jackets then took their hostages one by one from the vans, guided them down the beach and into the waiting inflatables. When everyone was aboard and the boats clear of the beach, the outboard motors were started. The noise was deafening in the silence as they finally set off through the rolling mist into the darkness.

TWO HOURS LATER, the inflatables approached the shore. As planned, Mac sent a text to their lookout. Scrump climbed aboard one of the vans and flashed the headlights. Offshore, Mac spotted the signal through the gloom. With the outboard motors switched off, they started paddling towards the beach. Ten minutes later, two inflatables silently emerged from the rolling mist and beached at the spot from which they'd set off.

The narrow beam of light from the lighthouse in the distance washed around every twenty seconds giving the beach an eerie luminous quality in the mist. The team worked in silence after beaching the inflatables, hauling the equipment up the beach back towards the waiting vans. The sun would rise in another hour and they needed to be away from the coast before any early morning fishermen or dog walkers arrived. Mac and his team loaded both inflatables and the rest of the gear into the vans. He would wash the salt-water off when they arrived back at the barn. They climbed into their vehicles and headed back to Mac's farmhouse. Their part in the operation was now complete.

26

The next day, after returning the vans to the hire company, Mac and his team sat in the boardroom waiting for Sir Duncan's arrival for the final time. At ten-thirty he entered and sat at the head of the table. He looked around Mac's team. He thought each of them had aged considerably since he'd last seen them just a few days ago.

"Gentlemen, I've asked you here because I wanted to thank you personally and to give you a cheque for your work as promised. As Mac knows, my lifetime mantra has been *don't get mad, get even*. Thanks to your hard work and professionalism, I think on this occasion we did more than get even." As he spoke, his Finance Director entered the room. "James, would you do the honours please." His accountant walked around the table handing each of the team an envelope.

Smithy was the last to receive an envelope but first to open it. He ripped open the envelope and took the cheque from inside. "And a little bonus. Thanks, guv." From his seat,

Smithy looked up at Sir Duncan's Finance Director. "James," he said in his most sincere voice, "I've always liked you accountants. Where would the world be without you lot?"

For a second the rest of the team stared at him in disbelief then burst out laughing. James stood impassive by the door. "Yes, a little bonus as thanks for a job well done," Sir Duncan said. "James, one last thing, please transfer a million pounds back to my investment account from the offshore account to replace my initial outlay."

James made a note of Sir Duncan's instructions. "And what about the remaining balance, Sir Duncan?"

"I have a plan for that, please sit down and I'll explain."

James returned to the boardroom table to await Sir Duncan's instructions.

"I want you to transfer the balance to my personal current account then close both offshore accounts."

"But you said you wouldn't profit from this," Mac protested.

Sir Duncan held up a hand. "Mac, you know me better than that, I haven't finished yet." He turned back to his accountant. "Is there any way I can draw cheques on my account without my name appearing on them?"

"Oh yes Sir, it's a little time consuming and the bank won't like it but there are a number of ways. The cheques would still show your sort code and account number but not your name. Or we could ask the bank to draw cashier's cheques."

"Good. I don't need to know the details of how it's done now but I'll be giving you instructions over the next couple of days of where I want the money to go, but please make the bank aware that there will be a considerable number of these cheques. If there are any problems let me know and I'll speak to the bank manager myself, I'm sure he won't want to lose our business. Once that's done this whole saga is at an end. Hopefully we can forget about it and get on with our lives as normal."

Sitting beside his boss, Mac wasn't so sure that he or any of his team would be able to *"forget it and get on with their lives as normal."* Sir Duncan didn't know what they'd done with the hostages the night before to ensure nobody would ever find out how they'd recovered the money, and he would never tell him.

"Please remember gentlemen, while we may have stopped these criminals committing theft on an unsuspecting public, I'm sure what we've done, and I include myself in this, is outside of the law. We don't want any of this to come out so not a word to anyone." Sir Duncan turned to his Finance Director. "And thank you for your help in all of this, James."

"My pleasure Sir, it's been an interesting experience, and one that appears to be not quite over yet." James stood and left the boardroom.

Sir Duncan pointed to Hassan's laptop laying in the centre of the table. "Is that their laptop, Mac?"

"Yes, Sir."

"I'll be needing that please."

"It's all yours Sir." Mac passed the laptop to Sir Duncan. "Please make sure it's destroyed once you have the information you need." Mac took a piece of paper from his pocket and handed it to Sir Duncan. "This is the password when you turn it on."

Sir Duncan placed the paper containing the password on top of the laptop. "Well thank you once again gentlemen, I'll let you be on your way."

Mac's team rose from the table. One by one they shook hands with Sir Duncan. "Drink anyone?" Smithy asked, waving the cheque over his head as he made his way towards the door. "My round."

"The Black Friar?" Taff asked.

"Good idea, that's where this all started so I think it's a good place to end it, and thanks again guv, see you around. If you need anyone for jobs in the future just get Mac to give us a call, mates rates next time." The team filed out, leaving Mac and Sir Duncan standing in the boardroom both smiling and shaking their heads.

"He certainly is quite a character. I'm not sure I could work with someone like that for long."

"You get used to him after a while. They're all good lads. They saw a lot during their time in the regiment, but I think this will have as much of an effect on them as anything they saw in Afghanistan or Iraq. They might look carefree now, but I think it will take them a little while to get it out of their heads, if they ever can. Something like this seems to affect you more the older you get."

There was a moment's silence as they stood staring at the boardroom door. Sir Duncan could only guess what Mac meant by "*something like this.*"

"I can see this has been difficult for you Mac, and I don't want to dwell on what you've had to do to ensure none of this gets out. You and your team have done a great job, not only for me and Sam but for everyone who's been scammed by these people, and those who would be in the future, so please don't be too hard on yourself. I don't want to know what happened to the people committing these scams, they deserved whatever fate you handed out to them. Think of all of the innocent people you've saved from the heartache and misery of having their money stolen in the future, not to mention the toll it takes on those people's mental health.

"Now don't hang about, after all, technically this is the last day of your holiday. You did this as a team and you should celebrate as a team, and goodness knows what that lot will get up to if you're not there to keep an eye on them.

"One last thing before you go, please remind them not a word of this must get out and ask them not to flash their money around."

"Thanks, Sir. I'll remind them of the need for secrecy but I'm sure they don't need telling. I'll be back at work as usual in the morning. We have our new guy starting tomorrow so I'll be here a little early." Mac headed towards the door to catch up with the rest of his team. He didn't need to rush and with his injured leg he couldn't, he knew where they were headed, and now each of them had enough money to buy their own drinks.

"Are you alright, Mac? You're walking with a bit of a limp. Did you get injured doing this?" Sir Duncan asked.

"I'll be fine Sir, thanks. It's just a scratch."

Mac's team stood at the bar of the Black Friar watched by a lone figure sat in the same alcove the team had sat in just a few days before. He hauled himself from his seat and headed towards the noisy group who were ordering. Just as he reached them, Smithy turned around. For a moment he stood staring at the man in front of him, for once speechless.

"Hello Smithy, how are you doing?"

"Gav, what the hell are you doing here?"

"Mac phoned me a week ago and said he had a security job for me if I wanted it. He called me yesterday and asked me to meet him here to go over a few final details. More to the point what are you and the rest of the team doing here? Holding a Regimental reunion without me?"

"No, we've been doing a little job for Mac's boss. It's great to see you looking so well, welcome to the team. This calls for a celebration. What can I get you?"

While Smithy ordered everyone a drink, Mac managed to get Gav alone. "Well Gav, it's good to have you on board. I'm glad you could make it today, there are a few things I'd like to go through before you start tomorrow."

"Thanks Mac. I've had nothing but dead-end jobs since I left the regiment. This is the chance I've been waiting for. You know about my injuries but now I've finished my treatment and rehab I can keep up with the best of them, I just needed a chance to prove it, that's all. Now you've given it to me I intend to grab it with both hands. I'll be there tomorrow at nine on the dot."

"That's great, you don't need to prove anything to me, I know you're more than capable, you just need to convince the other members of the team, and I know that won't be a problem once they get to know you."

LATER THAT MORNING a cross channel ferry alerted HM Coastguard that there were what they believed to be a number of bodies seen floating mid-channel. Twenty minutes after the call, a Border Force vessel arrived at the location given by the ferry and recovered the bodies of five men, one of whom had a broken nose and broken jaw. What puzzled the captain was that there was no sign of a boat. In his experience, when these accidents occurred there was always some sign of debris or a deflated dingy. It was also strange that none of the bodies were wearing lifejackets. Later autopsies couldn't explain the strange marks around the wrists and ankles of the bodies, although they looked as though they'd been bound hand and foot, possibly by people traffickers, or why one of the men had suffocated while the others had all drowned.

THE FOLLOWING MORNING, Mac picked up a newspaper as he did every day on his way to work before boarding his train. As the train pulled out of the station, he turned to an article about people smuggling. The article opened with news of five bodies recovered from the channel the previous day, a day that had seen record numbers of immigrants landing on the shores of southern Britain. The bodies were those of five men, one with a broken nose and broken jaw, none of whom were wearing life jackets. No inflatable boat had been spotted mid-channel by the captain of the ferry who first reported the sighting nor by the border force vessel that had recovered them, a fact that puzzled the authorities.

The article went on to speculate about the escalating violence involved in the people trafficking trade and calls from charity groups for help from both the French and UK governments to stop the violence. What really puzzled the authorities was the fact that these victims appeared to have been bound hand and foot. The people trafficker's involvement usually ended once the asylum seekers handed over their money and were on a boat heading for the UK. The article speculated on several issues. Had the people trafficking trade taken an even more sinister turn? Were the traffickers now taking asylum seekers money then throwing them overboard mid-channel to re-use the precious boats? Had the man with the broken nose and jaw been beaten by the traffickers before being thrown into the channel? Or had a fight broken out between the passengers of whatever craft they were using to cross the channel and all the occupants ended up in the freezing water? Why was there no debris or sign of an inflatable found at the site where the bodies were recovered? All newspaper speculation, Mac thought, none of which interested him. His only concern was for the body of a woman that had apparently not been recovered. He would keep a close eye on any news covering migrants crossing the channel. Hopefully, the body of a woman would be recovered somewhere along the coast of southern Britain in the next few days.

Wrapped in silver survival blankets, the most recent arrivals to Britain's shores stood in line waiting to be processed. After being picked up in the channel by a Border Force patrol, they were taken to Dover where they were given a rudimentary medical check then taken to a reception area where they would be asked some basic questions, they would then be transferred to a holding camp where the process of their asylum applications would begin. Each of them was checked for paperwork that may give a clue to their identity, as usual none had anything that might help identify who they were or their nationality.

Soaked from head to foot, one of the women picked up that day looked as though she had been in the sea. She also had a badly injured hand and marks around her ankles and wrists that indicated she had in some way been bound. The officers dealing with the woman were confronting an overwhelming flood of people trying to reach Britain, nobody made the connection between these marks and similar marks found on the five bodies recovered from the channel the previous day.

An immigration officer led the woman away from the others for a change of clothing and a hot drink. When she emerged from the changing cubicle, the officer led the woman to a small office. Once they were both seated, the officer began her interrogation. "Do you speak English?" she asked.

"Yes."

Without looking up from the paperwork in front of her, the officer continued. "Are you happy to continue without an interpreter?"

"Yes."

"We'll get some more medical attention for your hand later, but first I need to ask you a few questions and complete some paperwork. Once I've completed these forms, you'll be taken to a holding camp where more paperwork and investigations will be completed. You'll be detained there while your asylum application is considered. Firstly, can I have your name please?"

"Hadia," the woman replied. "But there has been a terrible mix-up. I don't want asylum. I want to go home."

The officer looked up in surprise. "You're not claiming asylum?"

"No, I want to go home," Hadia repeated.

The officer stared at Hadia in confusion, now unsure how to proceed. She'd never encountered a situation where someone arriving after the treacherous crossing from France did not want to claim asylum.

"Wait here," she said, "I'll get someone more senior to deal with you." She gathered the paperwork from the desk and left the office.

Hadia sat alone in the stark room, her uninjured hand clasped the hot drink in an attempt to rid herself of the cold that had permeated every part of her body after being in the freezing channel water. She knew she'd been lucky to be found so quickly before hypothermia set in, especially in the dark and fog. She'd read that boats crossing the channel were usually full to overflowing, the people traffickers making as much money as possible from each crossing. She'd been especially lucky that there was room in the boat for her. She'd heard nothing about the others and assumed they hadn't been as fortunate. She just hoped none of the other occupants of the dingy that had rescued her told the immigration officers they'd picked her up mid-channel. If they did, she would face some awkward questions and they may make the connection to her missing workmates.

Since being rescued, Hadia had thought of nothing but the situation she now found herself in. If she gave her real name, would the old man's intelligence network somehow be alerted and send someone to find her, even if she remained in the UK? If she chose to return home, would he have someone waiting for her when she arrived at the airport? Was it a risk she was prepared to take? Should she return to Pakistan and look for her uncle or tell the people asking questions she was from India? The text she'd received back at the unit said her parents were on a train headed for India, perhaps she should go there and look for them, even if the chances of finding them among its population of 1.4 billion were almost negligible.

After a few moments, the woman returned with her senior officer. He sat at the desk and stared at Hadia for some time before reading the notes his colleague had given him.

Hadia avoided his gaze, feeling uncomfortable under his intense scrutiny. Finally, he spoke.

"Before we start, my colleague tells me you speak English, are you sure you don't need the help of an interpreter?" He was certain his colleague had made a mistake. After crossing one of the world's busiest shipping lanes nobody had ever asked to be returned home. He was sure the woman sitting in front of him had misunderstood and probably didn't speak English quite as well as she thought she did.

"No, I understand English perfectly well." Hadia had to stop herself from telling the officer she'd spent three years in his country studying for her degree. In the situation she was now in, she knew she should reveal as little information as possible. For once, she managed to restrain herself and keep her headstrong nature under control.

"Very well, but if you feel you need an interpreter at any time please ask. Now, I understand from my colleague that you do not wish to seek asylum, is that correct?"

"Yes, that's correct. I don't want asylum. I want to go home."

The officer looked at Hadia sceptically. "Then can you explain to me why you have made such a dangerous and presumably expensive journey, only to ask to return once you've reached your destination?"

Slumped in her chair, Hadia looked down at the injured hand in her lap, avoiding the officer's intense stare. She wanted to appear broken and defeated. "I'm sure you are aware that in our culture arranged marriages are common-place. My parents have arranged for me to marry a man much older than myself, a man I've never met. I had no one to turn to, no one who could help me, so I decided the only way to get myself out of the marriage was to flee the country.

But now I'm not sure. I'd like to return home and respect my parent's wishes, or at least discuss it with them."

The officer continued to stare at Hadia, but still she wouldn't look him in the eye. He didn't believe a word she'd said. He let the silence drag on, hoping she would say more and possibly confess her story was a lie, but she kept her gaze fixed on the injured hand in her lap. "Very well," he said at last, "if you would give us some contact details for your parents, or someone else who can vouch for you in India, we can arrange a ticket home for you."

Hadia looked up, looking the officer in the eye for the first time. She sat up in the chair, crossing her arms in front of her. On hearing the news she would be sent home, she seemed to grow in stature. "You won't be able to contact my parents, they live in the country and have no access to a telephone, but you may be able to reach my uncle. Just ask him to confirm that Hadia Bukhari is his niece and that she is missing." She gave the officer the number and leaned back in her chair, trying to keep an outward appearance of confidence she didn't feel inside. She wondered if Omar had managed to escape the old man and if the British authorities managed to contact him that he would remember the identity they'd given her on the false passport, the name he'd told her to use to avoid anyone knowing she was his niece when he'd recruited her.

"When you were rescued you were soaking wet, you'd obviously been in the water. Would you like to explain to me how that happened?" the officer asked.

"I slipped as I was getting into the boat in France."

"Not thrown out of the boat mid-channel? Or maybe from another boat?"

"No, I slipped and fell into the sea before we left France."

"And the other occupants of the boat you were rescued from will confirm your story if I check with them?"

Hadia hesitated. "Yes," she replied. She knew she'd be in trouble if the officer questioned the others in the boat, but she'd come this far, she couldn't backtrack now. And would he even question the others?

The officer sat in front of Hadia still didn't believe a word of what she'd told him. He knew she was lying and if he questioned some of the other migrants who'd been in the boat, he may get to the truth. But what was the point in pursuing it when she wanted to return to India? Any investigation would result in a mountain of paperwork and the outcome wouldn't be changed. This woman would get what she wanted and would be sent back to India.

During his time processing asylum seekers crossing the channel, he'd never encountered anyone originating from India, and a woman travelling alone was a rarity from any country. But he was bound by regulations that meant he had to contact the number she'd supplied. Even if he couldn't reach the number the woman had given him such was the political clamour to extradite as many asylum claimants as possible, once the paperwork and various checks were complete, she would be on the first available flight to India.

27

For two weeks, Omar lived with Karachi's homeless and destitute under the bridge outside the city's main railway station. With his face partially covered and a dishevelled appearance, he blended in with the hundreds of other inhabitants of the city's poorest living in cardboard boxes. His only possessions were his mobile phone, the phones charger and his bank card. He went without food for almost the entirety of his stay, his emaciated appearance much as it was when he'd reached his brother's house after the long journey home from the war. Once confident he couldn't be recognised by the old man's network, he would head for the port where he hoped to persuade a captain of one of the small fishing boats to give him a ride to India. He knew it wouldn't be easy, the long running conflict on the Kashmiri border was restricting the flow of people between the two countries, but he thought if there was any way to make the journey undetected it would be by one of the port's smaller fishing vessels. He also knew if he was lucky enough to get a ride, it would be expensive and dangerous.

During his first week living on the streets, Omar's only movement was to visit the train station's toilets. While trying to appear destitute, he knew he had to keep himself in reasonable shape for his planned journey to India. Each morning he would use the station's facilities, timing his visit when the station was at its busiest. In his mind, this was the time when it would be most difficult for the old man's network to identify him, and for the station's security to stop him and the other inhabitants of the cardboard town outside the entrance from entering the station. After completing his morning ablutions, Omar would fill a bottle he'd found in one of the station's waste bins with water from the fountain, then return to his temporary home.

Worried his phone would run out of power and he'd have nowhere to charge it, Omar avoided turning it on during his first week hiding outside the station. He also worried that the old man may have some way of tracking him if he turned it on. On his eighth day in hiding, Omar decided to take the risk and turned his phone on while sitting in one of the station's toilet cubicles. During the time it had been turned off, he'd received two voicemails and one text message. The first voicemail was from the old man's number. Omar could only imagine the fury he was feeling and had no desire to listen to his rant about what he would do to Omar if he was caught. He deleted the message without listening to it. The second voicemail was from a number prefixed with 044, a message from the UK, but not from Hadia's number. He decided he would listen to it after reading the text message from his brother.

"Omar, I hope you managed to escape, and you are safe. We did as you said and escaped the city. We are living in a room in Mumbai, but our money is nearly all gone. I've found work in a textile factory which will tide us over for a short time but it's a temporary fix. If you've heard anything from Hadia please let me know, we are desperate to know that she's safe."

For a moment, Omar sat in the cubicle and thought back to his brother's warnings. Warnings he'd ignored. He wouldn't be hiding in a filthy train station toilet cubicle hoping to use all of his savings to flee to India if he'd listened to Salman. And his brother, who was the innocent party in all of this, wouldn't be living in a room in a foreign country, working in a sweatshop with no money.

Omar looked down at his phone. He tapped the screen to listen to the voicemail. "Good afternoon, this is HM Immigration Service in the UK. We are currently holding a Miss Hadia Bukhari who has informed us that you are her uncle. I wonder if you would call this number to vouch for her. We've contacted the Indian Embassy here in London and supplied them with a photograph, but they can find no trace of a passport issued to Miss Bukhari. She's currently being processed by our officers and will be repatriated to India in the next few days. We would like to know that a member of her family will be at the airport to meet her on arrival. Flight details will be sent to you by text once arranged. Thank you." Omar felt a huge sense of relief. Finally, some good news. Hadia was safe. Still feeling guilty after the death of his own family, he would never forgive himself if she'd come to any harm working for the organisation he'd introduced her to. He would take great delight texting his brother with the good news later.

Three days after receiving the messages, Omar looked up from his cardboard home at the station clock, a legacy of British rule shining like a beacon in the dark night sky. It was midnight, the time he'd decided to make his move. He walked into the station. Despite the late hour, the building was a hive of activity. He looked around to ensure no one was watching, then used his bank card to withdraw what he thought would be enough to entice a captain of one of the small fishing boats to take him to India. He didn't withdraw the whole amount he would be offering for his passage. He couldn't afford to lose that sort of sum if he was attacked on the dark streets. Besides, he wouldn't be handing over any cash tonight. He knew to do so would be foolish, but he needed to be able to demonstrate he had the money to pay for the journey.

He made his way to the port, stopping at each street corner he made sure he wasn't being followed. He knew he was being irrational. Anybody looking at the filthy, emaciated state he was in would never imagine he was carrying so much money, but in his mind, the wad of cash in his pocket acted like a beacon for any would-be thieves.

Evading security guards at the port, he waited in the shadows looking for a boat that appeared to be run down enough for the captain to need his money. Two hours later, he'd identified a boat he thought looked in need of invest-ment. To his untrained eye, all the smaller fishing boats looked in need of repair and a generous coat of paint, but the one he'd chosen looked particularly run down. As the crew stepped off the boat, Omar emerged from the shadows.

"Salam Alaikum, my friends. I need to speak to your captain."

The crew looked him up and down, wrongly concluding that the dishevelled man before them must be penniless, homeless and looking for work or a handout. "He's still on the boat, he lives on it. But if you're after a job you're wasting your time, we're fully crewed," one of them said.

Omar could sense their hostility. None of the crew could

afford to lose their precious jobs. "Thank you but I need to speak to your captain about another matter." The crewman who'd spoken shrugged, reassured the stranger was not there to take his job. After days at sea the crew were keen to get home. They turned and headed towards the security gate. Omar watched them disappear into the darkness before stepping onto the fishing boat.

"Salam," he called.

The captain emerged from the wheelhouse wiping his hands on an oily rag. Looking Omar up and down just as his crew had he came to the same conclusion. "How did you get past the port security? I don't need any more men, and I don't give money to beggars."

"I'm not a beggar and I don't want a job, but I do need your help. I need a ride to India and I'm willing to pay." Omar took some of the money he'd withdrawn at the train station from his pocket and showed it to the captain. "Forty thousand rupees. Half when we leave port, half when I get there."

The captain looked longingly at the money. He knew his boat was in dire need of investment, but the journey was long and if caught by the Indian navy he would be in trouble and could possibly lose his boat. "Fifty thousand," he said, "and you'll need to work for your passage as well, I can't afford passengers and I'll have to let one of my crew go. I'll drop you on a beach just south of Mumbai."

Omar nodded. "Agreed. When do we leave?"

"Come back in two days. Be here at midnight the day after tomorrow. We sail with the tide at first light the following day. If you're not here, we'll leave without you."

. . .

Six days after leaving Karachi, Omar stood on a deserted beach watching the small inflatable boat that had landed him in India row back to the fishing boat. Soaked from the waist down after wading the last few meters to shore all he had with him was his phone, it's charger, his bank card and a few hundred rupees. The sun was creeping over the horizon, and in the distance, he could see the smog laying over the city.

Setting off along the beach he wondered where he would live. He would contact his brother when he reached the outskirts of the city, maybe he would help him again, but he wasn't so sure after everything that had happened since he'd last asked for help.

Escorted by a member of the UK Immigration Service, Hadia arrived at Heathrow to await her flight to Mumbai. Bypassing the usual passport and customs checks, she was handed over to a member of the Indian police. Once on board, she looked out of the window as rain swept across the airport. The last time she'd made a journey from this airport she'd vowed she would never return. She wished she'd been able to keep the vow she'd made that day, but the decision to return had not been hers. It was a decision that, but for good fortune, would have resulted in her death in the freezing waters of the channel. She knew it was also a decision that had put her parents in terrible danger. As Hadia continued staring out of the window at the windswept airport a tear slowly worked its way down her cheek. Her father had been right all along, she should never have listened to her uncle's offer. Her headstrong nature had put the two people she loved most in the world in mortal danger. She closed her eyes and prayed they had escaped the old man's clutches and that she would see them again sometime soon. She looked down at her hand. The doctors had reset the bones and encased her hand in plaster. They could fix her broken bones, but no one could fix the terrible damage she'd done to her family.

THREE WEEKS after returning to work, Scrump sat in his office at the charity headquarters in Salisbury opening the post, his first job every morning. The last envelope he opened contained a cheque for a very large amount. A donation from an anonymous donor. Scrump smiled, he thought he had a pretty good idea where this donation had come from.

The same morning, charities throughout the country received similar generous donations, all of them anonymous.

ON THE SAME DAY, a postman delivered an envelope to a remote farmhouse on Dolwen Road, North Wales. Addressed to Major Andrew MacDonald, the envelope contained an anonymous cheque equal to half what the other members of the team had been paid. The envelope also contained a short unsigned note. It simply said, "thank you."

Now I really will need to go to the bank, Andrew thought. As he placed the cheque behind a photograph of his wife and son on the mantelpiece, Mac pulled on to the driveway. He got out of his car, opened the boot and took out the two shot-guns and drill his team had borrowed a few weeks before. His father opened the door to greet him before he reached the house.

"It's good to see you again so soon. Thank goodness you've brought my guns back. The bloody rabbits are running riot all over my veg patch."

AT THE SAME time the postman was delivering Andrew's mail, an anonymous call was made to the Metropolitan Police informing them of a scam and the address where they could find a computer used to transfer money scammed from innocent victims to a bank in Pakistan. It may help to break a worldwide scam operation, the caller said in a broad Scottish accent, before hanging up.

THE SAME DAY everyone on the list from Hassan's laptop received a cheque for the amount they'd lost to the scammers. Sir Duncan knew from Jock's presentation there was a good chance that some of the people on the list may have recovered the money the scammers had stolen from them but there was no way of knowing who, so a cheque was sent to everyone on the list. He decided that if they'd recovered their money what he was sending would be compensation for the upset and worry they'd been put through.

The only person on the list not to receive a cheque that day was his son. Sir Duncan had already replaced what Sam had lost. He didn't want to repay twice what his son had lost. After all, he wanted Sam to have the "*real uni experience*."

ACKNOWLEDGMENTS

Like many people during the pandemic I found myself with lots of time on my hands. During that time, I fell victim to a scam, the details of which are broadly outlined in Chapter 10. So, I suppose my first thanks, grudgingly, should go to the people who scammed me, without whom I would never have had the idea for this, my first book.

Thank you to my family for putting up with me over the last 18 months talking about and worrying whether I would ever publish. Thank you to Dan and Hannah for reading the first draft and coming up with some fresh ideas. Thank you to Helen for your endless enthusiasm. A special thanks to Alice who did a wonderful job on the final edit, any errors are mine alone, I tweaked the book after editing, sorry Alice. Thank you to Sophie Adams for the wonderful cover ideas and the final design.

A special thank you to my wonderful wife Jackie who has supported and encouraged me throughout this process, and who recognised the phone call I was on as a scam and helped recover the money before it was too late.

Finally thank you to everyone who takes the time to pick this book up and read it, I hope you enjoy my first novel.

Printed in Great Britain
by Amazon

79334484R20192